COOPER'S CORNER CHRONICLE

Twin Oaks Is Growing!

Twin Oaks Bed and Breakfast is turning out to be the hottest tourist spot in Cooper's Corner. Coproprietors Maureen Cooper and her brother, Clint, say bookings have been strong since their successful opening on Founder's Day weekend. Of course, all the excitement surrounding the disappearance and safe return of well-known travel writer William Byrd, a guest at the bed-and-breakfast, turned out to be a source of positive publicity. The glowing recommendation Byrd gave to Twin Oaks' hospitality and country charm in his latest guidebook hasn't hurt, either. Maureen says she and Clint are working on converting the attic space to create more rooms, and once again they've hired our very own plumber extraordinaire, Bonnie Cooper.

Of course, work is on hold this week. According to Bonnie's parents, Philo and Phyllis Cooper, their daughter is in New York visiting her aunt. "Bonnie's always on the lookout for vintage plumbing fixtures for her business," Phyllis says, "but we hope this time maybe she'll find a little romance in the Big Apple, too!"

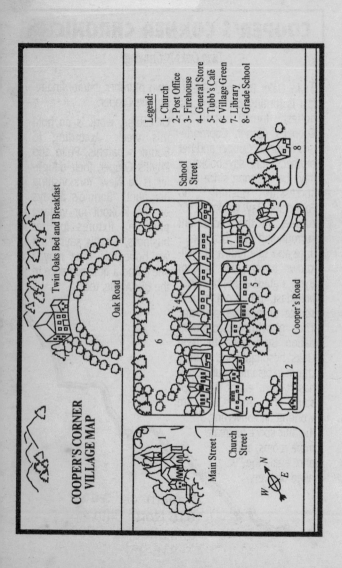

COOPER'S CORNER
VILLAGE MAP

Twin Oaks Bed and Breakfast

Oak Road

Main Street

Church Street

Cooper's Road

School Street

Legend:
1 - Church
2 - Post Office
3 - Firehouse
4 - General Store
5 - Tubb's Café
6 - Village Green
7 - Library
8 - Grade School

W N E S

C O O P E R ' S   C O R N E R

HEATHER MacALLISTER

After Darke

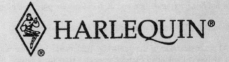

HARLEQUIN®

TORONTO • NEW YORK • LONDON
AMSTERDAM • PARIS • SYDNEY • HAMBURG
STOCKHOLM • ATHENS • TOKYO • MILAN • MADRID
PRAGUE • WARSAW • BUDAPEST • AUCKLAND

HARLEQUIN BOOKS
225 Duncan Mill Road, Don Mills,
Ontario, Canada M3B 3K9

RECYCLED PAPER

ISBN-13: 978-0-373-61253-6
ISBN-10: 0-373-61253-2

AFTER DARKE

Heather MacAllister is acknowledged as the author of this work.

Visit us at www.eHarlequin.com

Printed in U.S.A.

Dear Reader,

I'm pleased to be a part of the COOPER'S CORNER continuity series. As a writer, it's a challenge to weave my story into the setting, and as a reader, it's fun to see what the other authors have done with people and places I've come to know quite well.

In this book you'll meet the town plumber, Bonnie Cooper, and her unlikely blind date Jaron Darke, a satirical columnist from New York. How many of us have gone out with people our friends and relatives thought would be just perfect for us, but we knew better? We'd count the minutes until the date would end and we could feel virtuous. Bonnie and Jaron know instantly that they are completely unsuited for each other—and their date just never ends. Really. I hope you'll enjoy finding out how escaping from the mob, wearing plaid and fixing plumbing disasters is a recipe for true love.

Heather MacAllister

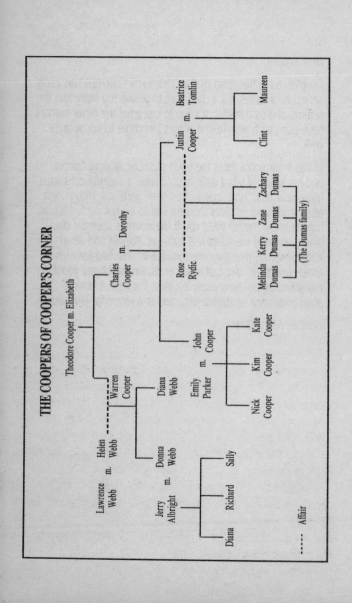

THE COOPERS OF COOPER'S CORNER

Theodore Cooper m. Elizabeth

Lawrence Webb m. Helen Webb — Warren Cooper — Charles Cooper m. Dorothy — Justin Cooper m. Beatrice Tomlin

Jerry Albright m. Donna Webb

Diana Webb

Emily Parker m. John Cooper

Rose Rydic

Diana — Richard — Sally

Nick Cooper — Kim Cooper — Kate Cooper

Melinda Dumas — Kerry Dumas — Zane Dumas — Zachary Dumas

(The Dumas family)

Clint — Maureen

- - - - - Affair

CHAPTER ONE

JARON DARKE RAPPED on the door of his mother's New York apartment. Life was good. He'd just been to a matinee reading of possibly the worst dreck ever to be foisted onto off-off—way off—Broadway. Bloated with conceit, Peter Edward Norris, or PEN, as he preferred to be called, had lost the vision of avant-garde and had delivered the merely banal. Even better, the members of the audience, fairly conceited themselves, hadn't figured it out.

Jaron would show them the way. There would be squirming, embarrassment, and above all, talk. PEN would denounce him.

Jaron could hardly wait.

After the performance, he had immediately gone to a little hole-in-the-wall eatery near the pretentiously shabby "theatre" to compose the scathing lead for his column. It was there that he'd discovered paradise on earth.

He bent his head to the warm, plastic-covered plate he held, and inhaled. If his mother would ever open the door, he'd share some of the paradise with her.

The handle turned, and his mother, talking on her cell phone, swept open the door and gestured him inside. Jaron blew her a kiss, went straight to the table by the window and set his offering on it. He had just turned on the lamps when his mother approached.

"Jaron, Cokie's niece is visiting New York this week.

It would please me if you would offer to take her out on the town one night.''

'' 'Out on the town'?'' Jaron gave his mother a sardonic look as he gestured for her to choose one of the selection of Hawaiian hors d'oeuvres he'd brought for her to sample. Jaron was not a blind-date sort of person. He never had been.

''You know what I mean.'' Nora Darke reached for a grilled pineapple-coconut shrimp. ''Pineapple?'' She examined the tidbit before popping it into her mouth. ''Mmm. Good. Pineapple hasn't been popular for a while. I can't think why not.''

''Two words—*fruit cocktail.*''

Nora's eyes widened. ''I *never* served you fruit cocktail!''

''But you didn't protect me from it, either.''

''Well, people *would* drown the stuff in garishly colored gelatin salads—and don't get me started on the horrors of whipped topping.'' She settled herself in her favorite overstuffed chintz chair.

Someday, Jaron would get her to change interior designers. ''You'll find no whipped topping at this restaurant,'' he assured her.

His mother examined the tray. ''Is this Thai?''

''Hawaiian.''

''Really! Hawaii is so early sixties.'' Nora cocked her head to one side. ''Though I must say, those Pucci prints are looking fresh and new again.'' She glanced at him and reached for a piece of fried coconut. ''You could use some color. Maybe a tie.''

''*Moi?* This is my trademark.'' He swept his hand down his black suit and shirt. No tie.

''Trademark or rut?''

"Now, Mother. I mustn't disappoint my fans. I'm working tonight."

It was Jaron's habit to stop by his mother's apartment several nights each week before he went out to collect material for his newspaper column, "After Darke." Part of the New York social scene herself, Nora Darke proved a reliable trend bellwether. Jaron liked to bring her his "finds" so she could introduce them to her "group"—a group that had proved fertile column fodder.

"The coconut is good, but missing something, I think," she said.

"The peanut sauce."

"Ah." Nora dipped the sliver of coconut into the sauce.

"Not too much—it's spicy," Jaron warned.

Nora took a tiny bite, then closed her eyes and let her head fall back. "Wonderful. What else have you got there?"

"Fish balls."

"Fish…balls?" She made a face. "Oh, how—"

"Take one."

She did. "Oh, my."

"A winner, you think?"

"Definitely. Who's the chef?"

Jaron's lips quivered. "Ron Ho."

"How unfortunate. And the name of his restaurant?"

"Blue Hawaii."

"Of course." Nora gave a slight shake of her head. "Do give him the option of changing it before we make him famous."

"*Are* we going to make him famous?"

Nora's fingers hesitated over the scallop and the crab claw, settling on the scallop and popping it into her mouth. She sighed and swallowed. "Oh, we must."

Good. Jaron smiled. That meant she planned to use Ron

Ho to cater a party. Nora Darke's gatherings were legendary and always gave Jaron enough column material for a week. "You should have your party quickly—he won't remain undiscovered for long."

"It's nearly October. There's barely time to squeeze one in before the holidays." She wiped her hands on a napkin and reached for her ever-present agenda on the lamp table.

Jaron toyed with the idea of getting her a PalmPilot for Christmas, but his mother's set was still assimilating e-mail. Maybe next year.

Scanning the weeks ahead, she made a slight sound of distress. "No openings while Cokie's niece is still in town. No, you'll just have to take Bonnie out on your own."

Jaron had hoped he'd distracted her from the blind date proposal. "*Bonnie?* Is that her name? Bonnie the bumpkin?"

Giving him a reproachful look, his mother said, "I've met her and I think she's very sweet."

"That bad?"

"Jaron—Cokie is my dearest friend, and I know she's wondering why I haven't suggested before that you and her niece get together."

"Because you know it will be a disaster?"

"Because you were dating Sydney."

He would have welcomed a break from Sydney. "Sydney and I did seem to be at the same places at the same times for a while there, didn't we?" They both knew that Jaron's mother had hopes of an art-gallery-owner daughter-in-law. They were terribly in fashion. Unfortunately, Jaron skewered the art world regularly in his columns, and Sydney had finally let it be known that he was persona non grata at her gallery.

He truly took no pleasure in the fact that her gallery had gone out of business shortly thereafter.

Nora sighed. "Well, I asked. My conscience is clear."

His mother had abandoned the battle far too easily, thus arousing Jaron's suspicions.

Eyeing the rest of the hors d'oeuvres, she took a banana chip. "Have you heard anything more about the Dettlings' divorce?"

Jaron tensed. In his column he'd reported rumors about Dettling leaving his wife for the Corlani widow. It would be a coup to report it as fact. "Have you?"

"No," said his mother. "They're more Cokie's friends than they are mine."

Ah. A not-so-subtle reminder that Cokie was one of his best sources outside of his mother, and that it would behoove him to stay on her good side.

Jaron chuckled to himself. He liked Cokie. Come to think of it, his mother wasn't so bad herself.

She hadn't been the mothering sort when he was growing up, treating him much the same as she treated him now. But he'd never felt neglected. Looking back, he decided he'd had an interesting childhood, if one could call it a childhood. Impulsively, he leaned over and kissed her cheek. "All right. I'll take Cokie's niece out and dazzle her with my wit and charm."

"Thank you, Jaron. And don't leave it too late because she's going home this weekend."

He leaned back and mentally rearranged his schedule. "I'll give her a call. Where is she from again?"

"Cooper's Corner, Massachusetts."

"Never heard of it."

"It's in the Berkshires. Cokie's sister married one of the Coopers."

"Ah. And what does she do in Cooper's Corner, Massachusetts?" What did anyone do out in the middle of nowhere?

His mother looked down at her agenda instead of meeting his eyes. A bad sign. "She's a plumber."

"BONNIE, DARLING," her aunt called. "Jaron is the son of my dearest friend. He's been kind enough to offer to take you to dinner tomorrow night. Please say you'll go."

Bonnie glanced toward the kitchen. "Sure, Aunt Cokie."

Her aunt beamed at her and spoke into the telephone.

If at that particular moment Bonnie hadn't been in the process of tipping the doorman for helping her cart some of the day's architectural salvage finds up to her aunt's apartment, she might not have been so quick to agree.

On the other hand, why not go out with this friend's son? After all, she *was* Bonnie Cooper, Berkshires' Blind Date Queen. She just hadn't realized her reputation had preceded her to New York.

Besides, maybe her aunt had other plans for tomorrow night.

Bonnie found yesterday's *New York Times* and carried it into the spare bedroom, where she spread several sheets over the carpet. Then she retrieved the paper bags from the foyer and emptied their contents onto the newspapers. What an incredible haul. She'd found just the right antique faucets, with intact connecting pipes, and even a cracked claw-foot tub with the exact feet she'd been searching for. What luck. She could ditch the tub, which she'd had shipped home, along with the larger items, and marry the feet to the tub her parents had been keeping for her in the basement of their hardware store. And then there were the two pull-chain toilets she'd bought on spec. They were in style again—who knew why, but they were.

This trip to New York was turning out better than she'd dared to hope. She'd found everything she needed for her next project—converting the attic of the Twin Oaks Bed and Breakfast to a fifth guest room.

She was sitting on the floor, happily measuring and cataloging plumbing fixtures and fittings, when Cokie appeared in the doorway.

"So you had luck at the excavation auction?"

"Oh, yes. Just look at this." Bonnie held up a blackened, curved metal faucet and rubbed it with her thumb. Brass gleamed back at her encouragingly. Taking the hem of her T-shirt, she rubbed at it again, looking up when her aunt gasped. "What?"

"Don't you have a rag for that sort of thing?"

"After today, my shirt *is* a rag."

"But you're still wearing it!" Cokie fretted. "And getting who-knows-what from that nasty thing all over it."

"This isn't just any nasty thing. This is an early twentieth-century faucet, and handles with the original escutcheons." She pointed to the china pieces.

"Is that good?"

"Decorators charge their clients big bucks to install reproductions. This baby is the genuine article and I've got all the fittings with it."

"Yes, I see."

Bonnie grinned up at her aunt. "I arranged for the rest to be sent back to the store, but I didn't trust the auctioneer not to be bribed to 'lose' this."

Cokie hesitated, then asked, "But, Bonnie…is it, er, clean?"

"Oh, no," Bonnie answered cheerfully. "That's why I put down the newspapers." Her aunt made a small sound of distress. "Do you have any other auctions tomorrow?"

"Yes, do you want to come?" Bonnie's type of auctions and sales were quick and dirty and involved climbing around in torn-down buildings or wandering through warehouses filled with architectural salvage. Cokie's type of auctions involved gilded chairs and discreet bidding paddles.

"I...I wondered about going to Elizabeth Arden's for a facial and a manicure." Cokie looked hopefully at her.

"A *manicure?*" Bonnie laughed and used her thumbnail to chip away at some sludge in the screw threads of the faucet. "What for?"

"You're going out to dinner."

She'd forgotten. "That's right. With...?"

"Jaron Darke." Her aunt's voice held a reverential tone.

Should she recognize the name? Bonnie couldn't remember hearing about him, unless her aunt had mentioned his name on a previous visit. "Are we all going?"

"Oh, no." Her aunt smiled benignly. "This will be a chance for you two to get to know one another."

Bonnie refrained from pointing out that it was unlikely there would be a future use for knowing Jaron Darke. This was clearly a case of two friends' wishful matchmaking, and she'd already agreed to go along with it. It was only for an evening and would make her aunt happy—inadequate repayment for all the times Cokie had welcomed her on her buying trips. "So tell me about him. Is he some kind of big shot?"

"Bonnie!" Cokie pressed her palm against her chest. "Everyone knows Jaron." She spoke in a near whisper, as though afraid someone might hear that her niece was clueless about Jaron Darke.

"Everyone in New York, maybe, but I'm not from New York."

Her aunt gave her that look of slight surprise, followed by the dismissal Bonnie was accustomed to seeing when New Yorkers were reminded that there was a world outside the city. "Jaron Darke is a newspaper columnist."

"Really? What's he write about?" Bonnie screwed together three sets of nuts and bolts, then reached for a pencil. Her fingers were dirty, so she looked around for something to wipe them on. Finding nothing, she used her shirt, then made a note.

Her aunt sighed, and when she spoke, Bonnie noticed her eyes were closed. "He writes about everything. Movies, plays, restaurants, music, personalities, the mayor, certain issues, crime, squatters... He's a social commentator."

"And why are people interested in his comments?"

There was silence, so Bonnie looked up.

Her aunt's lips were moving. She blinked several times. "They...they just are!"

"Oh." Bonnie went back to matching fittings. At least this Jaron Darke would be able to hold up his end of the conversation. All Bonnie would have to ask was, "What do you think about...", and he'd comment. She smiled to herself. She might even comment back.

The phone rang and Cokie went to answer it before she could tell her niece anything more about Jaron, not that Bonnie needed her to. She pretty much had this Jaron guy figured for a true-blue New Yorker very much of her aunt's social circle.

Bonnie was a small-town girl at heart and didn't fit in with her aunt's world, as much as Cokie pretended otherwise. She was always eager to have Bonnie stay with her and mingle with her friends, but after all these years she must know how unlikely it would be for Bonnie and a man like this Jaron person to hit it off.

It must have been because she was thinking of him, but when Bonnie picked up the pipe fittings for the faucet, there was the name, Jaron Darke, right in front of her.

He had a grease smudge across his forehead, but Bonnie brushed away the dirt from the newspaper and found herself looking at the picture above his column, "After Darke." Cute.

But cute only applied to the title. Jaron had a goatee and short, short hair and a supercilious expression topped by impressive cheekbones.

Bonnie had always wanted cheekbones to define her round face. Cheekbones would give her a haughty authority. She could use some haughtiness during negotiations.

Jaron Darke had haughtiness to spare.

Bonnie sighed and began reading his column.

When Dynasties Divorce and Competitors Comingle Rumblings from the Charity Circuit

With a possible split rumored between two titans of tithing, the question arises: Who gets custody of the contribution? Who ponies up payment for the pledge? What does it matter as long as the charity gets the money in the end, you ask?

If you do, indeed, ask, you are obviously one of that rowdy bunch consuming beer and pretzels at the twenty-five-dollars-and-under contributors' party. No, folks, we're talking serious giving here, which we all (except you with the warm beer in the plastic cup) know means buying. And what's for sale is no less than social position for the following year.

Now we have the hypothetical situation of Mrs. D. (I meant D for Dynasty—who did you think?) Mrs. D loves the ballet. Mr. and Mrs. D have underwritten the Spring Ballet Ball for a decade. But alas, only diamonds are forever. Enter Mrs. C (for Competitor— so there will be no misunderstanding and unsubstan-

tiated rumors resulting in boring legal threats.) Mrs.
C also likes the ballet. Because of her influence, Mr.
D continues his support for the Spring Ballet Ball.
Mrs. C achieves a spot on the top rung of the social
ladder next to Mrs. D, who wishes she could push her
off.

And she might. Mr. D pledged support on their
behalf. But he already made a contribution with Mrs.
C. Should the ballet call in the pledge or give credit
for monies received? At stake is nothing less than
quality of life....

The rest of the column dealt with the fight over whose
contribution should get credit—the one with Mrs. C or
Mrs. D—and how that credit affected restaurant ''A'' lists
and seats at fashion shows. And of course it was noted
how worthy these people were to be mentioned in Jaron's
column.

Like Bonnie cared *at all*. Oh, she appreciated the subtle
sarcasm, but people like Jaron, who clearly felt he was
superior to the rest of his world, made her nervous.

She looked down at her nails. A manicure couldn't hurt.

As IT TURNED OUT, Bonnie did not have her manicure and
facial, but she did find three wonderfully carved porcelain
toilets in superb condition, so no matter how her evening
with Jaron turned out, the day wouldn't be a total loss.
Working out the shipping details took longer than she'd
planned, but she took extra time with her appearance—and
wore her one and only black dress—to make up for missing the beauty treatments.

She finished dressing in enough time to scan the magazines in search of possible conversation topics. She also

read two more of Jaron's columns. One featured a commentary about a minor local political race, and the next was a follow-up containing blistering correspondence from the two politicians, protesting his column. Bonnie winced at how thoroughly Jaron skewered them in his rebuttal, even as she secretly admired his audacity.

She also had a horrible feeling she was about to become material for his column.

"Bonnie?" Cokie had arisen from her evening nap. She was off to play bridge tonight. "You're ready?"

Bonnie checked her watch. "It's after seven. You said dinner, right?"

"But it's only seven!"

"I guess I never nailed down the details, but he mentioned a drive through the city, so I assumed we'd be leaving around this time." Bonnie's stomach certainly wanted to leave around this time.

"Jaron wouldn't insult you by calling for you so early."

"I want to be insulted. I'm hungry."

Cokie headed for the kitchen. "Let me get you some bouillon and crackers."

Bonnie was way beyond bouillon and crackers. She followed her aunt into the compact kitchen. "I read Jaron's columns."

"Isn't he marvelous?" Cokie enthused, ladling out soup from the pot on the stove.

"He's sarcastic and snobby."

"He has a sophisticated wit."

Right. "I'm not sure about tonight, Aunt Cokie."

"Because of his column?" Cokie laughed. "Don't mistake his column persona for who he really is. He's actually quite charming."

"Sophisticated and witty."

Smiling, Cokie handed her a cup of chicken bouillon. "Exactly."

JARON WAS INTRIGUED by the thought of a date with a plumber, he had to admit. In spite of the Blue Hawaii restaurant discovery—now called simply Hawaii—and the horrible PEN play, life had seemed stale lately.

So he was mentally in a charitable mood as he greeted the doorman and made his way up the stairs to Cokie's apartment. He was taking the plumber to a tiny family-owned restaurant in Little Italy. Everyone liked Italian food. It was a safe choice and might become his latest discovery.

Yes, the evening was looking up.

IN SPITE OF COKIE'S assurances that the column Jaron was nothing like the real Jaron, the instant Bonnie saw him at the door of her aunt's apartment, she knew the date was going to be a disaster. She didn't normally judge people so strongly on appearance, but this Jaron Darke looked exactly like his photo in the paper. He was wearing a black, silk-knit T-shirt underneath a black suit. His equally black hair wasn't cut short, as she'd thought from the picture, but was combed back from his forehead. He *was* sporting the same thick goatee. Worst of all, he wore rimless sunglasses. At night.

Pretentious, pretentious, pretentious.

She stood in the open doorway and stared at the black glass covering his eyes. She didn't need to actually see his eyes to know that he'd given her a dismissing once-over.

"Hello." He smiled—maybe it was closer to a smirk. "I'm Jaron and...you're Bonnie."

He spoke as though she were unpleasant medicine he

had to take. It made Bonnie grit her teeth. Already. "Good guess." She stood aside so he could come in.

"Not a guess—who else could you be?" As he spoke, his gaze swept the interior of Cokie's apartment in a way that further irritated Bonnie, even though it wasn't *her* apartment.

"Since I don't have my name and picture plastered in the paper on a daily basis, I suppose I could be anyone." She retrieved her purse from the love seat by the mock fireplace.

He smiled, ignoring her snippy comment. "You've read my column."

"A few this week." Bonnie resisted the opportunity to say something derogatory. Anyway, his columns weren't bad—for what they were.

"Public recognition can be tiresome at times."

Though he sounded bored, Bonnie bet that Jaron loved every minute of it. "Oh, I get that all the time. Parties are the worst. People come up to you and want to discuss their running toilets. You know what I mean?"

He stopped studying the molded cornice and gazed down at her. She wished like anything she could see his eyes.

Then, very slowly, he unhooked the wires from around his ears and removed the sunglasses.

She almost wished he'd left them on. Obsidian eyes examined her with…interest? Bonnie wasn't sure she wanted to capture Jaron Darke's interest. What would she do with it?

And yet deep within her, *something* responded to the way he now gave her his full attention. *Something*… growled.

A smile touched the corner of his mouth and he gestured to the door. "Shall we?"

CHAPTER TWO

"JUST A MINUTE, you two!" Cokie DeGrace intercepted them.

And none too soon, Jaron thought. He couldn't believe Cokie intended to let her niece out on the streets in that getup.

He made his living by forcing people to confront their prejudices and pretensions, and he prided himself on not falling victim to the same. But there were limits, and he was only human. Prejudices came about because of the unpleasant fact that there was a tiny kernel of truth buried in each one. And the truth here was that this Bonnie Cooper fit every cliché he'd imagined.

He'd been taken aback when she'd opened the door. Yes, he'd made disparaging country bumpkin comments about her to his mother, but he hadn't been serious. Massachusetts was hardly the Midwest. In fact, he'd briefly considered the possibility that Cokie and his mother had been playing a joke on him. Thank God he hadn't said anything.

Her dress wasn't just out of style—it had no style to be out of. She might have a figure, but who could tell under that sack? The sack was encircled by a tiny string belt that did nothing to enhance the shape of the dress. And her shoes—walking shoes. *Walking* shoes. At night. Didn't she trust him to hire a car?

Topping off Bonnie's appearance was nondescript makeup

and hair, which Jaron suspected she cut herself one-handed while holding a tiny mirror. He sent a reproachful look toward Cokie.

Yes, he was early for a dinner date, but he'd thought Bonnie might like a drive around the city at night before they ate. He had said *drive,* hadn't he?

"Jaron!" Cokie tittered, and Jaron looked at her with alarm. "Naughty, naughty! Trying to steal my niece away without saying goodbye?"

Jaron inadvertently glanced over at Bonnie and saw that her expression was one of horror. Good. She, too, realized an alien was inhabiting Cokie's body. One thing on which they could both agree.

"Cokie, there was no stealing involved here." Jaron kissed her cheek in greeting.

"But I bet you'd like to!" She tittered again.

Prepared this time, Jaron maintained a fixed expression.

"Where are you taking her?"

"Lorenzo's in Little Italy."

"I don't know that restaurant."

Jaron smiled. "You will."

"I'm sure it'll be another of your—" Cokie gasped. "Bonnie, what have you got on your feet!"

They all looked at Bonnie's shoes. Bonnie sighed heavily. "Well, I was hoping you wouldn't notice."

"This is New York," Cokie said. "Everyone notices."

Hear, hear, Jaron thought.

"Too bad. I did a lot of walking today and I can't get into my dress shoes." She shrugged at Jaron. "You'll have to take me as I am. Or if Aunt Cokie has some gold spray paint, I could—"

"Oh, it'll be fine," Cokie said before Jaron could. "Jaron will probably turn sneakers at night into the latest trend!"

"There's a thought," Jaron murmured.

"In that case, I should add some sequins. Or beads. Designer laces at the very minimum." Bonnie met his eyes with complete guilelessness.

This one would take some watching. In spite of an unfortunate first impression, it appeared that the plumber had a few kinks in her pipes, kinks he might find interesting to, ah, plumb.

"Bonnie, you don't *want* to draw attention. It's just that you'll be with Jaron and he *is* fairly well-known, so—"

"So I've elected to take Bonnie to an out-of-the-way family-owned restaurant I've heard some good things about," Jaron interjected. "I hope you like Italian, Bonnie."

"Everyone likes Italian, Jaron. Now, you're sure your reputation won't suffer from being seen with me in these shoes?"

Jaron was ready to burn the shoes. "I believe my reputation can withstand a couple of crepe soles, Bonnie." He smiled, revealing his teeth. They were gritted.

She gritted right back. "How fortunate for me, Jaron."

The evening had not begun well, and Jaron was at a loss to pinpoint exactly where it had started to go wrong. No doubt at the moment either his mother or Cokie got the idea to pair up the two of them. What had they been thinking? In an instant, both he and Bonnie had realized they were mismatched.

At least he had the satisfaction of knowing that he was hiding the realization better than Bonnie was.

Cokie shooed them toward the door. "Oh, go on, you two. I'm on my way to bridge."

"May I drop you somewhere?" Jaron offered.

"You're a dear, but it's in the building."

"Goodbye, Aunt Cokie." Bonnie leaned over and kissed her cheek.

Jaron opened the door vowing to be a pleasant, entertaining—not overwhelming or patronizing—companion for the evening. The effort ought to be good for mega karma points.

WITH BOTH HER AUNT and his mother vouching for him, Jaron Darke must have *some* redeeming qualities, Bonnie thought as she stepped past the drive and climbed into the back seat of the black Lincoln Town Car. It was her mission to find them this evening.

It wasn't like her to react so negatively on first appearances. But there he was, all in black, Mr. Single-and-jaded-in-New-York. She knew the type. She didn't like the type.

She could tell that he wasn't impressed with her, either. And what had gotten into Cokie?

Well, Bonnie would offer the olive branch. After all, they were civilized adults; they could have a civilized evening. "It's very kind of you to take me out this evening. I can tell from reading your columns that you must work most nights."

"I do." Jaron lounged against the padded leather car seat in a way that told Bonnie he'd done it a hundred times before. "In fact, I'm working, if you will, tonight. I've wanted to try this restaurant, so you're actually helping me. We can order a wider variety of dishes."

Okay. Not too bad. A little patronizing if she wanted to get picky, but maybe they'd make it through the evening without inflicting bodily harm on each other, after all. Bonnie relaxed slightly.

Time to lob the conversational ball. "Do you often review restaurants?" She knew how to cook; this should be a safe topic.

"'Review' isn't the word I'd use."

And that took the conversation right into the net. Bonnie would serve again. Maybe right at him. "What word *would* you use?"

"Among other things, I occasionally comment on exceptional meals."

"'Comment' meaning you write about the food."

"Yes."

"'Exceptional' meaning either good or bad."

"Precisely." He'd left off his sunglasses—presumably due to the car's tinted glass—and Bonnie could see his eyes swivel her way, a hint of amusement in their dark depths.

What was so funny? She hated it when people acted as though they knew a joke and she didn't. "Isn't commenting on meals what a restaurant reviewer does?"

He shook his head and went back to scanning the ever-changing scene outside the car windows for who-knew-what. "A reviewer would go into much more detail about the food and the chef as well as tag the entire piece with cutesy dollar signs indicating the cost. I'm concerned with the total experience as well as who's doing the experiencing."

The total experience. Just the way he spoke grated on Bonnie, but there was no reason why it should.

Jaron leaned forward and said something to the driver, who immediately changed lanes with a typical New Yorker's disregard for vehicles behind him.

Reminding herself that she didn't know Jaron, but both Cokie and Nora liked him, Bonnie vowed to stop attributing hidden meaning into everything he said. She was reacting to a few columns and the goatee and sunglasses. And he had agreed to take her out, meaning he was considerate of little old ladies. Bonnie smiled to herself at the thought of either Cokie's or Nora's reaction to being thought of as "little old ladies."

"You find that amusing?"

"Find what amusing?" Why couldn't he have just said, "What's so funny?"

"My comment."

"About the total experience?"

"That *was* what we'd been discussing."

"Oh." Bonnie mentally backtracked. "No. I didn't find that funny."

"Good. It wasn't meant to be. Except for the remark about the dollar signs. I had hopes for that."

Bonnie smiled politely. "I kind of like the little dollar signs."

Your kind would. Jaron didn't say that aloud, but he didn't have to. Bonnie could hear him think it.

"I guess they do have their uses, though it always seems that one person's dollar is another's twenty." Jaron's smile was a twin of hers. In other words, all for show.

Silence fell. They both turned to look out their respective windows. Bonnie shifted on the leather, very aware of the stilted conversation and the awkward gaps. Perhaps that was why, when Jaron pointed out that they were approaching Times Square, which she'd seen on every single trip to New York, Bonnie reacted with more enthusiasm than the blinking sign deserved.

"Oh, wow. It looks just like it does on television!" She craned her neck to see out the windows.

There was more stiff silence, then Jaron observed, "Seen it before, have you?" When Bonnie looked over at him, he was rubbing his temple. He gave her a tight smile.

Caught. "I come to New York a couple of times a year," she admitted.

"Well, you know, Bonnie, I live here and I don't know

whether it's the lights or the theater marquees or the people, but I never get tired of seeing a revitalized Times Square at night.''

Bonnie was embarrassed. What was the *matter* with her?

He turned his head to look out the window again. ''I love this city,'' he said with quiet sincerity. ''I can't imagine living anywhere else.''

Just for a moment, seeing his profile illuminated by the garish lights of Times Square, Bonnie thought there might actually be something behind the Jaron Darke persona, something that might make the man worth knowing—if she could dig it out.

Maybe he was like the vintage fittings she bought—not much on the outside, but after a little buffing and tapping out of dents, they became things of beauty.

Bonnie tried to visualize Jaron as a thing of beauty. Nope. Wasn't happening. ''If you like New York so much, then why do you write such nasty things about it?'' she demanded.

''Because I'm not blind to the faults of the city or the people who live in it.''

''But what gives you the right?''

''Anyone has the right to express an opinion. I just happen to get paid for mine.''

''And how did that happen?''

''A friend of my mother's is an editor of a weekly magazine here, and she started buying blurbs I'd submit for their 'About Town' column.''

''Oh, *connections.*''

''That's the way of the world.''

''Not for everyone. Some of us make our own way.''

Bonnie had been talking to Jaron's profile all this time. At her last remark, he turned his head away from the city lights and fastened his gaze on her. He let the silence lengthen, and Bonnie was tempted to break it, but it became very important to her not to give in. Why, she couldn't say. Maybe because she wanted him to realize that he was a grown man still trading on his mother's influence. She struggled not to let her lips slide into a sneer.

"And I understand that you're a plumber?" he verified mildly.

"Yes," Bonnie replied, ready to defend her profession.

"And your parents?"

"They own a combination hardware store and grocery in Cooper's Corner."

"A hardware store." His expression didn't change. "How convenient for you."

He didn't have to say anything more. Bonnie felt her face heat even as she mounted an oh-so-weak protest. "It's not the same thing." But it was.

"You mean no one ever buys a…a toilet thing and asks if your parents know a good plumber to install it?"

"No." Everyone in town already knew who she was.

He gave her a half smile she would have found sexy on any other man. "Bonnie, Bonnie, you disappoint me. I expected better. You've clearly lost this point. Give up and attack me on another subject."

"What?"

He gave her an impatient look. "Obviously, I'm right and you're wrong."

"I don't think it's so obvious!" Bonnie's voice sounded shrill to her own ears, probably because her mind was bombarding her with evidence supporting Jaron's claim. The fact that she used her parents' storage space and bought all her supplies through them, the fact that the desk and phone in the store's basement constituted her office… rent free. And her mother sometimes answered the phone….

"Oh, all right!" she snapped.

"There's no need to apologi—"

"I wasn't going to!"

"Not to me," he said dryly. "For using connections to establish yourself."

"I wasn't going to apologize for that, either!"

"You don't have to. That was my point."

"But your points always seem so…so superior!"

After a moment, Jaron asked in a different tone of voice, "This isn't working, is it?"

"Did you think it would?"

His gaze flicked over her. To her complete disgust, she felt a warmth kindle in her stomach. Of course, that could be hunger. It better be hunger.

"It's just one evening, Bonnie."

She hated—*hated*—that he'd already cataloged her as a "not possible." She hated knowing it. And she hated that she hated it. He hadn't even given her a chance.

But why should she care?

"Would you like to go back to your aunt's?" he asked.

It was very tempting, but would result in too many questions. Or really, only a few questions asked many, many times.

She shook her head. "I think it would be best to carry on."

He stared at her for a long moment. "I'm not sure it's worth the effort."

If he'd slapped her, Bonnie wouldn't have been more surprised. "What a nasty thing to say!"

"Come on. We can't even carry on a civil conversation."

A tiny inner voice started to point out her less-than-stellar behavior this evening, but since Bonnie already knew what it was going to say, she didn't bother to listen.

She couldn't think of anything to say to Jaron, either, and just sat there and goggled at him like the hick he seemed to think she was.

"What I hope you'll explain before we part is why you agreed to this date if you'd already made up your mind that you didn't like me," Jaron said at last.

"I agreed before…" She trailed off.

"Before you read my columns?"

Bonnie nodded. "But the instant you saw *me,* you sneered."

"I don't sneer."

"Yes, you do. And it's a great sneer."

"Is it?" He looked pleased.

"Oh, yeah. You just barely move your lips, and your upper lip on the left side rises just the tiniest bit." She indicated the distance with her thumb and forefinger. "An outstanding sneer. First rate. The best I've ever seen. You don't even need the glasses thing to go with it."

"The glasses thing?"

"Oh, you know. The whole dark glasses at night. Staring at a person, sneering, then taking off your glasses as though you're looking at an insect. Trust me, the glasses are overkill."

There it was again, that flicker of amused interest in his eyes.

And just as before, it caused an answering warmth within her.

There was something about him that got to her and she sure wished it didn't.

"I'm not my columns."

"I guess I'll never know."

He stared at her some more, his lips curving sneerlessly this time, then leaned toward the driver. "Little Italy. Mulberry Street."

"Changed your mind?" Bonnie asked. *Stop feeling relieved.*

"You changed my mind."

His voice had dropped a notch, and Bonnie's heart picked up a beat or two in response.

Settling back against the plush seat, facing her this time, Jaron said, "And now you must tell me all about being a plumber."

"Why must I tell you?" She was cross because she did *not* want to feel attracted to Jaron Darke.

"Because it was what intrigued me about you. I've never known a plumber socially, and you must admit that it's an unusual occupation for a woman."

Bonnie inhaled, not ready to admit any such thing, when that little voice inside shouted—screamed, actually—and what it screamed was, "Shut up!"

So she heeded it, something she should have done much earlier.

She exhaled, and began to tell the story she'd told countless times before. "As you know, my parents own the town hardware store. People would buy replacement ball cocks..." Jaron's left eyelid flinched and she smiled inwardly. A girl could have fun, couldn't she? And that *was* what they were called.

"...or faucet washers, and I'd earn a little money by installing them. Pretty soon, I learned that the more I knew how to do, the more money I would earn."

"Yes, but that's true of most situations. *Something* had to draw you to plumbing." His tone implied that he couldn't imagine what.

"I think it was that plumbing drew me *away* from teaching—that's what I studied. I do like living in Cooper's Corner and I suppose I just got caught up in the whole teaching mystique."

"Hmm." Jaron looked into the distance. "I need some help visualizing this 'teaching mystique.'"

"Well, I didn't, and that was the problem. First of all, you must paint a mental image of Theodore Cooper Elementary." Bonnie used her hands to indicate an imaginary canvas. "Think little red schoolhouse surrounded by colorful fall foliage, think wood-burning stove—"

"No—really?"

Bonnie nodded. "But only in the foyer. The rest has been modernized, but not too much, you know? It's still so picturesque, it hurts. I swear, the ghost of Norman Rockwell haunts that building."

Jaron laughed. "That's pretty good. I might steal that line sometime."

"Go ahead, I probably heard it somewhere myself." Bonnie tried not to be pleased that she'd made him laugh. "Now imagine little girls in pigtails and crisp plaid jumpers, and little boys with slicked-back hair, new jeans and plaid shirts, all sitting eagerly at their polished oak desks, listening as I, dressed in a white blouse, pearls and a full skirt—"

"Plaid?"

She grinned. "Probably."

He grinned back. He didn't look half-bad when he was really smiling. "So the teaching mystique is wrapped in plaid."

"Only in the fall. In winter, there are cute sweaters and velvet. I think I was mentally casting a long-distance telephone commercial. Anyway, the point here is that I thought teaching was all about happy little kids bringing me apples." She was silent for a moment. "I lost a child my first day in charge of a class."

He grew still. "It…ended well?"

"Eventually. The little girl just decided she'd had

enough school for the day and wanted to go home. So she did. I, however, thought she was in the bathroom. The whole incident taught me that regimented bathroom breaks are not all that barbaric.''

He laughed. Bonnie managed a halfhearted chuckle and shook her head.

''Hey, it was a beginner's mistake,'' Jaron said when he noticed she wasn't laughing.

''That's what my aunt Gina said. She's a teacher there. Except it was a spectacularly *huge* mistake.''

''It could have happened—''

''No, it couldn't. And I did *not* want to see what other spectacularly huge mistakes I could make, so I cut short my teaching career.''

Jaron seemed at a loss for words. Bonnie suspected it didn't happen very often, and was doing a little internal gloating when he quietly spoke and caught her off guard.

''I'm sorry.'' He looked as if he meant it.

She didn't want him to mean it because that would indicate he had *some* redeeming characteristics. If so, there was a possibility that she might actually begin to like him in addition to being attracted to him, which would be awful, because he clearly didn't like her. So she would just continue to think of him as a pretentious urban snob.

''Don't be sorry,'' she said. ''I don't know what I'd been thinking. And since that reality check, I've been called to unclog the school bathrooms about once every six weeks, which not only provides a semiregular source of income, but reinforces my decision.''

Bonnie could see him grappling with the concept of her unclogging school toilets. She couldn't fault him. Sometimes she had to grapple with it herself.

''Your path from teaching to plumbing isn't clear to me yet.''

"I already was halfway there." She didn't want to talk about her occupation anymore. "I worked as an apprentice all the way through school. Emergency weekend calls paid great. So I just kept going with the training. I still am."

He nodded. "Okay."

"I'm glad my life plan meets with your approval," Bonnie snapped before she could stop herself. Honestly, something about him just brought out the worst in her.

"I thought we had a cease-fire," he stated mildly. "I enjoyed hearing your teaching story. And I realize that it wasn't funny at the time."

She turned her head to look out the window, wishing she hadn't told him about the little girl. Bonnie didn't know why she had. She hardly ever told anyone, and revealing her ineptitude to a man who didn't think much of her to start with was just asking for it.

The fact that Jaron hadn't taken advantage made it worse.

"You're embarrassed," he said.

Bonnie whipped her head around. "I'm not!"

"Yes, you are. You revealed something of yourself to me, and to balance the relationship, I must confess something of equal gravity."

"We don't have a relationship."

He gestured with his hand. "Temporary association, then."

"Whatever."

Silence followed, which told Bonnie what she needed to know. "You've never done anything worse than ordering the wrong wine with a meal, right?"

"I was endeavoring—"

"*Endeavoring.* Why do you talk like a British stage actor?"

"Why do you talk like a character in a network sit-com?" he retorted.

"I talk like a real person!"

"A real person with no education or class."

Bonnie gasped.

Jaron looked pained. "Congratulations. You've made me sink to your level."

They glared at each other.

He didn't apologize, and she didn't, either. Clearly, civility was beyond them, and the more time they spent together, the worse it would get. They rubbed each other the wrong way. That's all there was to it.

"Take me home." She turned back to the window and told herself that this was the best thing that could have happened to quash any growing feelings she might have for him—other than dislike. That one could grow.

The car kept moving. Bonnie could swear she'd seen this street before. Maybe more than once.

She felt Jaron lean forward. "Lorenzo's."

The car turned at the next corner and slid to a stop by a green scalloped awning that stretched over the sidewalk. In gold script, "Lorenzo's" curled along the side.

"This is the restaurant," she said.

"Yes."

"I asked you to take me home."

"To be more accurate, you *ordered* me to take you home."

"That is because I want to go home now." She spoke very distinctly, biting off each word.

"And I want to have dinner now." He was just as distinct.

"So have dinner."

"I intend to."

The driver got out and started around the car to her door.

Actually, Bonnie was relieved. This way, she wouldn't have to endure an awkward ride back with Jaron. "I'm not hungry, so could you please have your driver take me home while you eat?" There. That was polite. She added a smile for good measure. It would be his last image of her and all that.

Jaron smiled back just as politely. "No."

CHAPTER THREE

"WHAT DO YOU MEAN 'no'?"

Jaron stared into the angry face of his date.

It wasn't a bad face, actually. Attractive in a wholesome sort of way. Not his usual style, but her lips were on the full side, and Jaron acknowledged a fondness for full lips—especially when the lower one was slightly larger, as hers was.

Yes, he did like a full lower lip. He'd been fooled in the past when he'd mistaken a pout for a larger lower lip, but Bonnie didn't strike him as a pouter. No, she came right out and said what she thought, which made her interesting to Jaron. Maddening, but interesting. Also irritating and annoying. It was obvious she harbored a visible contempt for him. But she wasn't boring, and that made up for all the rest.

Who would have thought Bonnie-the-plumber would prove intriguing?

So, no, he wasn't ready to give up yet. She would go home when he was ready to take her home.

The driver opened the door, and her jaw tightened in a way that gave Jaron second thoughts.

He might be ready very soon.

"Jaron?"

"I offered to take you home. You declined."

"I've changed my mind."

"So have I." He gestured for her to get out.

She glared at him.

He desperately hoped she wasn't the type to make a scene, a possibility he should have considered earlier. "Please?"

Something changed in her expression, and without a word, she climbed out of the car. How about that? *Please* really was the magic word.

He spoke to the driver, giving him an approximate time to pick them up, and warily turned to Bonnie.

"You really want to go through with this?" she asked, her chin tilted up belligerently.

"I really want to go through with this."

"Because I'm finding it very difficult to be nice."

"I've noticed."

"That's not like me."

"Nice is boring."

"Well, I can guarantee you won't be bored."

Jaron gave a bark of laughter. "I'm going to hold you to that."

"Why did you change your mind?" she asked as they walked toward the door.

He had no idea and would no doubt regret it. "Call it pride," he admitted, and exhaled. "I've never run off a woman yet."

"There's a first time for everything."

"And tonight's first is going to be dinner with a plumber." He opened the dark green door.

Bonnie swept past him. "I'll try not to let down the profession."

He grinned at that, but she didn't see it.

They walked into a smallish room. Three ficus trees strung with white lights stood by a podium and served as a makeshift foyer.

He gave his name to a teenage boy in an oversize white

shirt who sat on a stool behind the podium. The boy put down a schoolbook and took them past a lovely empty table by the window to one smack-dab in the middle of the room.

Great. They'd be on display. Jaron started to ask if they could be seated by the window, but it occurred to him that if they were so visible, it might keep future disagreements from escalating. Bonnie looked like a shouter. Come to think of it, so did the burly redheaded man at one of the window tables. He and the older man seated with him were talking in low, but intense, voices. Perhaps this was the better location, after all.

As the boy seated Bonnie, Jaron glanced at the other tables. Each had a white cloth and napkins, which was good. Jaron wasn't into red-and-white-checked oilcloth, straw-covered Chianti bottles as candlesticks, and Italian flags stuck into cheap bud vases. There couldn't be more than a dozen tables in the place, and only a third were occupied.

No one paid the slightest bit of attention to them. Other than the two men at the window table, there was only a young couple holding hands in the corner and a party of four laughing and talking rapidly in Italian.

It was on the early side for dinner, but not *that* early. The place should be hopping.

Well, if Lorenzo's was as good as he'd heard, by the time he wrote about them, they'd cram another five tables into the room and still be full every evening.

"Pellegrino *con gas, per favore*," Jaron said to the boy, and a bottle of water appeared almost instantly, along with the menu. Excellent.

"Shouldn't you be taking notes?" Bonnie asked dryly. She'd been silent ever since they'd walked in the door.

"I generally don't when I'm entertaining a guest."

"Entertaining? Oh, please. We are so beyond that. Take your notes. Then at least the evening won't be a total loss for you."

All righty, then. Jaron withdrew a leather-covered notebook from his breast pocket. "And the evening isn't a total loss."

"How do you figure?"

Jaron glanced past her and quickly counted the tables. Twelve, just as he'd thought. "Your aunt and my mother would have kept after us to go out together. Now we've done so and they'll leave us alone."

"Yeah, right." Bonnie rolled her eyes.

"You're leaving for home this weekend, aren't you?"

She nodded.

"Problem solved." At least temporarily. "Now, tell me your first impression when you walked in the door."

She lifted a shoulder and allowed the change of subject. "White tablecloths and dark wooden floors. Garlic. I'm guessing it's a two-, maybe three-dollar-signs place."

He smiled as he scribbled a possible lead for his column. "Just for you, I'll try to work that in."

She fingered the red flower set between two votive candles. "The carnation is real."

"Good."

"Yeah. At Tubb's Café back home, they use plastic flowers that get all dusty. It's really gross."

Tubb's Café. Plastic flowers. What must the kitchen be like? "You actually eat there?"

"Sure. The food's okay, and there's not a lot of choice in Cooper's Corner."

Jaron made a mental note to avoid Cooper's Corner as a waiter brought focaccia and drizzled herbed olive oil on a plate, then presented him with the wine list.

Jaron glanced over the card. Lorenzo's offered a small

selection of Italian wines, with a few very reasonably priced, most in the moderate range, and a couple for *very* special occasions. Smart. "Would you care for wine?"

"Definitely."

He made eye contact with their waiter, who'd been unobtrusively standing by. "Do you have a preference?" he asked Bonnie.

"Large."

He'd meant red or white. "A bottle of the Leverano and a big gulp for the lady."

"Pardon?" The waiter bent forward slightly.

"Never mind, he's making a joke," Bonnie said to him. Jaron nodded and the man took off.

Bonnie gave Jaron a scathing look, opened the menu, then closed it almost immediately.

"I know you said you weren't hungry, but please order something. To be fair, I need a good sampling."

"I am ordering. I've already made up my mind."

Jaron looked at the modest menu. One side held the usual Italian offerings, but the other was a handwritten description of the day's specials. That meant half the menu changed daily according to what the chef had found at market. Jaron began to suspect the reason for the raves he'd heard about the place. "How can you possibly have read the menu and decided that quickly?"

"I want spaghetti and meatballs. I was just making sure they had it here."

"Did you see the daily specials? There are four different fish dishes, not to mention the lamb. And the Veal St. Francis—"

"You eat veal?" She looked horrified.

"You'd order spaghetti and meatballs when you could have anything from Crab Claws Venetian to prosciutto with melon and figs?"

"I like spaghetti."

"You might like one of the other dishes."

"Or not."

"But...spaghetti?"

"*With* meatballs. It's an extra charge. I didn't think you'd mind."

"You can have spaghetti anywhere."

"And I do." Her lips thinned. "Consider me a spaghetti-and-meatballs expert. It'll be the control dish. If they cook the basics well, then think what they'll do with the fancy stuff."

She had a point. A very valid point. He hated when that happened. He should admit as much, but didn't have it in him.

"You aren't one for culinary adventures, are you?" He scanned the entrées and was tempted to order more than one.

"I don't see the point."

"You don't see the point?" He was astounded.

She shook her head.

"You might find something you like better. What if you'd never tasted spaghetti and meatballs?"

"I didn't see fried chicken on the menu."

Bonnie's intrigue factor plunged. Jaron ordered two appetizers and the sea bass with capers—not really an Italian dish, but he wanted to see what the chef did with it. He ordered the calamari because he thought it would be amusing to see if he could get Bonnie to try some, then watch her face as he told her she'd eaten squid.

At that moment, their waiter appeared bearing a bottle of one of the expensive wines, which Jaron hadn't ordered. "I asked for—"

"Compliments of the gentleman by the window."

Jaron looked over, and the older companion of the gruff redheaded man inclined his head. Jaron did likewise.

Showing more deference than before, the waiter poured the wine. Jaron raised his glass to the man, then sipped the wine. Ah. *This* was worth the entire evening. The wine caressed his tongue as he swallowed, leaving oaky memories in its wake. Jaron closed his eyes and savored another sip.

"Does this happen to you often?" Bonnie's question interrupted the words of praise Jaron was mentally composing for his column.

"More often than not," he admitted.

She looked over her shoulder. "Who is he?"

Jaron shook his head. "I don't know. Maybe the owner, or more likely, just a fan."

"Or maybe it's somebody you insulted in one of your columns and the wine is poisoned. That's what *I'd* do."

Jaron blinked.

"Kidding," she murmured, and lifted her glass.

He sat back and regarded her as she sipped her wine. "Good," she pronounced, though he wasn't sure her opinion—the opinion of someone who ate at Tubb's Café—carried much weight.

On the other hand, the wine—a nice strong red—*was* good. Better than good. Sublime. Reminiscent of the rolling hills of Tuscany, where its grapes had been gently crushed by the feet of virgins....

"Have you ever been to Italy?" he asked Bonnie, already guessing the answer.

She shook her head.

"So your lack of culinary adventurousness extends to other areas of your life, as well?"

Wincing, she asked, "Do you get paid by the word, or something?"

How could this woman be related by blood to the elegant Cokie? Jaron spoke very slowly, gesturing with his hands. "You no likee travel?"

Bonnie gave a short laugh. "I haven't traveled much, no. I'm not really interested."

"How can you not be interested? Aren't you curious about other countries?"

"Well…it isn't like I don't know anything about them. I mean, I've been to Disney World."

For the life of him, Jaron could make no response.

"You know—Epcot? The nations exhibit? World something-or-another?"

"You've got to be kidding."

She grinned. "Yeah."

Jaron took a sip—actually, a large swallow, which was not at all fair to the wine.

"Except I really don't have any desire to travel," Bonnie continued. "I like coming to New York, though. Everything seems to be here."

"As much as I agree with you, I have to admit that the rest of the world has much to offer."

"So what am I missing?"

Everything. "Well…art, for one thing."

"I've been to the museums here."

"But…but…the *Mona Lisa.* It's in France."

"Is there anyone on earth who can't draw the thing from memory?"

"But to see it in person…" How could he explain? "The brush strokes, the nuances of color…"

Bonnie tore off a piece of foccacia and dipped it in the oil. "Isn't the painting behind Plexiglas—roped off and everything? Just how personal is that?" She eyed him as she bit into the bread.

Infuriating woman. "All right, not the *Mona Lisa.*"

He'd been trying for something she might recognize. "There are a lot of other artists." Jaron tore off a hunk of bread for himself. He usually skipped the bread. Look what she'd done to him. "There is just something about, say, being in Madrid at the Prado and looking at the work of El Greco."

Bonnie swallowed. "Isn't he the guy who paints the gray people with long faces?"

"He has a certain recognizable style, yes." Jaron refilled his wineglass. Look at this—already on his second glass and the appetizers hadn't even arrived.

"All his paintings look alike." Bonnie demolished more bread.

"They do not. How can you say that?"

"Because he used the same models for most of his work."

Jaron narrowed his eyes.

"Hey—I'm not stupid. I'm just not interested."

"Not interested in travel or art." Jaron drew a deep breath. "I am. In fact, those are two of my favorite activities."

"What's another?"

"The theater."

"Hmm. Both plays Aunt Cokie took me to were boring. I mean, I understand about using my imagination, but in this one play, there were two chairs on the stage. That's it. The actors mimed everything else, and I'm sorry, but it just didn't work for me. And then there's the way they talk—nobody really talks that way."

That was it. Absolutely it. For a while he'd thought there was the slimmest possibility of finding something in common with her, but no.

"So what *are* you interested in?" he asked.

"I like hiking," Bonnie offered. The bread plate was empty. "Do you?"

"No." Jaron couldn't think of another woman of his acquaintance who'd eat that much bread—or any bread.

"Cross-country skiing?"

"No. I do a little downhill."

"At the right resort, naturally."

"I'm not sure what you mean by the 'right' resort."

"One you'd write about in your column."

Jaron spread his hands. "Everything is grist for the mill."

Her face froze and she stared at him.

"What?"

"Don't you dare write about me."

"It hadn't occurred—"

"Then it will. You'll be sitting in front of your computer and you won't be able to resist a little dig about the country bumpkin in the big city. It'll be one of those gauche–tourists–contaminating–New York bits."

"Not a bad idea." The calamari arrived, along with an eggplant dish. Good. The wine was giving him a buzz he was afraid would loosen his tongue.

"Don't you dare."

"What?" Jaron was making a note about the length of time from order to first course.

"Write about tonight."

"I wouldn't use your name." He picked up one of the fried rings and popped it into his mouth. Hot and crispy.

"Aunt Cokie and your mother would know, and how do you think that would make them feel?"

"I could disguise it." He ate another calamari ring and nudged the plate toward her. "Try one."

"No, thank you."

Jaron looked from the plate to Bonnie. "Tell you what.

You try this one new food, and I'll promise not to mention you in my column.''

"Jerk."

"I'm trying to broaden your horizons."

"You're trying to make me eat squid."

"You might like it."

"I don't *think* so. If God had intended for us to eat squid, he would have made it say 'moo.'''

She wouldn't try the eggplant, either.

When her spaghetti and meatballs arrived, she pronounced them outstanding and did let him try a bite. They were good—as good as spaghetti and meatballs can get— but not worthy of the raptures she went into over the meatballs. Were meatballs ever worthy of rapture?

"There's no filler in these babies," she said knowingly. "Write that down."

As Jaron dutifully paraphrased, there was an exclamation from the table by the window.

"I tell you, the man's not gay!"

"Sonny—"

"He's a slimy little weasel, and I'll see him in hell!" Standing, the redheaded man dragged the napkin from his collar, threw it on the table and stormed out.

Bonnie raised her eyebrows.

There was an unnatural hush. "My apologies," said the older man, a hint of an Irish lilt in his voice. "More wine?" he asked Jaron.

"No, thank you. It's wonderful."

The man nodded his acknowledgement. "Enjoy it as I enjoy your work."

"Don't forget to mention the floor show in your column," Bonnie murmured.

"Shh!"

Unfortunately, after the blowup, their dinner conversation had more duds than a string of wet firecrackers.

Bonnie didn't like foreign films—big surprise—fashion or cooking—another big surprise.

He didn't like camping—just the thought made him shudder—flea markets, or pretty much anything on television.

To her, wines were red, white or bubbling.

To him, wines were…well, they were really important, damn it.

The two of them had nothing in common.

But they'd known that. The surprise was that his mother and Cokie hadn't.

Still, he and Bonnie had made a valiant effort, and rewarded themselves by skipping dessert and coffee.

Jaron glanced over the bill, then put his credit card in the folder. "Well, Bonnie, it's been…"

"Interesting," she suggested.

"Yes. It has." Everyone needed a little character-building experience now and then.

"Even better, we got through the evening without killing each other."

"Always a plus."

The waiter returned with the credit card receipt. Jaron figured the tip and scrawled his name, half expecting the chef or the owner to appear. Or both. If he hadn't previously been recognized, his name on the credit card usually tipped off the management. But other than the man at the window, it appeared he wasn't known to them.

Standing, Jaron glanced around.

"Looking for someone?" Bonnie asked.

"I did want to speak with the owner, but I'll come back another time."

"Nonsense. You're here now. I don't mind waiting."

Jaron glanced at his watch. "I don't think there's time." He gestured for her to precede him to the door, nodding to his fan on the way out. "I promised I'd catch a band that's playing at a club not too far from here." Hell. Now he'd have to invite her. As he opened the door for her, he injected his voice with as much enthusiasm as he could. "You game?"

"Jaron, you are too darn polite." Bonnie sighed. "We tried. Let's just call it an evening."

Relief washed over him as they stepped onto the sidewalk under the awning. Yes, it was past time for the evening to end. He'd had enough of Bonnie and he was sure she'd had enough of him.

A lone woman, attractively middle-aged, passed them and entered the restaurant. It was the first customer he'd seen enter since he and Bonnie had arrived. Well, that would soon change. The place was an undiscovered treasure.

"Go on to the club and hear the band," Bonnie told him. "The driver can take me back. I don't mind. Truly."

Good manners warred with expediency. "Cokie would never forgive me if I didn't escort her niece home."

"Cokie won't know—she'll still be playing bridge. Please. Go."

He looked down at Bonnie, tempted to do as she asked. It was nice of her to offer to go home alone. She could be very attractive when she was being nice.

But she wasn't nice often, and he should take advantage while he could. "Thanks." Looking up and down the street, Jaron didn't see their car, but they were running ahead of schedule. He pulled out his cell phone and called the driver. "He'll be a few minutes," he told her.

"You don't have to wait here with me."

"Yes, I do." Having the driver take her home was one

thing, leaving her standing on a street at night was entirely different.

"Pooh. I'm a big girl. I tromp all over New York by myself."

"Indulge me." Not that she would.

She waved an arm. "There are people all over the place. What could happen?"

"This is not Cooper's Corner."

"Right. This is the big, bad city. Just look." She gestured to a man walking toward them carrying a bouquet of red roses. "That's a scary sight."

Jaron noticed the name of the trendy florist on the bouquet sleeve. The flowers had set the guy back a hundred bucks, easy. "I realize you're eager to escape my company, but I'm not giving in on this."

Giving him a direct look, she said, "Oh, you're not so bad. In fact, I'm glad you insisted on dinner."

She was being nice again. That was twice in five minutes. A record. Jaron looked down at her. She wasn't so bad, either—now that their time together was nearing an end. And he could honestly say that he was glad he'd met her. He was debating telling her when he caught sight of their black Town Car turning the corner, and the moment passed.

The tires squealed as their driver completed the turn and sped up.

"Whoa. What did you say to the guy?" Bonnie took a step toward the curb.

"Just that we were ready and waiting out front."

The car careened toward the sidewalk. Jaron took Bonnie's elbow. "Hang on a minute."

She didn't argue with him, which was good because something wasn't right.

The car finally slowed, but not enough to stop in front

of the restaurant. A window lowered and Jaron saw the profile of a man with excruciatingly red hair as the car passed them.

"Hey! That's the guy from the restaurant!" Bonnie tugged on Jaron's arm. "What's he doing in your car?"

"That's not our car." Jaron felt his heart give an extra thump as adrenaline spurted through his body a split second before a dark object appeared out the window.

A gun.

He flung himself at Bonnie, pushing her across the sidewalk all the way to the brick wall of the restaurant, where he stood, eyes closed, covering her body with his. She was apparently too stunned to struggle. Two pops sounded and the motor revved. Tires screaming, the car roared around the corner.

Everything had happened so quickly.

Jaron's heart pounded harder than it ever had, and he had to consciously tell himself to breathe. He took several deep breaths while he was at it, then became aware of his body smashed up against Bonnie, who was smashed up against the wall.

It felt kind of good, except that he was disgusted he'd even noticed, considering the circumstances.

"Ouch?" Bonnie's protest was a small sound in the eerie silence.

Jaron took a shaky step back and looked down the street. Less than a dozen yards away, the man who'd been carrying the roses lay on the sidewalk. Blood pooled around his head.

Jaron just stared, not believing what he saw. Things like this happened in movies and on television, not in real life.

"Did somebody throw firecrackers?"

"No." Jaron shifted to the side so Bonnie wouldn't see.

"The car backfired?" Her voice was small and thin.

"No." Jaron drew a monster of a breath and forcibly exhaled. If he didn't watch it, he was going to hyperventilate.

"It…it couldn't have been a gun. Guns are loud. That was…was like popcorn." She sounded wobbly. And with good reason.

"Bonnie—"

"Can you move a little?" She touched her hair. "I hit my head."

Jaron stepped back, careful to block her line of vision. He was still a little wobbly himself. Bonnie's face was white and he had a feeling he didn't look any too great, either.

He gently moved her unprotesting fingers aside and found a lump already forming. Her cheek and temple were scraped.

He reached for his handkerchief.

"You carry a handkerchief? I might have known."

"Hold this against your cheek."

"Jaron—"

"Let's go back inside the restaurant."

Distant voices grew louder.

"But, Jaron, what's going on? What happened?"

He was trying to figure out exactly how to tell her when she ducked around him and gasped.

"The rose man! He's—" With an inarticulate cry, Bonnie started running toward the guy.

Jaron snapped out of his daze. "Bonnie, no!" He raced after her and grabbed her arm. She shook off his hand and knelt beside the man.

"Call 911," she ordered, pressing Jaron's handkerchief against the neat little hole in the man's temple. A few curious folk came to see what was going on, took in the situation and retreated inside the other buildings and restaurants. In fact, the foot traffic on the street virtually disappeared. Music grew fainter as the windows of the apartments above were slammed shut.

Jaron had a bad feeling about this. "Bonnie, we have to get out of here."

"Why? The car's gone."

"But it might come back and we don't want to be here when it does. We're witnesses. The man who did this doesn't want to leave any loose ends. And right now, we're as loose as they come."

"Call 911."

"Bonnie. This is one leak you aren't going to be able to fix." Jaron didn't have to check for a pulse to know that the man was dead. "I don't want my cell phone traced. I'll call 911 from a pay phone. *Come on.*"

"No!" she snarled up at him. "I can't believe you can be so heartless."

A faint siren sounded, very gradually getting louder.

"There," he said. "Somebody has already called the police. Let's leave."

"Without talking to the police?" She looked at him as though *he'd* shot the rose guy.

"It's not going to make any difference to him."

"We might help them catch his killer."

"We don't want them to find his killer! From what I know, which isn't much, this looks like a hit, and the only people who do that kind of thing have friends in low places. They are not nice people, Bonnie. You would not find them living in Calico Corners."

"Cooper's Corner."

Lights announced the approach of an emergency vehicle.

"Well, go on if you want to," she told him.

It would serve her right if he did. Instead, Jaron made

a last attempt to drag Bonnie away from the body. He literally seized her shoulders and pulled. She turned her head and opened her mouth.

"You bit me!" More surprised than hurt, Jaron dropped her, and Bonnie scrambled to resume her vigil by the dead man as a police cruiser zoomed toward them. "Oh, hell."

"I am *so* sorry you're feeling inconvenienced."

"Bonnie, I just hope we survive long enough to be inconvenienced."

CHAPTER FOUR

"I CAN'T GET OVER how much the police station looks like it does on TV." Bonnie's voice sounded loud in the bare interrogation room.

Without moving his head, Jaron rolled his eyes her way, then went back to staring at a crack in the gray-green plaster wall.

He'd been doing that for a while now, she realized.

He hadn't said much since the police cruiser had arrived at the restaurant and she'd babbled their story to the two officers who'd emerged.

That had been the first time she'd told the story. There had been three other times, and Bonnie was no longer babbling. In fact, she could barely remember what she'd said.

She was sure Jaron could remember everything *he'd* said because he'd said so little—at least in her presence. At first, they'd been separated for a time, presumably to make sure their stories matched. She'd told her story to a man and a woman. Then they'd asked questions. Then she'd had to tell it all over again to another man. And he'd asked more questions—or, rather, the same questions once more. And if Bonnie didn't answer exactly the same way she had previously, there were even more questions.

And that was another thing. It was nearly midnight and she was tired. The way she and Jaron had been treated, a person would have thought *they'd* shot that poor man.

Bonnie shuddered.

"Are you cold?"

Not as cold as your voice. "Just from sitting so long."

Jaron didn't look at her as he spoke. "Get up and walk around our cell—excuse me, interrogation room."

He was angry with her. Well, tough. Citizens had a duty, though Bonnie wasn't quite as patriotically gung ho as she'd been a couple of hours ago.

She'd expected to have to "come to the station and make a statement." Everyone who'd ever watched any police action in a movie expected that. What she hadn't expected was to be shoved, along with Jaron, into a smelly police car with sticky seats and left to sit for more than half an hour.

All the blinking vehicles—eventually there were three police cars and an ambulance—had drawn people out of the buildings. They'd stared at her and Jaron sitting in the police car. Bonnie had wanted to make sure they knew she and Jaron weren't suspects, but the police wouldn't let anyone near the car. And with Jaron slumping down and concealing his face with his hand, they'd looked really guilty.

They'd been brought here, to the Fifth Precinct on Elizabeth, and questioned by people with unsmiling faces and hard eyes.

Bonnie was getting nervous and could have used a little reassurance from Jaron. "You know, you don't have to be so grumpy about this. At least you'll have plenty of material for your column."

"You know, I didn't take you for an airhead." Jaron shifted on the metal folding chair. "Hasn't it occurred to you to wonder why we're still here?"

Bonnie bristled. "I assumed that either the paperwork was taking awhile, or they were trying to find that red-haired man for us to pick out of a lineup." When Jaron rolled his eyes, she added, "Or the news media has discovered that you're here and a crowd of paparazzi is blocking the door."

"Or maybe, just maybe, the guy who was killed or the guy who did the killing is somebody big."

"No, duh. That redheaded guy must have weighed close to three hundred pounds—oh, stop looking at me that way. I know what you meant. I'm just scared," she admitted.

"Bonnie, I'm not scared. I'm terrified." And Jaron went back to studying the crack in the plaster.

Well. That wasn't quite the reassurance she'd hoped for.

She slid a glance his way and was caught by the expression on his face. Blank. No, that wasn't right. It had a lack of the seen-it-all cynicism and made him look like a younger version of himself. She had a fanciful thought that she was seeing the man behind Jaron Darke.

"Why are you staring at me?" In an instant Jaron Darke had returned.

Bonnie didn't know if she was sorry or not. "You said you were scared."

"I said I was terrified."

The door opened and a heavyset man with a gravelly voice spoke. "It's good to know I don't have to convince you two that we've got a serious situation here." He strode forward, trailing underlings in his wake. "I'm Captain Frank Quigg with the detective unit," he announced when he reached the table. He jabbed a thumb behind him. "Detectives Slade and Falco."

Slade—or was it Falco?—positioned himself by the door. What? Did he think they'd try to escape? Falco—or maybe Slade—sat at the table and stared silently at them. He wore an earpiece and occasionally got a vacant expression that Bonnie guessed meant he was listening to something.

And speaking of listening... "You—how did you know...? Is there a microphone in here? Have you been eavesdropping on us?"

Captain Quigg gave her an incredulous look as he dumped files and binders on the table and dragged out a chair. "Of course."

"She's from out of town," Jaron said.

"Ah." Propping both hands on the table, Quigg lowered himself onto the chair. "I do apologize for keeping you two waiting."

Bonnie was mollified somewhat, even though he didn't sound particularly sorry.

"I've got some pictures for you to look at." Opening one of the file folders, he tossed photos on the table as though dealing a hand of cards.

Bonnie gasped. "It's the red-haired man!" She recognized him even though the pictures were in black-and-white.

Captain Quigg looked at Jaron.

Reluctantly, Jaron turned in his chair and picked up the mug shot. He stared at it, then picked up another shot of two men walking along a street.

"Jaron—"

Quigg interrupted her with a raised hand. "Not so sure, are you?"

Closing his eyes, Jaron exhaled heavily. "I'm sure. I just don't want to be."

"In your situation, I wouldn't want to be, either." Quigg gathered up the photos, then tossed some more at them.

Both Jaron and Bonnie shook their heads.

Quigg tried again. Bonnie figured she was staring at major riffraff. She shook her head again.

"How about him?"

It was a fax of a driver's license photograph. The dark-haired man looked vaguely familiar. "I don't know," Bonnie said.

Jaron snorted. "May I?" He gestured for a pen. Quigg handed it to him and Jaron drew a small, dark circle on the left side of the head.

"Oh." Bonnie covered her hand with her mouth.

"Who was he?" Jaron asked.

"Maurice Fenister."

"Was he a criminal?" Bonnie asked.

"He was an interior decorator."

"Same thing," Jaron said.

"Jaron!"

"I know the name. He never met a chintz he didn't like."

Quigg tapped the picture. "This one's got us puzzled. The man you've identified as the shooter—"

"Neither of us saw the actual shooting," Jaron pointed out.

"No, but you saw a man with a gun, you sensed danger and ran for cover. And the man you have identified is Sonny O'Brien."

The name meant nothing to Bonnie. She looked at Jaron, who shook his head.

"We've linked him to the McDormand clan. Irish mafia, if you will."

"I knew it." Jaron rubbed his forehead with both hands.

"Now, what's so strange here is that Sonny is above doing actual hits. And he's certainly rusty if he left you two standing there."

Bonnie felt the chill of the room seep into her bones. She'd been shaken when Jaron had pushed her up against the wall, but everything had seemed unreal. Even after two hours in the police station, she felt distanced from what was happening.

Now she felt it. Now she understood why Jaron had been so tight-lipped.

And why he'd tried to drag her away.

Quigg was talking. "My best guess is that Sonny got a little hotheaded and this is an old-fashioned crime of passion." His lips curved and Bonnie realized he was attempting to smile. "Sonny must have really hated chintz."

"I know exactly how he feels," Jaron said.

Quigg consulted some notes. "You say that you first saw Sonny O'Brien in Lorenzo's Restaurant and that he was dining with another man."

"The other man sent Jaron a bottle of wine."

Quigg raised his bushy gray eyebrows and Jaron gave Bonnie a long-suffering look.

"I have no idea who the man is," Jaron told Quigg.

"Let's see if he's in the family album." He took one of the binders, opened it and turned it around to face them.

Bonnie glanced at the other binders and knew she wasn't getting back to her aunt Cokie's for a long time yet.

They flipped through the first binder, which had page after plastic page of surveillance photos and mug shots, and two more binders just like it, without seeing the man who'd sent Jaron the wine.

"Must not have been a family member," Quigg said with audible disappointment. He stacked the binders and stared at them, tapping his fingers against the tops. Blowing out his cheeks, he exhaled, then looked toward the detective with the earpiece. "Get me a photo of McDormand."

"There's just the one," the detective said.

"So go get it." From the look he gave the younger man,

Bonnie figured that Captain Quigg wasn't used to being questioned.

"Are we nearly finished?" she asked. "I don't know anything else."

"We didn't know that much to start with," Jaron said.

Quigg gave him a look. "You know enough."

The detective returned to the room with a file folder and handed it to Quigg.

Quigg opened the folder and extracted a photograph. There was only one other piece of paper in the file. "Saint Patrick's Day three years ago." He carefully placed the photo on the table, turned it around and slid it toward them.

The man, wearing a green bowler with a shamrock in the hat band, was getting into a car. He'd glanced toward the photographer, a look of irritation on his face.

The picture had been enlarged and wasn't clear, but Bonnie recognized the man from the restaurant.

Jaron groaned and thunked his head on the table. "Why me?"

Quigg tensed and leaned forward. "You've seen this man?"

Bonnie nodded. "He was the man at the table with the other man."

"You mean Sonny?"

"Yes, she means Sonny!" Jaron snapped.

"Are you sure?"

"She's sure. *I'm* sure." Jaron shoved the picture back across the table. "We're dead."

"We'll try to make very sure that won't happen." Quigg smiled, creasing new lines in his seasoned face. "This was worth missing the end of *Law and Order*."

"Why? Who is that man?" Bonnie asked.

Still smiling, Quigg nodded to the detectives, who

melted from the room. "Seamus McDormand, head of the McDormand crime ring."

Bonnie's jaw dropped. She'd eaten spaghetti and meatballs just feet away from...from... "But he sent Jaron wine! He's a fan of Jaron's—Jaron writes a column."

Jaron moaned.

"We know," Quigg told her, and gathered the binders and files. "And unfortunately, so does McDormand. You say he was sitting at the table in the restaurant when you two left?"

"Yes!" Flinging up his arms, Jaron pushed himself out of the chair. "Yes, he was still there. Yes, we waited for my car right in front of the window, where he no doubt saw us. And he probably saw as I played hero and flung myself at Bonnie—which I will point out for the record she has yet to thank me for—and then, if he'd bothered to hang around, he saw Bonnie run toward the body...oh, God." Jaron ran out of steam and slumped back onto the chair.

Bonnie gasped. "You don't think he'd come after *us,* do you?"

Jaron made an elaborate show of checking his watch. "Look at that. She's finally connected all the dots and it's only taken her three hours."

"She *is* from out of town," Quigg said.

"And I have had enough of New York, thank you very much." Bonnie had had enough of everything at this point. She stood and picked up her purse—which had been searched earlier. "Goodbye."

As she walked toward the door, she half expected Jaron or Quigg to stop her, but they didn't.

That could have been because the door was locked. "The door is locked," she said without turning around.

"She's from *very* far out of town," Jaron said.

Bonnie marched back to the table. "Why are we being treated like prisoners? We have cooperated fully. You have everything you need to know and I want to go home—or back to my aunt's apartment, then home. And I want to go *now*."

"No can do." Quigg didn't look sorry, either.

What was it with men ignoring her requests all of a sudden?

"You're going to be guests of the city of New York tonight. Maybe several nights."

Oh, no, she wasn't. "Nice try, but just call me a cab and I'll consider us even."

Quigg laughed.

Jaron looked at her pityingly.

The door opened and one of the detective duo stuck his head in. "One bed or two?"

Quigg glanced at them. "Two. Did you really have to ask?"

The detective held up two fingers to someone, then nodded at the captain. "All set."

"Good work." Quigg was once more all business. "Okay, listen up."

Bonnie listened, but she didn't like what she heard. "You've got to be kidding." She'd said it before and she'd probably say it again. Captain Quigg actually wanted to keep them in protective custody.

"For how long?" she asked. "I've got a renovation I'm due to start on Monday."

"As long as it takes."

"You've got to be kidding."

"No, Bonnie, he's not kidding, so you can stop saying that."

Bonnie ignored Jaron. He'd done nothing but glare at her and make derisive remarks for hours. Well, she was *glad* she'd seen this side of him. Yes, Jaron had now revealed himself in all his sarcastic glory. Her first impression of him had been right on the money. Oh, for a time there during dinner she'd thought he wasn't so bad. Rub away that cool exterior and there was a gleam of an attractive man beneath. Actually, the man on the outside wasn't too bad, but she was going to ignore that. She would have even been willing to tolerate another date if Aunt Cokie had insisted on it, but not now. Uh-uh. No way. The sooner she got away from him, the better.

And then the Cooper's Corner blind-date queen was going to turn in her crown.

"So how long *do* you think it'll be until we're free to go?" Jaron asked.

"We'll need a positive ID on Sonny O'Brien. But first we've got to find him. And until then, we're going to keep you two under lock and key."

"*We* are not the criminals here!" Bonnie couldn't believe this was happening. "You can't do that."

"I can and I will." Quigg laced his fingers together and leaned forward, looking up from under those bushy brows. His voice was deadly earnest. "We have been after McDormand for years—even before we knew who he was. Before we knew he existed. You've seen our only picture. The man is like a ghost. And now he's slipped up, and you two are the best chance we've ever had of getting to the guy. If you think I will jeopardize that chance, then you are very much mistaken."

"No good deed goes unpunished, eh, Quigg?" Jaron patted Bonnie's chair. "Sit down, Bonnie."

The look he gave her was sympathetic—for him. Bonnie sat just as the door opened and a *very* large, florid-faced man in street clothes entered.

Quigg nodded to him. "Officer Sorenson. How's the diet going?"

"Not so good." Sorenson clutched his belly. "Millie's got me eating cabbage. Tonight it was cabbage rolls with ground turkey. Whoever heard of such a thing? It's unnatural."

"But that's what it's going to take to get you back out on the street. In the meantime, I understand you'd like to get out from behind the desk."

"Yes, Captain." He jerked a thumb toward Bonnie and Jaron. "Are these the two I gotta baby-sit?"

"They are."

Jaron leaned toward her. "Hey, Bonnie, think we can outrun him?"

"I wouldn't advise you to try," Quigg said.

"What's he going to do if we try to escape—shoot us?"

"He'll aim for your leg. Sorenson, how'd you do on your last firearms proficiency test?"

Sorenson shrugged.

Quigg turned back to Jaron. "So he might miss your leg."

Bonnie stared at Quigg. "I don't believe this conversation."

"Then believe this—if we don't shoot you, one of McDormand's men will."

"But...Jaron's a celebrity." That ought to give his ego a lift. "I can understand hiding him, but they don't know who *I* am."

"They can find out."

"Bonnie, your esprit de corps touches me deeply," Jaron drawled.

Oh, that was it. That was just *it*. "You're right, Jaron. What was I thinking? I *should* stick by you night and day for goodness knows how long."

They stared at each other and then Jaron actually smiled. "Thank God you're not boring."

"Did you two used to be married or something?" Sorenson asked.

"No," Bonnie answered.

"God, no," Jaron said, which Bonnie thought was totally unnecessary.

She had a horrible thought. "Is my aunt in danger, then? And I have to call her and tell her what's going on."

Quigg stood. "We'll prepare a statement for you."

"Like I'm a hostage? That's what we are, isn't it? Hostages."

"What kind of statement?" Jaron asked. "Her aunt and my mother are friends, so anything Bonnie says to her aunt will be repeated."

"We need to kept this quiet for now, so we want Bonnie to just say that she's staying with you tonight. Stick to the truth whenever possible."

Bonnie felt her face drain of color, then her cheeks grew warm. "I don't— We just met!"

"Contrary to what you may think, I don't on short acquaintance, either," Jaron said.

"So this time you two hit it off," Quigg said.

"No!" They both spoke at the same time.

"She'd never believe it," Bonnie added.

Jaron made a disgusted sound. "Yes, she would."

Bonnie gaped at him. "What?"

"Cokie and my mother would love it. You know they would."

They *would* love it, Bonnie knew. In fact, Cokie and Nora would be pricing caterers by tomorrow morning.

"You don't want them to worry, do you?" Quigg asked.

Bonnie shook her head.

"Then we'll retrieve Jaron's cell phone and you can

make the call." With that, Quigg headed for the door, gesturing for them to follow.

"Just shoot me now," Jaron muttered.

Bonnie glared at him. "Before this is all over, I just might."

CHAPTER FIVE

JARON HAD NEVER REALIZED that hell was in New Jersey, but here he was, in New Jersey, and he was definitely in hell.

Hell consisted of a tiny World War II vintage hotel room, one bed, one too-short-to-sleep-on love seat, and a two-hundred-fifty-pound policeman with a bad case of gas.

Oh, yes. And Bonnie Cooper. Bonnie "By Gum I'm Going To Do My Civic Duty If It Kills Me" Cooper. And it just might.

If Jaron didn't get to her first.

"We're both supposed to stay *here?*" she exclaimed from the doorway, pretty much echoing his thoughts.

The odor of rancid burritos and sweaty fear hung in the air, though if their experience in the car was anything to go by, Sorenson would clear that up pretty quick.

"The taxpayers, they don't like puttin' folks up at the Waldorf." Sorenson prowled the tiny room, presumably checking for any mobsters who'd managed to follow them, guess their room number and race ahead to lurk in the shadows.

He clicked on the lights and pressed the button on an ancient clock radio. "…have Jennifer, who is in a hotel room with the best man. Her wedding's in twenty-four hours. Should she call it off? You're listening to radio 780 WTKX, the voice of Extreme talk radio in the Big Apple. This is your host, Emma Hart. It's 2:37 a.m." Sorenson checked his watch and shrugged, then clicked the radio off. The clock part said 1:45.

"There's only one bed. We'll need another room." Bonnie still hadn't crossed the doorway.

"There's only one of me," Sorenson said.

But there's enough of you for two. Jaron happened to catch Bonnie's eye and knew she was thinking the same thing. It was a little bonding moment that caught him off guard. He didn't want bonding—he wanted unbonding.

Bonnie dragged her gaze away. "Connecting rooms, then?" She was sounding desperate.

"This is all they've got tonight. Come in and shut the door." Satisfied that they were alone, Sorenson manually locked the door, pulled the desk chair over in front of it, belched and sat heavily. "I got your standard-issue prison toiletry kit right here." He zipped open a duffel bag and tossed them little bags with toothbrushes, toothpaste, soap, a disposable razor and deodorant.

Bonnie looked from her bag to Jaron. Then they both looked at the bed. It was a double—not even a queen.

"You know what? I just don't care anymore." Bonnie sat on the bed and untied the shoes that Jaron and her aunt had disparaged. She pulled them off, then stood and ripped off the spread and got into the bed on the side closest to the wall, which she faced. "Sleep where you like—here, there, anywhere. It's two-thirty in the morning and I'm just too darn tired to care."

Jaron looked from Bonnie's back—she wasn't even taking up half the bed—to Sorenson.

Sorenson leaned over to the table that had the TV remote control device bolted to it, and punched the channels until he found one he liked. The image on the screen started to waver, so he lurched out of the chair, went over to the TV and banged the top. The wavering stopped. He grunted and audibly released another cloud of sulfurous gas. Clutching his belly, he shook his head. "Millie's cabbage rolls. Don't ever eat 'em."

"Thanks for the tip," Jaron said.

Sorenson heaved himself onto the chair and turned the sound down on the TV. "You can sleep easy. I'll be guarding you all night."

Oh, joy. Jaron considered his choices. There was the love seat by Sorenson, there was the floor and there was the bed with Bonnie.

Fumes from Sorenson's latest emission wafted over, making his decision for him.

Slipping off his shoes and jacket, Jaron, fully clothed as Bonnie was, got into the bed, careful to hug the side as she was doing. He didn't know how long it would last, since the mattress dipped in the middle, but he wanted her to see that he was making a good-faith effort.

He pulled the sheet over his shoulder.

Bonnie pulled back. The edge barely covered him, so he tugged. So did she. He held on to his edge until the sheet stretched tautly between them.

"I need more sheet," he said in a deliberately pleasant tone. "Shall I move closer?"

The fabric immediately went slack and he smiled, then drifted off to sleep.

Roaring woke him before dawn, and he roused enough to realize that Sorenson had fallen asleep, head tilted back against the door, and was snoring. The sound even drowned out the television.

Momentarily forgetting where he was, Jaron pulled on the sheet and felt a warm body roll into him.

Lifting himself on an elbow, he saw a sleeping Bonnie on her back, clutching her edge of the sheet. He started to roll her over, then stopped.

The night was cool and the heating hadn't been turned on yet. She was warm and she felt good. Surprisingly good, actually.

Jaron eased back down. She felt very different from Sydney, the last woman he'd had a serious relationship with. Sydney was fashionably thin and clothes looked great on her. In other words, his usual type. He'd liked the way Sydney looked, and if her naked body lacked a certain lushness, he'd gladly accepted the trade-off.

Sydney was always cold and liked to spoon herself next to him. And while he hadn't minded, it wasn't a particularly sensual experience. Not the way it would be with Bonnie, which was not a thought he should be having.

And why was he having that thought? It wasn't the only one, either. He'd had a lot of thoughts about Bonnie. He'd never known a woman to take up so much of his mental energy. Sydney certainly hadn't; even at the end, he'd expended all his negative emotions in his gallery-skewering columns and that had been the end of it.

He didn't even remember what had provoked him— aside from Sydney's infatuation with the work of an artist with execrable taste—and even then Jaron hadn't been roused to the point Bonnie had managed on just a few hours acquaintance.

In other words, she got to him.

Jaron didn't want her getting to him. So she wouldn't.

He consciously relaxed the muscles he'd held taut against her, and her warmth seeped into him. She was soft and round and...

Lush.

The word popped into his mind and, once there, refused to go. He did not want to think of Bonnie Cooper in terms of lushness. Warmth was okay. Soft was okay. But lush, no. Not okay. Because all he really had to go on was the feel of her molded against him, the way the curve of her hip fit into the small of his back. Perfectly. Soft and warm. He didn't need to see anything to know this.

But lush. To be *absolutely* certain of her lushableness—lushability?—he'd have to *see* her body. And since he couldn't see it, he'd have to imagine it, and that way led to disaster.

Because sooner or later he'd have to know whether or not reality matched imagination, and by then it would be too late, because reality would be the two of them in bed together under very different circumstances. Which wasn't going to happen. Never. Ever.

So for now, since he couldn't ignore them, Jaron was going to concentrate on soft and warm.

He eased about a centimeter closer to her, and because he wanted to make sure the sheet was properly covering her, he stretched his arm behind him and smoothed it into place, in the process learning that her curves did indeed indicate a very lush body.... *No!*

He liked sleek, sculpted, straight lines in his world and on his women. Very aesthetic. Lush was...too much. It too easily became overblown. Blowsy. Rubenesque.

That was it. He'd think of art. Fat pink cherubs floating in an aqua sky. Women who looked as though they'd bathed in fettuccine Alfredo.

Her elbow was poking his back. How was he supposed to sleep with her elbow poking him in the back? He reached behind him again and nudged her, hoping she'd roll onto her side.

She barely moved. Jaron pushed—harder this time. Bonnie made an annoyed sound in her sleep and rolled.

Toward him.

She still held the edges of the sheet—stubborn woman. Jaron sat up, pried her fingers off the sheet, tucked it around her shoulders and tried to reclaim as much of his half of the bed as he could. Since Bonnie was now plastered up against him, he abandoned any hope of actually sleeping.

He could feel her warm breath through his shirt. Felt even more of her softness against him.

He decided to take off his shirt because he couldn't stand the thought of having a great big drool spot on his back.

Sitting up, he began unbuttoning his shirt. As he did so, he gazed down at Bonnie in the flickering gray glow of the television set. The light sculpted her cheekbones and lips, especially the full lower one, which thrust out even more in her sleep.

Desire pierced him swiftly, but not altogether unexpectedly. Jaron swallowed, fighting the urge to bend down and take that lower lip into his mouth. He didn't know which bothered him more—the urge, or that he had to fight it.

Ripping off his shirt, he flung it on the floor beside the bed—something he'd never done in his life—and punched the pillow. If she woke up, good.

She didn't, because she was ever contrary, even in her sleep. Jaron sank onto the bed and yanked the sheet. Two seconds later, unable to overcome his innate courtesy, he gently spread part of the sheet over Bonnie.

She sighed in her sleep and settled against him.

Taking off his shirt had been a mistake, because he now felt Bonnie's soft, warm body even better than before. Her warm, soft, *lush* body.

And, so help him, it felt good.

BONNIE WAS NOT ACCUSTOMED to awakening with her face pressed against a bare male back.

She wasn't accustomed to awakening in police protective custody, either, but first she'd deal with the issue of the male back.

It was Jaron's, she knew. How she'd gravitated toward it in the night, she didn't know. It could be because his skin held the faint scent of sandalwood—he probably used some trendy bath soap. But though she mentally scoffed, she had to admit that she liked it.

It sure beat the musty smells in this room.

She was contemplating a move that would take her back to her side of the bed while still feigning sleep, but she was too late. He was already awake. The side of her head felt cool and her sore cheek began to ache a bit as he slowly shifted away from her. He was getting up. Now she really had to pretend to be asleep to preserve what little dignity she could. It wasn't helped by seeing the pink spot on his back that her face had made.

Bonnie clamped her eyes shut and was totally surprised when she felt him tuck the sheet over her shoulder.

It was such a...*nice* thing to do. She didn't associate the word *nice* with Jaron.

Giving in to curiosity, she opened her eyes the tiniest bit when he stood. He bent down to the floor and rose with his shirt, which he shook out and draped over the lamp.

He picked up the plastic toiletry bag and stared at the contents, tilting his body toward the window, where a strip of light cut into the room.

Bonnie opened her eyes more, then involuntarily widened them. Holy cow. Whose body had he stolen? He had muscles. Subtle ones, to be sure—so subtle, she hadn't noticed them beneath his jacket.

She forced herself to close her eyes to slits in case he looked over at her.

She liked construction worker types. Farmer types. Beefier types who worked outside without their shirts. Men who worked with their hands. That was not to say that men of this type came her way very often. She'd already dated or written off the eligible male population of Cooper's Corner by the time she'd finished high school. As for her blind dates, the hunky types didn't go for vacations that consisted of looking at the scenery, antiquing and staying in picturesque B and B's. Hunky types generally didn't go for blind dates at all.

Once upon a time, she'd had a thing for Seth Castleman, the local carpenter—talk about muscles—but that was over long ago. Seth's physique had become her male template.

But Jaron...Jaron was supposed to be skinny and pale and gangly. Jaron wasn't supposed to have *abs*. Or shoulders with defined muscles that moved attractively in the morning light. And arms that looked as though they'd have no trouble throwing a punch or two.

They were fake muscles, she told herself—muscles gained in a gym, not from honest labor. But Bonnie was beginning to think that muscles were muscles and they looked good no matter how they'd been acquired.

He had chest hair. Bonnie tried to tell herself that she liked the smooth-skinned look, and failed, because Jaron had enough chest hair to enhance his torso without invoking the ick factor.

Drat. But she could admit that Jaron looked okay without his shirt. That didn't mean she was *attracted* to him. There was a lot more to attraction than a few muscles and a flat stomach.

Flatter than her stomach, if she wanted to get technical. And if that wasn't an attraction killer, she didn't know what was.

Jaron headed for the bathroom and Bonnie clamped her eyes shut.

And she'd slept with him. She drew in calm, deep breaths....

But along with the mustiness from the ancient mattress, she inhaled the faintest scent of sandalwood.

The sound of the shower was loud enough that Bonnie figured she could pretend to awaken. She made a show of gradually moving and sitting up.

She needn't have bothered. Sorenson was asleep, breathing heavily, his head at an angle that told Bonnie he'd have a crick in his neck today. The TV was still going and one of the morning news shows was on. She didn't know which channel, but she recognized the hosts. The weather report promised the rest of the week would be bright and clear. That should bring out the tourists and make Maureen and Clint happy. They ran the Twin Oaks B and B in Cooper's Corner, and this was their first leaf-peeper season. They were booked throughout the fall, but bad weather brought cancellations, and Bonnie knew they couldn't afford many of those. She moaned softly. She was supposed to start work on Monday to convert the attic to another guest room. And all the fixtures she'd found were back at Aunt Cokie's.

Cokie hadn't answered the phone last night, and Bonnie had left her lying message hurriedly in case her aunt picked up. Fortunately, she hadn't, but Bonnie was going to have to talk with her sometime and she wasn't looking forward to it.

She wasn't looking forward to facing Jaron, either. But he didn't have to know that she knew how much of the bed she'd hogged last night.

Speaking of which... Bonnie swung her legs out of the bed and got up, then immediately made it. She wasn't a neatness freak or anything, but it seemed better to cover the scene of her crime.

The shower stopped as Bonnie smoothed the spread into place. She hoped Jaron didn't linger in the bathroom, and she hoped Sorenson planned to take them somewhere for breakfast. Or coffee. She'd settle for coffee. Even black. Bonnie wasn't a heavy coffee drinker, but she wanted it in the morning as fast as she could get it.

Now would be a good time.

With nothing to do, she sat on the bed and watched the TV. She watched short vignettes on cooking, stain removal, a new movie, a new novel and a Hollywood divorce. She watched the weather again, after which came the local news. And she watched that.

There had been a murder in Little Italy. *And we were there last night,* she thought. A couple of beats went by before she realized the newscasters were talking about *their* murder, the one she and Jaron had seen—nearly seen. Close enough.

She leaped off the bed and pounded on the bathroom door.

"Jaron! Our murder is on TV!"

With a snort, Sorenson awoke. "Police! Nobody move!" He patted himself, searching for his weapon.

Jaron came barreling out of the bathroom, face lathered, thin, short towel wrapped around his waist. "What's—" He stopped and gathered his towel tighter.

Bonnie pretended not to notice—a good trick, since it was a *very* short towel—and pointed to the TV.

There was a picture of Maurice Fenister and then a clip of the crime scene. People were gathered around and there were the usual man-on-the-street interviews where folks who spoke with double negatives expressed their surprise that such a thing could happen in their neighborhood.

The camera panned the area as the ambulance pulled

away, and then zoomed in on a police car. Bonnie gasped. "That's us!"

There was her white face, pressed up against the window of the car. The picture cut to another angle and zoomed in through the back on Jaron, who had turned his face from the side window leaving his recognizable profile available for the telephoto lenses.

The reporter spoke. "Police will neither confirm nor deny that columnist Jaron Darke and a companion witnessed…"

"Did you hear that?" Jaron demanded. "Don't the police have any connections with the media to prevent that sort of speculative reporting?"

"Well, there is that pesky first amendment dealing with freedom of the press." Bonnie paused. "And aren't you a member of that same press?"

"I'm print. We have standards."

Sorenson shook his head. "Captain isn't gonna like this."

"I don't like it much myself." Jaron stormed back into the bathroom.

"It's time for me to call in, anyway." Sorenson heaved himself out of the chair and rubbed his neck.

"After that, I'm going to have to call my aunt," Bonnie said. "And Jaron will want to call his mother."

"I don't know…."

"Ask. And also—coffee?"

"My relief will bring it."

"Tell him to hurry."

The bathroom door opened then and Jaron emerged, fully dressed. Bonnie had to acknowledge a pang of disappointment, though now that she knew what was under the loose-fitting shirt…. It made no difference. None. He could be Hercules for all she cared.

He was fastening his cuffs, and jerked his head toward the bathroom. "All yours."

Bonnie found her toiletry kit. "Keep the pressure on for coffee."

"How do you take yours?"

"With milk, but I'll settle for anything."

"Gotcha."

He didn't meet her eyes. Instead he seemed to be staring at her mouth as though lip-reading. Was he embarrassed? Jaron? Hardly.

JARON WAITED UNTIL he heard the shower start, then strode over to Sorenson. "You are going to get us a room with two beds—no, make that a two-bedroom suite."

"In this place?" Sorenson chuckled and changed the channel on the TV.

"No, not in this place. In a decent hotel. I don't care if it's in Idaho, but I'm not staying another night in this room." Or another night in the bed with Bonnie.

"We've put in for a room change."

"I want a hotel change. I'll pay the difference myself."

"I don't think you're going to be going anywhere, not with your mug all over the TV."

"If our accommodations are not to my satisfaction, then I will leave."

Sorenson didn't even look at him. "I don't think so."

"What are you going to do—shoot me? Go ahead. I don't much care."

Sorenson regarded him soberly. "There are a lot worse things than spending the night in a bed with her." His eyes rolled in the direction of the bathroom, where Bonnie was still in the shower.

And Jaron was ninety-nine point nine percent certain that she was naked.

BONNIE GINGERLY PATTED her cheek with the rough towel. It wasn't too bad and looked worse than it felt. A bruise that resembled the plum eyeshadow she used to wear—and why had she?—spread underneath her eye.

All in all, she'd looked better.

But that wasn't what was really bothering her. Seeing her face brought home what Jaron had done. *Which I will point out for the record she has yet to thank me for.*

It was true. Bonnie swallowed and gingerly touched her cheek. She was going to have to ask Sorenson for another bandage—and she was going to have to thank Jaron.

Without any trouble, she recalled the feeling of being pressed against the brick of the restaurant, with Jaron's body covering hers. He didn't even like her, yet he hadn't hesitated to try to protect her. True, they weren't the targets, but he hadn't known that.

And he hadn't left her when she'd insisted on staying, either. She'd done the right thing, and the police would have questioned him eventually anyway, but she'd been glad of his steadying presence during those first few minutes.

The phone rang and she started. The thing sounded as though it was in the room with her. Sorenson was talking. Quietly, Bonnie finished drying off and dressed, listening.

It was apparent that Captain Quigg had seen the morning news, and as Sorenson had predicted, he wasn't happy. Big surprise. There was mostly uh-huhing and okay-bossing and sure-thinging from Sorenson.

Bonnie emerged from the bathroom and shot a glance toward Jaron, who was staring out the window, hands shoved into his pockets. He was fully dressed, complete with jacket. Somehow, though, the solid black didn't look as intimidating this morning. Maybe that was because she had a pretty good idea what was under the black.

Sorenson hung up the phone.

"You didn't ask him about the room," Jaron said, without turning around.

"Couldn't work it into the conversation," Sorenson mumbled, rubbing his neck.

Jaron gave him a disgusted look over his shoulder.

"How about coffee? Is it on the way?" With Jaron in an understandably foul mood, Bonnie wanted caffeine fortification before delivering her thanks-for-saving-my-life speech. Though he hadn't actually *saved* her life, the thought had been there.

"Uh...they're shorthanded and I'm gonna have to pull a double shift."

"So relief isn't coming with the coffee," Jaron stated crisply. He strode toward the door. "I'll get it, then."

"No!" Sorenson could really move fast when he was motivated. "I'll get it." Huffing, he jerked open the door. "You two, *stay here*. You don't open the door for anybody but me."

"Aren't you going to give us a secret code word or something?" Bonnie asked.

"Huh?" Sorenson stopped rubbing his neck and stared at her. He could probably use some coffee, too.

"Cabbage roll," Jaron said. "The password is cabbage roll."

Muttering, Sorenson closed the door. "Lock it," he called.

"Like a stiff wind wouldn't blow it down." Nevertheless, Bonnie locked the door.

Jaron walked over to the window. Well, caffeine or not, now was the time.

"Jaron?"

"What?"

Bonnie approached him. "About last night..."

"Ha! What *about* last night?"

"Well...thanks. For pushing me into the wall, I mean."

He was still watching out the window, but she saw him smile. "That sounds really bad."

"Look—you were protecting me and I haven't thanked you, so, thanks."

He turned to her then. Reaching out, he gently touched her cheek. "I may have been too enthusiastic."

Bonnie felt a warmth that had nothing to do with her injury. "You just don't know your own strength." She was thinking of his muscles. She shouldn't have been thinking of his muscles.

"Right." Still smiling, he went back to staring out the window, then straightened. "Bingo." He headed for the door.

"Where are you going? Sorenson said we were to stay here."

"Sorenson just went into the coffee shop down the street. What he doesn't know won't hurt him. But you should stay here."

"I don't want to stay here. It stinks. Where are you going?"

"To bribe the desk clerk for another room."

"So why do I have to stay here?"

Jaron stopped, hand on the doorknob. "Because if I ask for a room with two beds and he sees you, he'll think I'm out of my mind." And then he was gone.

It took Bonnie a few moments to realize that she'd been complimented. Sort of. Was Jaron implying that she was the type that appealed to clerks at seedy hotels? Bonnie took inventory: bruised cheek and rumpled clothes. No makeup. Sleep-crinkled hair. Maybe it wasn't a compliment.

While she waited, she looked at the telephone, tempted

to call her aunt. Sorenson hadn't forbidden her to use the phone, but he hadn't said she could, either.

With Jaron off doing his thing, perhaps Bonnie shouldn't push the boundaries. Because she couldn't think of anything else to do, she took up Jaron's perch by the window and kept a watch for Sorenson.

It appeared they were in the downtown area of somewhere. They'd crossed a bridge last night—maybe two. She didn't know where they were—Brooklyn? That had a bridge, didn't it?

"Hey, Bonnie." There was a tap on the door and Jaron opened it. Oops. She should have locked the door behind him.

Grinning, he crooked a finger at her and disappeared. Bonnie grabbed her purse and followed him. He heard her, turned around and held up a key.

"You got us a different room?"

"Yes, one miraculously became available."

Bonnie followed him to the very last room at the end of the hall, where he was unlocking the door.

"They didn't give us this one because of the fire escape." He indicated the hall window, where a fire escape obstructed the view.

"Well, in case of a fire, wouldn't that be a good thing?"

"In case of someone trying to sneak in, it would be a bad thing. This room isn't 'secure.'" He stepped inside and Bonnie followed him.

"Two beds. Two wonderful, glorious beds." Jaron looked extremely pleased with himself.

"Was I that awful to sleep with?"

He glanced at her. "You stole the sheet."

"I did not!"

"Not once you fell asleep and I could steal it back," Jaron retorted. "Anyway, I like to spread out more."

And she'd crowded him. How embarrassing. Bonnie decided that it was a good time to check the bathroom. Same as the other one, except that the sink was stained with a rusty stripe and the faucet dripped. If there was one thing Bonnie hated, it was a dripping faucet.

"Well, there's something to keep you occupied," Jaron said from behind her.

"I don't have tools with me." Bonnie took one of the washcloths, stuffed it into the faucet and arranged the rest of the cloth so the water would silently run down it and into the drain.

"Is that a plumber trick?"

"Oh, ha, ha."

"Listen." Jaron checked his watch. "I'm going to call my editor. I have a noon deadline I'm going to miss."

"You could dictate your column."

"Sure. If I'd written it already." He stood by the phone. "Would you look at this? It's a rotary. The dark ages." He dialed a number. "Once I get my laptop, I'm going to have to have an Internet connection, and I'd really like my cell back.... Angela? Jaron." His voice dropped. "Yeah." He chuckled. Purred, actually.

Bonnie didn't want to hear him flirt with his editor, or whoever that was. She went over to the window. It was the same third-floor view as their other room, but from a slightly different angle. There was a stone ledge outside the window, blocking out the sidewalk directly beneath, but Bonnie could see traffic and watch for Sorenson to come out of the coffee shop, assuming he hadn't already.

On the phone, Jaron was assuring his editor that he was fine, but that he was going to be involved with the police for a couple of days.

A couple. Right. By now, Bonnie could see that this was going to drag on even after they caught the red-haired man.

Maybe it was because she was thinking of him that Bonnie focused on two men stepping out of a car that was double-parked.

One had red hair. It wasn't their redhead, but something inside Bonnie tightened. "Jaron, come here."

He didn't argue or wait, but was beside her in an instant. "Quick—those two guys coming toward this place…"

"That's not Sonny."

"I know, but…"

They looked at each other. "You've got a bad feeling?" Jaron asked.

Bonnie nodded. "I'm probably being paranoid—"

"Oh, no. I have the utmost respect for hunches." He crossed to the telephone. "Later, Angela."

"What do we do?" Bonnie asked when he hung up the receiver.

"Open the window." Jaron went to the door and opened it a crack.

Bonnie shoved the window up, not liking the implication. The only reason to open a window in the city was to climb out.

They heard knocking on a door down the hall. "Hey, you two, soup's on."

Sorenson. "Do we let him know we're down here?" she asked.

Jaron hesitated.

"Hey!" Sorenson knocked again, this time with his foot. "Lemme in. Uh…cabbage roll."

"He's making too much noise," Jaron murmured. He pulled open the door, then shut it quickly.

Bonnie didn't have to ask why. Jaron quietly locked the door, then ran to the window as shouts erupted. "Let's go."

"Go where?" Bonnie wailed, but Jaron had already stepped out onto the ledge.

CHAPTER SIX

BONNIE GULPED great breaths of air. She could do this. She *had* to do this. She arranged her purse bandolier style across her shoulders and drew one more breath.

She had one leg over the dusty window ledge when Jaron turned toward her.

"Okay, back inside. There's nowhere to go, unless you've got a flying gene I don't know about."

"What are we going to do?" Bonnie was so scared she could hardly think. No, she was being generous. She couldn't think at all.

Jaron closed his eyes briefly. "Fire escape."

They'd have to go out into the hall. "They'll see us."

"We'll have to be quick."

Bonnie's heart was hammering so hard she could barely hear him. Swallowing, she nodded dumbly.

Jaron stared at her a moment, then took hold of her upper arms. Warmth seeped into her muscles. "You can do this. You *will* do this."

He held her gaze with his until Bonnie found herself giving him a quick nod. Amazingly, she felt better. Not great, but better.

Jaron unlocked the door and opened it the slightest crack.

There was a loud crash. "They've kicked in the door."

"Why? It wasn't locked."

"Come on." He touched her arm. "And don't look back."

Naturally, she did, and saw a large lump—Sorenson—and the spilled coffee in the hallway. Was he all right?

"Don't even think it." Jaron used the muscles she'd admired to jerk open the window. "Go!"

And Bonnie went. It was her first time on a fire escape, but she managed okay.

"Hurry!" Jaron urged her.

She was going to have to do better than okay. Blindly climbing down step after step, she prayed her feet wouldn't slip.

"Keep moving. You're doing great."

It sounded as if they were making enough noise to alert the whole building that they were clattering down the old metal stairs. Bonnie zigged, then zagged. Jaron was right above her, and if the circumstances weren't enough to convince her to hurry, the thought of him stepping on her head was. He would, too.

She got to the end. The last section of stairs lowered to the ground and she jumped off. They were in an alley between two buildings, and no one was in sight.

"Move!" Jaron landed beside her, took her arm and propelled her to the wall of the hotel. *Not again,* she thought, bracing herself in time to prevent injury. After listening for a moment, Jaron put on his sunglasses and nodded.

Bonnie started to run down the alley but he grabbed her, then looped his arm around her waist. "Running attracts attention. We're going to stroll to the front of the hotel and then blend in with the crowd."

It was just a few feet, but it seemed like miles. Purely to keep pace with Jaron, Bonnie put her arm around his waist, too. They might have been a couple returning after spending the night together.

Which, in a way, they were.

They strolled past the building next to the hotel, then kept going. Jaron's arm felt like the restraining bar in a roller coaster—padded, but all steel beneath. With every step, Bonnie strained to hear the sounds of pursuit—or gunfire. There were a few people on the street this morning, but not enough for them to be lost in a crowd.

She couldn't stand it. She *had* to know if they'd been discovered.

"Don't look back," Jaron instructed, reading her mind.

"I'm so scared," she whispered, not sure if he'd hear her over the traffic and the street noise.

"Adrenaline is great stuff, though, isn't it? Damn, what a high."

Bonnie actually laughed. "Terrific." She was still breathing hard.

Jaron tightened his arm around her, and for a moment, if she didn't exactly forget about their situation, she was able to ignore it and enjoy the feel of his arm around her waist and his body against hers.

She didn't know why she did, and to be honest, didn't much care. Life was too complicated at the moment. She'd just go with the feelings and worry about the repercussions later. Assuming there *was* a later.

She glanced up at Jaron. Staring straight ahead, his expression determined, he seemed totally focused on making sure there was a later. Who'd have figured he'd be great in a crisis?

They crossed the street with a knot of people. "Do you think Sorenson is okay?" Bonnie asked.

"Yeah."

"Why?"

"Because I didn't hear any gunshots and because he *is* a policeman and because killing police attracts attention they don't need."

"But he wasn't wearing a uniform."

"He didn't have to. Who else would be guarding us?"

Bonnie decided to accept Jaron's reasoning. "What about their car? Is it still double-parked?"

"I don't want to look."

"I do. I want to look." She had to know.

"People who are going about their business don't look over their shoulders while they walk down the street."

"I don't care. I have to know."

Jaron dropped his arm from around her waist. "Okay, then I'll have to kiss you."

"What?" She stopped right in the middle of the sidewalk.

Instead of explaining, Jaron stepped in front of her and lowered his head.

It all happened so fast, Bonnie didn't have a chance to pull back. At least that's what she told herself. It was less complicated that way. Her lips tingled in anticipation.

But pulling away became unnecessary. Jaron's mouth stopped an inch away from hers. Bonnie opened her eyes and found him looking behind her. Oh. It was a ruse. And later—again, assuming there was a later—she'd have to face this completely inappropriate disappointment she felt.

"Are they still there?" she asked.

"Can't tell. Tilt your head."

"Right or left?"

"Right."

She tilted, which brought her even closer to him. He smelled like hotel soap instead of sandalwood. She kind of missed that.

"The car's still there," he said. "Let's boogie."

But he didn't move. Behind the dark glasses he wore, his gaze dropped first to her eyes, then slid to her mouth.

Bonnie's heart, which apparently hadn't been given enough of a workout this morning, started beating faster. And harder.

His lips crooking in a grin that made her stomach do a flip-flop, Jaron kissed her. For real.

In spite of her curiosity, Bonnie admitted that she thought Jaron would be a prissy kisser. Especially since they were in the middle of a sidewalk in downtown…somewhere.

Part of her wanted a prissy kiss, one of those dry-lipped, closed-mouth, pressing-lips-together deals. That would kill this inconvenient attraction she'd developed for Jaron. Considering that he had just rescued her from a nasty situation, well, the attraction was understandable.

And part of her—the man-starved part—was so very, very glad that the kiss wasn't prissy. Not that Jaron was trying to say hello to her tonsils. She should have known he'd have too much class for that. However, this was, indeed, a full-fledged kiss, the kind that established him as a man with certain manly appetites. A man that made her glad she knew how to cook—and had a full pantry.

At the same time, it was not enough to presume— Though, come to think of it, kissing her in the middle of a sidewalk was pretty presumptuous. In fact she should— She should quit thinking and just go with it.

His lips were firm and his beard was not really noticeable, especially since Jaron was doing things with the tip of his tongue that made her lips extra sensitive. This was a man who'd kissed before and enjoyed it.

Bonnie had been kissed before. Heck, she'd even enjoyed it—but that was before she'd learned what enjoyment was.

Jaron tugged her lower lip into his mouth ever so slightly, and her stomach, still dizzy from its recent flip-flop, quivered.

She sighed into him, going all boneless and melting, then felt the vibrations of his chuckle before she heard the sound.

"Like I said, adrenaline's great stuff." Looking self-satisfied, he set her aside.

Well, Bonnie wasn't satisfied. Not at all. When she didn't start walking, Jaron put his arm around her waist again and urged her onward.

She gathered all the scraps of outrage she could—not much, since most of it was on its back, purring. "What did you do that for?"

"I was in the neighborhood and thought I'd drop in."

"So…so you kissed me just because you could? You took advantage of the situation—oh!"

"What?"

Bonnie had been thinking that if he'd taken advantage of that situation, then what other situations—specifically the one where they'd been sleeping together—had he taken advantage of? She eyed him speculatively.

"I wouldn't have kissed you if I hadn't thought you'd enjoy it."

"That's very cavalier of you. Treat the little country hick to some big-city lovin'?"

He glanced down at her. "But you did enjoy it, didn't you?"

Well, yes, but that wasn't the point. Bonnie felt a murderous rage well within her. She was so angry she was seeing beyond red; she was all the way to purple. Jaron didn't know it, but he was in more danger from her than any pursuing thugs.

She stopped walking. She didn't want to be with Jaron

any longer. "Okay, I think we're safe. We'll say goodbye now."

"Why?"

"Because..." Bonnie became aware of her surroundings. She'd conveniently stopped in front of a drugstore with a coffee counter. "Because I'm going to get a cup of coffee."

"Are you completely insane? We're still within sight. We've got to put as much space between us and the bad guys as we can."

As of now, *he* was a bad guy. "You go ahead."

"I will not. If you insist on coffee, then we'll both go in."

"You go somewhere else."

Jaron reached around her and opened the glass door. "I can't believe you."

Bonnie didn't really want coffee—well, she did, but not enough to endanger her life. But Jaron was storming over to the counter, where he stared stonily at the older woman behind it.

She stared back.

"Two coffees to go. You like milk, right?" He tossed the question over his shoulder at Bonnie.

"Yeah."

"We don't offer 'to go.'"

A muscle moved in Jaron's jaw as he gritted his teeth. "Just bring the two coffees, please."

Bonnie edged toward the door. She'd slip out while he was occupied with paying the tab. Beside the door, there was a newspaper vending machine. Bonnie had her hand on the glass door before the front-page story registered. With horror, she saw Jaron's picture blown up three columns wide under the headline Columnist Witnesses Murder.

In the picture, he wore sunglasses, a beard, and was dressed all in black. In other words, he looked exactly the way he did now.

Bonnie raced over to the counter and grabbed his arm. "We've got to get out of here!" she whispered.

"I'm glad you realize it." He slid a five-dollar bill across the counter as the woman put down two cups of coffee.

In Bonnie's opinion, she'd stared at Jaron as though she recognized him. Suddenly everyone in the world was a suspect. "Come *on!*"

"Drink your coffee. I'm not going through this again."

Bonnie poured in as much cream as she could to cool it off, then drained the entire cup. Jaron got in a couple of sips before she jerked on his arm.

"My cha—"

"Leave it." She dragged him to the door and pointed meaningfully to the local New Jersey newspaper displayed in the vending machine window.

"Sh—"

"Take off the glasses."

Jaron ripped them from his eyes as Bonnie pushed through the door.

"You look too much like you," she said. "We have to fix that."

"And just how are we going to do that?"

Bonnie spied a store selling camping gear. "Follow me."

BONNIE WAS QUITE PLEASED with herself. "I think wearing the cap backward is the perfect touch."

"It is so last century," Jaron muttered. "And I hate these shoes." He stuck out a foot encased in a casual athletic walking shoe. "They're too big."

"They change the way you walk. Be glad I haven't put a rock in them. I learned that from the 'Master of Disguises' special on PBS. You see, TV does have some value."

No more than thirty minutes had passed since Bonnie had discovered that Jaron was front-page news. She was now walking down the street with a different person. She wasn't worried that anyone would recognize her—after all, she was wearing the requisite black and blended in with the natives. But Jaron wasn't the type to blend in with anyone.

So while he'd tried on and bought jeans, a T-shirt and a flannel shirt that Bonnie told him to wear unbuttoned, she'd gone back to the drugstore and bought a razor.

Then she'd made him shave off his beard.

He hadn't argued, only grimly disappeared into the store's rest room and emerged clean-shaven.

Bonnie couldn't believe how good he looked without the Jaron Darke trappings. He had a well-shaped jaw. She hadn't ever considered the relative merits of jaw shapes before, but after seeing Jaron's, she knew what a good one was.

They'd also used the ATM machine because Jaron knew that if he wanted to avoid being traced, he wouldn't be able to again. Bonnie wished he could, since he casually withdrew more than she had in her entire account.

Never mind.

"So where are we going?" she asked.

"Down the street." He walked hunched over with his hands in his pockets. His own mother wouldn't recognize him.

"But where?"

He exhaled. "I hadn't got that far. Damn, I wish I had my cell phone, even though it would be risky to use it."

"Who are you going to call?"

"Captain Quigg, I guess."

"Not the police!"

"Why not the police? They'll protect us."

"Well, they've done a lousy job so far! It took the bad guys about six hours to find us at a hotel the police consider safe. Sounds like a leak to me."

"And that would be your specialty."

Bonnie tilted her chin up. "Laugh all you want, but I'm not going back to the police."

Jaron didn't say anything for a few minutes. They turned down the block, now several streets over from the one their hotel was on. "What do you want to do?" he asked finally. "I have to tell you, I know New York, but I don't know New Jersey."

"You can't go back to New York. Even without the goatee, someone will recognize you." Bonnie stepped into the street and hailed a cab. "So you're coming home with me."

"Oh, right. Like they won't look there."

Bonnie climbed into the cab. "Then we'll know about it. That's the beauty of small towns. They thrive on gossip."

"I don't know...." Jaron shook his head.

"I do. Get in."

Looking none too gracious, Jaron climbed into the cab. "This is a bad idea."

"A bad idea is better than no idea. Take us to the train station," she said to the driver.

Bonnie enjoyed being the one in control. So far they'd been in Jaron's world and look what had happened.

Now they were going to her world.

She could hardly wait to find out what would happen there.

FOR TWELVE HOURS, he'd jounced around in buses, trains and taxis. After reluctantly agreeing to go to Cooper's Corner with Bonnie, he'd insisted that they take an indirect route. So they'd been to Atlantic City, Philadelphia and then some town in Massachusetts. At least they were in the right state now. They'd paid cash, and each time Jaron had felt as though he were sinking deeper and deeper into the world of people who operated in the gray areas of the law.

The first ticket agent had met Jaron's eyes as he'd handed over money for their fares. Jaron had actually sweated for a few moments in case the guy recognized him. After that, Bonnie bought their tickets, delighting in the fact that Jaron never knew where they were headed.

The closer they got to her little village, the brighter and happier she became, and the more morose he got. Jaron was not a country person. The country was fine when he was a houseguest for an occasional weekend, but he'd seen way too much of it today.

The last stop was a bed-and-breakfast in New Ashford. They'd wangled a ride on the private shuttle from Pittsfield. It was dark, which appealed to Bonnie, who had taken this business of outwitting the bad guys very seriously. He should be glad, but now he was just tired. "Is this it?" he asked.

"No, this is New Ashford. We're going to Cooper's Corner."

"I was hoping Cooper had a corner here."

"Nope." She walked off.

There was nothing much down the street that he could see. "Where is Cooper's Corner?"

"A couple of miles north of here. We can walk."

Walk? Two miles? At night? In the country? "Bonnie,

wait.'' He jogged to catch up to her. ''Why don't we pay the driver to take us?''

''Jaron! What he doesn't know, he can't tell. Besides, I don't want anyone in town to know I'm back.''

True, but she wasn't the one going hiking in shoes that were too big for her. ''I understand being careful, but we shouldn't go to extremes.''

The lights of New Ashford—and there weren't that many—were already behind them when Bonnie whirled to face him. ''Extreme? I consider being shot at extreme.''

''No one shot at us.''

''They wanted to and that's close enough. Look, Jaron. I'm cold and tired and cranky and in no mood to argue. We're following a bike trail that I've ridden about fifty bajillion times. Just pretend you're on a treadmill at some fancy club and walk!''

She marched off.

Fine. Whatever. They trudged in the eerie silence. Jaron had always found country silence unnatural. The only noise he heard was the occasional car that passed. And the cars never honked. Now *that* was unnatural.

At one point, he saw Bonnie rub her arms, and he dug his black jacket out of the plastic bag with the rest of his clothes. She took it with a gruff, ''Thanks.''

He decided to count that as a conversational opening. ''What's the plan for when we get there? Where do you live?''

''In about thirty seconds, I'll show you.''

They'd been gradually climbing uphill, and now reached the crest where the bike trail curled toward a scenic overlook. Bonnie headed for the railing. Jaron wasn't into scenic overlooks that added extra steps to their journey, but knew better than to argue.

"There." She swept her hand and indicated a small collection of lights.

A very small collection. It looked like someone had taken Monopoly houses and hotels and scattered them in a valley.

"There's the church." Bonnie pointed to the far end. The building was easily the largest structure and had a narrow, sharply pointed steeple. Landscape lighting illuminated the arched windows and the bridge behind it. "And there's Main Street. The big two-story building in the second block is my parents' store. I live in one of the cottages on the street right behind it, next to the village green. The cottages were originally intended to be part of a hotel, but the builder ran out of money in the land bust of the eighties."

Jaron couldn't make out much in the dark, but he'd heard the word *cottage*. That meant small. And Jaron had already done small with Bonnie. He wanted to avoid it again, if at all possible. "Are you planning for us to go there? Won't your neighbors notice?"

She sighed. "No. I rented it out for the leaf season. We're going there." She pointed to a large farmhouse up on a rise overlooking the town. "Twin Oaks Bed and Breakfast. I'm doing a remodel of the attic and I was going to stay there for the next few weeks anyway."

"I'm supposed to hide out in an attic?"

Bonnie gave him a cool look and started back toward the trail. "You can if you want to. Or not. Frankly, I don't care what you do, Jaron."

He was taken aback by her hostility, which was a huge contrast to the softly pleased expression she'd worn when pointing out her picture-postcard village. He caught up with her and pulled abreast instead of walking behind, as he had during most of their nocturnal hike. She walked faster. He did, too. They were practically jogging down the gentle slope.

"Hey." He took hold of her upper arm.

She snatched it back. *"What?"*

"What's this all about?"

"I don't know what you're talking about."

"All day you've been bossy—which I'm willing to think of as 'self-assured'—as well as snippy, prickly and curt to the point of rudeness. There's an all-purpose word that covers that, too."

"And that's the word you use to describe women who are immune to the Jaron Darke charm?"

Jaron stared at her profile. "You're still mad that I kissed you, is that it?"

Bonnie made a noise. "I'd forgotten all about it."

"Shall I remind you?"

He heard her breath whistle between clenched teeth. "That is *such* a lame response. I expected better of you."

"I might say the same."

She stopped and stared up at him, and though her face was softly illuminated by moonlight, her expression said she wanted to strangle him.

"Okay. We need to hash this out if we're going to be cooped up together." She drew a breath. "I don't like being kissed the way you kissed me."

Ha. And they said men didn't understand women.

"Oh, and it wasn't anything technical," she continued. "Your technique is fine."

"Thank you," he said dryly.

"But kissing is more than a technical exercise. It's supposed to mean something. Yours didn't. You don't even like me."

"I do like you." He realized it was true. "Surprises the hell out of me."

She looked down at her toes. "Well, me, too—when you're not being a jerk."

He knew how she felt. He wasn't her type and she wasn't his. But when they weren't annoying each other, each thought the other was okay. The problem was, they were usually annoying each other. They might even be semi-attracted to each other, but that was no doubt due to the circumstances.

And lighting, Jaron thought, as Bonnie raised her head and the moonlight created those magic shadows on her face. "I'm sorry if you felt…"

"Used."

"Ouch. That makes me feel about two inches tall."

"Good. You should." She jerked a thumb over her shoulder. "We're going to go through the fields."

"Wait a minute, we're not through here."

"Why not? You apologized. I accepted. Let's move on." She stepped off the bike trail.

"I want to kiss you again."

She froze, one foot on the trail, one foot off. Without turning around, she said, "I thought I made it clear that I don't go in for meaningless kisses. Or meaningless anything elses, for that matter."

He took a step toward her, encouraged when she didn't start tearing across the field. "This will mean something."

"Something more than assuaging your masculine ego? I don't think so."

"You used 'assuaging' in a sentence. *Very* good." He took another step. "I hardly ever hear that word used in conversation."

"We are not having a conversation!" she said irrationally. But she still hadn't moved.

"Bonnie." One more step and Jaron took hold of her shoulders, slowly turning her around to face him.

"What?" She glared up at him. "You still want to kiss me?"

"I still want to kiss you." A lot, he discovered. He probably shouldn't tell her that. Wouldn't tell her that.

"Why?"

"Because I'm sorry you didn't like the other kiss. I want another chance. And I'm glad to be away from the bad guys. And I'm glad you aren't the type to crumble in a crisis. And you've got quite a mouth on you, which I've discovered I like. You aren't intimidated by me. And..." he drew her closer "...you look damn good standing in the moonlight."

Bonnie hadn't blinked. "Okay."

Ah, victory. He lowered his head as he asked, "And what will your kiss mean?"

"I want to compare how it feels to kiss you without your goatee."

Couldn't leave well enough alone, could he? Jaron mused. Not only was he *not* victorious, he'd lost an important battle. He might have salvaged a little pride by making her admit that she wanted to kiss him, too.

And he would have, if she hadn't stood on her tiptoes just then, bringing her mouth within kissing range. Suddenly, making her admit anything seemed unimportant.

So he kissed her. Not too hard, not too soft. Not too long, not too short. He was aiming for something meaningful, something that conveyed emotion. Mostly the emotion was a we've-been-through-some-major-stuff one, but he was also careful to work in a hint of apology and an echo of the technique she'd admired, if *admired* wasn't too strong a word. Since she'd mentioned his technique, he'd take the compliment.

He most definitely avoided any you-turn-me-on emotions, while still letting her know she was being kissed.

Quite tricky. There was a very narrow line between passionless and passionate.

This morning had been pure adrenaline-fueled desire. He saw, he wanted, he took.

Banked passion. That was the tone he was going for now, though with the feel of her softness against his newly shaved skin, things wouldn't be banked for long.

All in all, Jaron was very proud of this kiss. First, that he was kissing her at all, and second, that he'd figured out what she wanted. Yes, he *was* the man.

It was tough, but he avoided pulling her full lower lip into his mouth. He felt it beneath his lips and mourned the lost opportunity, but virtuously ended the kiss before any passions became "unbanked."

Bonnie blinked up at him.

Look at that. She was dazed and he hadn't even given it fifty percent. How would she respond if he unleashed a full one-hundred-percenter on her? Maybe he'd find out. Not now. He'd make her wait for it. And just when she couldn't stand—

"*That's* the kiss you want me to remember?"

Now *he* blinked. "Yeah. You wanted meaningful."

"That dry little pucker was your idea of an emotional communication?"

"Yes."

"So with you, my choices are hot and meaningless or aridly emotional?"

He was becoming…no, there was no becoming about it. He was seriously annoyed, a familiar emotion where she was concerned.

"Maybe I was wrong about meaningless kisses," she mused. Turning, she stepped off the path and kept walking. "Makes me wonder if I've been wrong about meaningless sex, too."

CHAPTER SEVEN

JARON WATCHED AS BONNIE used her key to open the back door of Twin Oaks Bed and Breakfast. "We'll go up the service stairs."

She sounded very matter-of-fact—"professionally pleasant," he believed, was the tone she used. But he knew she was enjoying this, enjoying being the one who called the shots.

He should never have kissed her—either time. By revealing that he'd regretted hurting her, he'd shown weakness in the face of the enemy. Instead of kissing her, he should have told her to get over it.

As they climbed the two flights of stairs, he kept telling himself the same thing.

Bonnie pushed open the attic door and felt for the light switch. After flipping it on, she stepped into the attic. "Seth's been busy while I've been gone. There was only one light up here when I left. I brought my things and a sleeping bag before I went—oh, Maureen, you sweetie."

Jaron had been only half listening as he looked around what was a partially demolished attic. It was cold in the room, so he shut the door. The light was dim in spite of the extra bulbs strung across the roof beams like mutant Christmas lights.

Bonnie was making cooing sounds, so Jaron turned his attention toward her. In one corner, a quilt was tacked up over the insulation on the walls, with a cot set up in front of it. A piece of blue toile covered a crate on which sat a small Tiffany-style lamp that was hooked up to a yellow extension cord that followed the outer wall until it plugged into a nasty-looking exposed outlet with multiple adapters. Jaron hoped this Seth person knew what he was doing.

When Bonnie turned on the lamp, a small warm pool of red, gold and green light spread over the cot, which was covered with another quilt, and the rag rug next to it. "Look what she did—isn't that sweet?" Bonnie was beaming.

"Very sweet," Jaron agreed, keeping an ear out for suspicious sizzling electrical sounds.

"I was going to sleep on the floor in my sleeping bag. Now you can." She handed him a dark green roll that had been sitting next to a suitcase.

Jaron had slept in sleeping bags before. Sure, they looked cushy, but he knew from experience that his hip and shoulder would be sore by morning.

Well, so what? He should be grateful he was in a safe place that was not in the same room as Sorenson. Jaron did feel safe here and thought he might even be able to sleep tonight. "Could I borrow your rug for some extra padding?"

"Sure. I'll go raid the linen closet for quilts and blankets."

After she left, Jaron dropped the rolled sleeping bag on the floor and sat on it. He was worn-out from being on constant alert. Now that she was in her element, Bonnie looked bright and cheerful. He felt old and creaky.

Why shouldn't she be happy? She had her life back. This was exactly where she'd planned to be, just a couple of days early. In contrast, Jaron's life was blown to bits. A little over twenty-four hours ago, he hadn't even *met*

Bonnie Cooper. Now he was hiding out in a town named after one of her ancestors.

He'd missed his column deadline and had left Angela, his editor, hanging. His mother was probably sick with worry. He visualized her opening the morning newspaper and seeing his picture. His friends would be calling her. His enemies would be gloating.

Not that his picture looked anything like him now. He was wearing plaid, for God's sake. He'd shaved his beard just after he'd paid seventy-five dollars to have it professionally trimmed. He stared at his shoes, then untied the laces. His feet were swollen enough that they weren't flopping around in the shoes anymore, but he had blisters on his heels.

And he'd thought he was in shape. It was too much fresh air, that's what it was. He heard Bonnie's footsteps on the stairs and went to open the door for her.

She bustled in, looking all bright-eyed and bushy-tailed. "Here you go." She handed him a stack of blankets and quilts that smelled like pumpkin-pie spice, then dragged the rug by her bed over a few feet. Then a few feet more.

Jaron pulled it toward the wall so that her crate table was between them, and began making his pallet.

Bonnie started working on the knots in the string wrapped around the sleeping bag.

"You realize that at some point we will have to contact Captain Quigg," Jaron said. "And your aunt must be frantic." Not to mention his mother.

"I already called my aunt."

"Just now?"

"No. Hours ago at some bus station. She'll call your mom. I said we'd explain later."

"You…and you didn't think to call Quigg?"

"I didn't want to call Quigg!" She jerked on the knots.

"We *have* to! We can't hide here for the rest of our lives. I can't believe this." Jaron stood. "Is there a public phone downstairs?"

"Can't it wait until morning?"

"We have no idea what went on today. For all we know, Sorenson was just dazed or faking it, and single-handedly captured the baddies and is now basking in glory. They might have brought in Sonny what's-his-name. We might be free and clear."

"Or not."

"Or not," he acknowledged.

Bonnie stared at him, then heaved a great sigh. She reached for her purse and unzipped it. "If you really insist on calling Quigg—here." She handed him a cell phone.

Jaron stared at the phone as though he'd never seen one before. Then he looked at her in astonishment. "You've had a *cell phone* all this time?"

She nodded.

He couldn't believe it. She'd had a frigging cell phone the whole time and she'd never said a word. "Why didn't the police take yours away?"

She shrugged. "I leave it turned off. It's only for emergencies."

"*This* is an emergency, Bonnie." Jaron turned the phone on and listened as it chirped to life.

"Not now."

"Back in New Jersey—that was an emergency! You don't get much more emergent than that!"

"I know, but there would have been roaming charges."

"You mean you'd rather be thrifty and dead?"

"Of course not! But you would have called Quigg and he would have told us to come to the station and we would have gone through everything all over again! Besides, you're one of those people who uses a cell phone all the time. You would have called your editor and who knows who else, and by the time you'd finished it would have taken me three months to pay the bill.''

Incredible. "I will not dignify that by a response. Except to point out that *I* paid for our tickets today.''

"I *had* a ticket, and I would have used it if you hadn't taken me to a restaurant frequented by gangsters.''

"I didn't know it was frequented by gangsters.''

"You didn't know anything about it! You took me there so we wouldn't see anyone you knew!''

Since that was very close to the truth, Jaron went on the offensive. "How has a discussion that started about a cell phone deteriorated to this?''

The look she gave him said she wasn't fooled. "Just call.''

Jaron started to punch in 911, then stopped. He wouldn't get New York, he'd get the local emergency response center.

After making a disgusted sound, Bonnie went back to her purse and withdrew Frank Quigg's business card.

By calmly stating his business, Jaron managed to get put on hold three times. "I want to speak to Captain Frank Quigg," he repeated for the fourth time. "And he will want to speak to me. Trust me, this isn't a normal operating-hours kind of call.''

Bonnie grabbed the phone. "Tell Quigg I have pictures and I'm going to the press.''

"What are you doing?''

She held up a finger. "May I have your name? They'll want to know who was responsible—yes, I'll hold.''

Jaron rolled his eyes. "It's late. He's probably not even there.''

A smile bloomed across Bonnie's face. "Captain Quigg?

This is Bonnie Cooper—yes, he's here with me. We're fine. I don't want to tell you—''

It was Jaron's turn to grab the phone. ''Some protection you provide, Quigg!''

''Ask how Sorenson is,'' Bonnie whispered.

Jaron nodded. ''How's Sorenson?''

Quigg's gravelly voice sounded in his ear. ''Bump on the head. Scalded his hand on coffee. He'll live.''

Jaron gave Bonnie a thumbs-up. ''But the question is, will we?''

Bonnie started making cutting motions by running her finger across her neck. ''They're tracing us! They do it on TV all the time!''

''Where are you?'' Quigg asked, as Jaron knew he would.

''We went to Bonnie's home—Cooper's Corner.''

''Oh, great!'' Bonnie threw up her hands and started circling him. ''You told him! What did you do that for? After all the trouble I went to so nobody would know where we—''

''What's the matter with her?'' Quigg asked.

''Too much television.'' Jaron cleared his throat. ''She's worried that someone in the police department tipped off the guys who came looking for us this morning.''

''Yeah, so am I,'' Quigg said.

What? ''You're not supposed to agree with her.''

Quigg sighed heavily. ''I gotta consider it, but I think it's more likely that you were recognized.''

''Yeah, thanks for alerting the media.''

''I didn't have anything to do with it.''

''So what do we do now?''

''I'm packing and getting out of here,'' Bonnie said.

''And going where?''

''Somewhere *else,* and nobody is going to know.''

Quigg spoke. "Tell her to hang loose for a bit. I'm looking up something. Darn computer."

Bonnie grabbed her suitcase. "Adios." She stepped over the sleeping bag and headed for the door.

"Go. I don't care," Jaron said. She'd said it to him once.

"Don't let her leave," Quigg warned.

Jaron swallowed the first word he'd thought of, because it wasn't the brightest thing in the world to swear at the captain of detectives. He ran past Bonnie and leaned against the door.

Giving him a filthy look, she returned to her cot, sat on it and crossed her arms over her chest. Yeah, that lower lip was definitely in pout mode.

Jaron stayed by the door, just in case.

"Ask Bonnie if she knows the Twin Oaks Bed and Breakfast," Quigg said.

"We're hiding out in the attic as we speak." This place must have a good reputation if somebody like Quigg knew about it. He didn't look like the B and B type.

"Does Maureen know you're there?"

"Who?"

"Maureen Cooper. She owns the place, along with her brother, Clint."

Didn't anyone in this place have a different last name? "Relatives of Bonnie's?"

Bonnie dropped her arms when she heard her name.

"I guess. For now, you two stay put and let me talk with Maureen."

"Why? Why do you want to talk with Maureen?"

"He wants to talk with *Maureen?*" Bonnie echoed.

Jaron shushed her with a wave of his hand.

"This will have to be on a need-to-know basis," Quigg said.

"I need to know! What's going on?"

But Quigg ignored him. "It's late now, so until we know what we're dealing with, lie low. I'll call Maureen in the morning."

"So we're still at status quo? You haven't caught Sonny or his minions yet?"

"No."

After Jaron punched the off button, Bonnie lit into him. "How could you tell him where we were?"

"He's on our side, Bonnie." Jaron crossed the room and flipped her phone to her.

She caught it and put it back into her purse. "What's going to happen now?"

Jaron squatted and finished untying the sleeping bag. "He said to stay right here. He knew the place."

"He *did?*"

Nodding, Jaron unrolled the sleeping bag. It looked like a veteran. He imagined he could smell smoke from a long-ago, or maybe not-so-long-ago, campfire. Great. So not only did he look the part of an L.L. Bean fanatic, he'd smell like one, too. "Quigg will call Maureen in the morning." Jaron unzipped the bag. "Is she your sister?"

"Distant cousin. I wonder why he wants to talk with her." Bonnie absently slipped off her shoes and Jaron's jacket. "I really hate to get her involved with this."

"What did you think was going to happen when you came here?"

Bonnie unzipped her suitcase. "I guess I thought all the bad stuff would go away. Stupid, huh?"

"Yeah, but I understand completely."

She gave him a tired smile, at last losing some steam. "There's a rest room off the gathering room downstairs. I'll just be a minute."

It was more than a minute when Bonnie, clad in a fleece robe with sheep on it, came padding back into the room.

The robe covered her from neck to ankles, and Jaron stalled, wondering what her sleepwear looked like.

In a second, Bonnie removed the robe and tossed it across the foot of the cot. She was wearing matching flannel pajamas with enough sheep to count a person into a deep sleep.

He should have known. Smiling to himself, Jaron crept down the stairs.

"FRANK!" Maureen Cooper hadn't been expecting to hear from him, and was jolted as always when her former life as a New York City police detective reached out and touched her new life. In fact, it was precisely because she didn't want that former life that she and her brother had moved here.

Automatically, her eyes darted to the breakfast table, where her twin daughters were eating their cereal and playing with their Super Slide Kelly. Maureen had no illusions that as soon as she turned her back, Super Slide Kelly would take a dunk in the milk. If only that was all she had to worry about. If anything happened to the twins...

"Is this about Nevil? Have you heard back from forensics? Did he send the letter?" Owen Nevil was an ex-con and brother of a man she'd sent to prison for murder, Carl Nevil. Carl had vowed revenge, and Maureen believed he would try to get it through Owen.

The envelope, with no return address and marked "personal," had arrived at the station after she'd moved to Cooper's Corner. Even now she could hear the heart-stopping message Frank Quigg, her former boss, had read to her: "You can't hide from me. I will find you."

A strand of hair had come loose from her ponytail. Maureen tucked it behind her ear as she cast another look at her daughters. She smiled as they sent Super Slide Kelly into a bowl of milk.

"Sorry, Maureen. We couldn't tie it to him. But don't worry—"

"Oh, right."

"We're keeping tabs on him. And the note was addressed to your married name here at the station. He doesn't know you're living in Massachusetts."

"I hope that's true." She paused a moment. "If you weren't calling about Nevil, then what's going on?"

Frank cleared his throat. "I need a favor."

"I am not coming back to work. My first responsibility has *got* to be my daughters—"

"Whoa, whoa."

Maureen was surprised at how hard her heart was pounding. She'd considered herself tough when she was on the force, but now she had the twins to consider, and that made her vulnerable.

"We had some trouble in Little Italy."

"I heard."

"We've got witnesses."

"I knew about that columnist, but who else?"

There was a beat of silence and Maureen braced herself.

"A relative of yours—Bonnie Cooper."

Maureen gasped before she could stop herself. "*Bonnie?* What was she—"

"She and Darke had been out for dinner and happened to be in the wrong place at the wrong time. And they didn't see just any hit, they saw Sonny O'Brien take out Maurice Fenister. He was Sonny's interior decorator, and the scuttlebutt is that he was having an affair with both Sonny's wife and his daughter. Now, personally, I gotta sympathize with the guy, but he got all hotheaded, and lucky for us, he wasn't discreet. He made the hit himself.''

"And Bonnie saw it? Is she okay? Can I talk to her?"

"In a little bit." Frank cleared his throat again.

Maureen narrowed her eyes. "Allergies acting up, Frank?"

"Yeah. Must be it."

"You don't have allergies and you've never minced words with me before. Talk."

"They were recognized. Before he went off, Sonny was having dinner with Seamus McDormand. McDormand is apparently a Jaron Darke fan. Sent him a bottle of wine.''

Maureen listened in growing horror as Frank related the events of the past twenty-four hours. "Where's Bonnie now?''

"Staying very well hidden, if you don't know. They called me last night from your B and B.''

The room reeled around her. Two people had sneaked into her home and she hadn't even known it. She hadn't even been gone from the force a year and she'd already lost her edge.

"And I want them to stay there where you can keep an eye on them," Frank continued.

"They can't stay here! I've got children to consider. Bonnie and her friend have got *Seamus McDormand* after them. I want you to send them far, far away and assign your best people to guard them.''

"I am. You."

"I can't."

"Maureen—ten years. Ten. That's how long we've been after him. You know what I'd give to get to McDormand?''

She did. "You know what I'd give to keep my kids safe?''

There was another beat of silence, and Maureen realized Frank was changing tack. ''Bonnie and Darke successfully escaped or they'd be dead by now. Moving them will only draw attention to them, and to you. Besides, you've got to know that this is huge and is going to take precedence over Owen Nevil.''

''Frank—''

''Now, you know I'll try my best, but having to worry about my two star witnesses and tracking down a possible leak in the department will take time away from the Nevil case. That's just the facts, Maureen.''

''No, that's blackmail.'' But she did see Frank's point. And, too, she'd been unable to relax completely for months, always watchful and always nervous, especially after the threatening letter and the disappearance of one of her guests on the B and B's opening weekend. That had proved to be unrelated to her own situation and the man had been found safe, but Maureen was still wary.

As long as she was on guard, she might as well be looking after the columnist and Bonnie, too.

Quigg had been silently waiting, knowing that she had to work it out first. Knowing she'd see things his way. ''In exchange for them staying here, I want the Nevil case on the front burner.''

''Absolutely. In fact, I'll run checks on all your guests. Just fax me the info.''

''Okay.'' That would be a relief.

''Now, here's the cover story we've worked out for them.''

After hanging up the phone, Maureen stared at it before turning to discover that a milky sea had swamped the table and was dripping onto the floor.

"Uh-oh." Randi nudged her twin.

"Uh-oh," echoed Robin.

But to their surprise, their mother swept them into a huge hug.

"BONNIE, are you in there?"

Bonnie awoke with a start and sat straight up in bed. From somewhere nearby she heard Jaron do the same. What time was it?

"Bonnie?"

"Maureen?"

The door opened and Maureen strode in. "Bonnie, are you all right?" When she got closer, her eyes widened. "Your face! What happened?"

"Ran into a wall." Bonnie touched her cheek. It didn't hurt as much this morning. "Maureen, I—"

With a hard, quick hug, Maureen cut off what she'd been going to say. "I've already spoken to Frank Quigg this morning." Peering over the crate table, she said, "You must be Jaron Darke."

"Only if you're one of the good guys." Jaron raked his fingers through his hair. It responded by arranging itself into perfect layers. He didn't even have hat hair from the baseball cap he'd worn yesterday.

Bonnie tried dragging her fingers through her own hair, but they got stuck in the tangles and she gave up.

"I need to tell you both something and it can go no further than this room."

"Sure."

"I mean it, Bonnie." Maureen looked over at Jaron, who nodded.

"Okay. What is it?"

"Before Clint and I came here, I was a detective with NYPD. A sergeant. Frank Quigg was my boss."

"Small world," Jaron said.

"But that's great!" Bonnie was only half-surprised.

She'd met Maureen a couple of times before she moved back to Cooper's Corner, and had had the impression of a very strong, self-confident woman. "Why wouldn't you want anyone to know?"

"Because I was very good at what I did and there are people who would like revenge. One of them is after me now."

"So you're also a member of the small but exclusive club of people suffering for doing the right thing," Jaron said.

Maureen shrugged. "I accepted threats as part of the job, but that was before my husband took off and left me to raise the girls. I'm all they've got. So when Uncle Warren left Clint and me this place, it was literally the answer to my prayers. Nobody knows what I did before except Clint and one other man who needed to know. And now you two."

"So why are you telling us now?" Bonnie asked.

"Because Frank wants you to stay here. You managed to elude the McDormand clan and he figures I can keep an eye on you."

"And what does Quigg want *me* to do?" Jaron asked.

"He wants you to stay here, too."

"I don't think so." Jaron extricated himself from the sleeping bag. He still wore his T-shirt and jeans and looked attractively rumpled.

Bonnie figured she just looked rumpled. "Why not?"

"I would rather take my chances with Sonny than stay in this attic for days on end."

"You don't have to stay in here," Maureen said.

"I can't go wandering around now that my face has been plastered all over New England."

"You know, you don't look a whole lot like your picture," Maureen said.

Bonnie beamed. "I *told* you! He's got his Jaron Darke clothes with him, but I made him shave. Believe me, he looked *exactly* like his picture before."

"Well, this is good. It fits in with the plan," Maureen said. "As far as we know, McDormand doesn't know who Bonnie is, and since she planned to stay here during the renovations and is from Cooper's Corner anyway, she's set. But Jaron is the problem."

"I've heard that before." Jaron wandered over to the attic window.

"You can't be yourself, so Quigg is setting up a new identity for you."

"I like my old identity," he grumbled.

"You're going to be Jay Drake, computer expert from Syracuse. Shaving the beard was good. You should also wear glasses—"

"Hold it." Jaron turned.

He was backlit by the window and Bonnie couldn't read his expression, but she didn't really need to.

"I don't know much about computers and even less about Syracuse."

"Learn," Maureen told him.

He stepped away from the window, and Bonnie saw that his expression was grim. "Oh, sure, I can read up on Syracuse. I do use the Internet and write my columns on a laptop, but that's my total knowledge. What if someone asks me to fix a computer?"

"Say okay, take it with you and drive someplace and get it fixed," Bonnie said. Didn't he have any imagination?

"That's the idea," Maureen said. "Since Jaron will be staying here, we'll tell everyone that he's your fiancé."

"What?"

"Is that really necessary?" Jaron asked.

Bonnie hooked her thumb toward him. "I'm with him. Just how am I supposed to convince my parents that I'm engaged to a man they've never met or heard me talk about? And besides, everyone will want to meet him."

"That's exactly the idea. We want to get Jaron accepted in the community with a rock-solid cover as fast as we can."

"Can't I just be a friend of Bonnie's?"

Maureen shook her head. "People will try to find out about you and wonder why you're here for so long. If we tell them you two are engaged, then they'll accept all their information from Bonnie and her family."

Bonnie moaned. "She's right. I hate it, but she's right."

"Okay, so I'm accepted. Then what am I supposed to do?" Jaron asked. "How long does Quigg think this is going to take?"

Maureen stood. "We've been after McDormand for years. Since you two can place McDormand and Sonny together right before the hit, and since you have identified Sonny as the gunman, Quigg thinks it's possible McDormand authorized the hit. He's hoping that's what Sonny will confess when they find him. And as soon as they do, they'll push for an early trial."

"That will take months," Jaron said.

Maureen gave him a direct look. "If not years."

"Wait a minute." Bonnie protested. She was not going to have a fake fiancé for *years*. How was she supposed to meet her one true love if she was engaged? "This is not a good plan."

Maureen started for the door. "I've got to help Clint with the breakfast. Change whatever you don't like about the plan."

"I don't like anything about the plan," Jaron said.

"Then come up with a better one. You'll have all day."

CHAPTER EIGHT

JARON COULDN'T COME UP with a better plan. The best he could do was refine this one—and there wasn't much to work with, because, except for the fake engagement, it *was* the best plan.

And since the object was to weave him into the fabric of the town, having him be a B and B guest or a friend of either Clint's or Maureen's really didn't work as well.

It looked as though Jaron had acquired a temporary fiancée.

He and Bonnie had wrapped themselves in blankets and quilts and griped about the situation at length after fortifying themselves with the excellent breakfast Maureen had brought them. Not that Jaron could eat like that every day, but he felt he deserved all the eggs, sausage and hash browns he could manage this morning. And the bread basket was incredible. It contained a selection of homemade toast, English muffins, croissants, cinnamon rolls and blueberry muffins. If that wasn't enough—and Jaron felt it was—the specialty of the house was walnut griddle cakes prepared by Maureen's brother, Clint.

If Jay Drake stayed here long, he was going to look the part of a soft, slightly pudgy computer expert.

Once the B and B guests had left for their day's activities, Bonnie used Maureen's shower and Jaron used the one in the suite her brother, Clint, shared with his son, Keegan, who was at school.

It looked like that would be the setup until Bonnie the Wonder Plumber hooked up running water to the attic. Since Jaron had had some experience with remodeling jobs, he wasn't going to hold his breath.

When he returned to the attic after his shower, he found another cot, and Bonnie and Maureen stringing sheets to allow for a modicum of privacy.

As if a sheet would protect her virtue. Jaron hadn't imagined Bonnie's response to his kiss—at least not the first one—and no matter what had been said since, that first one counted. Man, did it count.

But she was safe. Jaron had no interest in her virtue, not after last night's little display on the bike trail, lower lip or not.

She wasn't interested in him; he wouldn't be interested in her. And that was final.

Just then, she reached up to hand a clip to Maureen. Today, Bonnie wore jeans and a shirt that rode up when she lifted her arms. It was the first time Jaron had seen her in clothes that fit, and boy, did those jeans fit. Designer clothes might not hang perfectly on that body, but Jaron was beginning to think that the designers had got it all wrong. He exhaled faintly.

It was going to get awfully boring in the attic.

He was wearing his new, now day-old clothes. Plaid did not improve with age. "I'm going to need to buy some more clothes," he said to their backs.

"We should drive down to Pittsfield and go shopping there," Bonnie suggested to Maureen, who was standing on a stepladder.

"Good idea," Maureen replied to Bonnie. "People here would wonder why he didn't come with extra clothes. And this way, we can make sure he dresses the part."

"Do you think we can sneak out today?" Bonnie to Maureen again.

"No. Too risky. You'll have your official arrival tomorrow. You can buy everything before you roll into town," she answered.

"What about the stuff I left with Aunt Cokie?" Bonnie asked Maureen.

"Quigg will clue her in," Maureen informed her. "She'll be part of the setup. It'll explain about Jay."

Jaron was not part of the conversation. "Hey!" He snapped his fingers. "Remember me?"

Both of them looked at him blankly.

"I'd like a say in this, too."

"What do you want to say?" Bonnie asked.

And damned if he could think of anything. "I want to pick out my own clothes," he managed to state.

"Sure." Bonnie went back to arranging sheets with a noxious floral pattern across the clothesline they'd strung.

If he had to wake up to that every morning, he'd puke.

And she'd capitulated far too easily about his clothes, which told him the shopping in Pittsfield was really the pits.

The sheets bugged him. One was okay to block her cot from the rest of the room, but they were making entirely too much of a fuss.

It was insulting, that's what it was. As though they felt he couldn't control his baser instincts, that the sight of a sleeping Bonnie in her sheep-covered flannel would kindle passion's flame, or some such rot.

He must have revenge. "Bonnie, will you be doing the renovations by yourself?" He already knew the answer, since she'd told him once before.

"No. Seth Castleman will be working on the carpentry and doing the wiring."

"My brother likes to do carpentry, so he'll probably be up here, too," Maureen added.

Jaron smiled. "Your brother knows the score, but Seth will think we're engaged." He waved his hand at the sheets. "He'll wonder why we're not sleeping together, or at least in the same vicinity."

"If he knew you, he wouldn't," Bonnie retorted.

"Tut, tut, Bonnie, is that any way to talk to your fiancé?"

"You are not my fiancé!"

"Jay has a point," Maureen said.

"Do you have to call me that?" Jaron asked.

Bonnie shrugged. "So we'll just tell Seth what's going on."

Both Jaron and Maureen shook their heads. "The more people who know, the greater the risk," Maureen told her.

"Well…well, does chastity count for nothing anymore? What ever happened to the charming custom of waiting for the wedding night?" Bonnie clearly wanted her sheets.

Jaron gave her a lecherous grin. "Have you, uh, waited for the wedding night so far?"

Bonnie blushed bright red, which told him nothing except that she was embarrassed.

"Jay, stop baiting her."

"Don't call me Jay."

"I have to. Bonnie, you should, too, so you'll get used to it. We don't want any slips. And something else—you two are not only going to have to get along, you're going to have to convince the world that you're madly in love."

"This isn't going to work." Bonnie was still flushed. "No one is going to believe that I'd want to marry *him*."

"Ditto," Jaron said.

They glared at each other.

"Well, *make* it work." Maureen closed the stepladder

and leaned it between two wall studs. "I'll be back at teatime." There was the implication that they'd better behave themselves while she was gone. When she reached the door, she looked back at them. "I really don't understand you two. Your lives depend on this." She closed the door.

Good exit line. "She's right," Jaron said.

"I agree."

They warily looked at each other. "All right, I'll go first so I can be the magnanimous one here," he said.

"That is *so* typical."

He gave her a mock bow. "Thank you."

Bonnie grimaced when she realized what she'd said.

"After last night, we can call things equal between us. Let's go from here."

Bonnie threw up her arms. "Go where?" She slumped down on her cot and stared at her shoes.

Jaron knew she didn't expect an answer, but he gave one anyway. "I don't know, but it'll be a hell of a ride."

MAUREEN HAD CALLED Bonnie's parents the following morning and offered to pick her up from the train station in Pittsfield. So, when things slowed down at the B and B, Jaron and Bonnie hid in the car as Maureen drove out of town, which took no time at all.

Now they were on their way back from their shopping trip, and Jaron had a suitcase full of clothes that were perfect for sawing logs, should the urge ever strike him.

He grimaced at the thought of wearing khaki pants. It was just not his style. His style was black—solid, sleek black. He hardly recognized himself in colors. But that would be the point.

And wonder of wonders, he had his laptop, courtesy of Cokie, who had actually arrived on the train. She'd brought his computer, along with Bonnie's things, and was now sitting next to him in the back seat.

"You wouldn't believe the nice young man Captain Quigg sent to watch my apartment. Such a sweetheart—too young for you, Bonnie."

"It figures."

"He's having girlfriend problems and I've made a few suggestions—just a little more polish and he'll be a gem. A woman is watching your mother's apartment, Jaron. Nora hired a Mercedes for her to sit in so she wouldn't be so conspicuous."

That sounded like his mother. Both Cokie and his mother seemed to be taking this all in stride. In fact, Cokie seemed in remarkably good spirits for someone who was going to perpetuate a lie to her sister.

"Bonnie engaged." Cokie sighed. "Phyllis will be so thrilled." She'd said it several times and Jaron was getting uncomfortable.

Apparently so was Bonnie. "Aunt Cokie, you do know that this is just a charade? Jaron and I aren't really engaged."

"But you and Jay are."

Bonnie's gaze skittered to his and then away.

Cokie smiled at her fondly, then reached into her purse. "I've had the best time making up a family for him." She leaned forward and whispered, "I even wrote them in my address book." She withdrew several pages of her elegant stationery.

"We already have a rough background for him," Maureen told her.

"Oh, *that*. I've thought through all those little things a mother wants to know about the man her daughter is going to marry."

Jaron suppressed a shudder. "You will give me a copy, won't you?"

"Now, Jaron—or I should say, Jay—don't you take that tone with me." Cokie handed him one of the sheets. "This scam will be made or lost on the strength of the details. And Phyllis and Philo—Bonnie's parents—are detail connoisseurs."

"She means gossips," Bonnie said matter-of-factly. "They know everything."

"And they'll be the perfect way to spread your story," Cokie explained. "If Phyllis and Philo pass it on, you can take it to the bank."

Funny how that ran in the family, Jaron thought, remembering all the tidbits Cokie had fed him for his column.

Bonnie shook her head. "I really hate doing this. This is lying to my parents."

Jaron felt an unwanted pang of sympathy. "You're keeping them safe. If they knew who I was, they'd be targets."

"And who's to say that it'll stay a lie?" Cokie added archly.

"I do," Bonnie said.

"There you go. Two little words in the right context and—"

Jaron interrupted her. "Cokie, what's NMNCNLTRGE?"

"Never married, no children, no long-term relationship, gainfully employed. It's a code mothers of marriageable children use."

"Where's the *H*?"

"'*H*'?"

"Heterosexual."

"Well, if you're engaged... But you never know these days. Everyone, add an *H* to Jay's bio."

Jaron read over the elegant handwriting. "This makes me sound like a nerd."

"News flash," Bonnie announced. "Jay *is* a nerd, which is why no one will believe I'm marrying him."

"I'll do my best to be my usual studly self."

"You'll have to do better than the best I've seen so far."

"Children, children," Maureen said from the driver's seat. She sounded like she was trying not to laugh. "You two need to kiss and make up."

"No way." From the front seat, Bonnie looked back at him.

Was that fear in her eyes? Or hope? Whichever, Jaron obligingly blew her a kiss.

She made a face and turned back around. If he moved a little to the left, he could see that her lip was jutting out a bit more than usual.

He smiled to himself, then became aware of the unnaturally silent Cokie, who was watching him with a dangerous smile of her own.

THEY STOPPED on the outskirts of town to change seats, because Cokie thought it would look better if Jaron and Bonnie were sitting together.

Maureen turned the car onto School Street, and Jaron saw the elementary school where Bonnie had had her short teaching career. A block farther, Maureen turned onto Main. "Heads up. It's show time."

In response, Jaron put his arm around Bonnie's shoulder. She shrugged it off.

He was being juvenile to get such a kick out of harassing her, but if she didn't make such a big deal out of it, he'd let her alone.

So. This was Main Street. It looked even smaller in the daylight. To cater to the tourists, the merchants had preserved as much of a late-eighteen-hundreds look as they could. Period streetlamps stood on the corners. Someone had decided on a forest-green, cranberry-red, federal-blue and white color scheme, and the buildings were all painted in one of the colors or a combination. Very appealing, if a person went in for that type of thing. Jaron did not. Faux history was one of his pet peeves. His opinion was to either restore something accurately or leave it alone.

"That's the library on the left."

A library. *There is a God,* Jaron thought.

Maureen was giving them the guided tour—actually more of a tourette, since the place was so small. "And our favorite eating spot—Tubb's Café."

"It looks like the only eating spot." Jaron vividly recalled Bonnie's description of the plastic flower centerpieces.

"Except for tea at Twin Oaks," Bonnie said.

Tea had possibilities. He'd eaten some wicked chocolate chip cookies yesterday.

Just past the café, Maureen parked in front of a building with a typical old-timey facade and a sign in script announcing Cooper's Corner General Store. One side was the grocery, the other the hardware store.

"Everybody ready?" Maureen asked.

"How do I look?" Cokie gave a movie-star smile. "Does this look like an I'm-happy-my-niece-is-getting-married smile?"

"It might be a bit much," Bonnie said.

"Any less and it'll be a something's-wrong-and-I'm-trying-to-put-a-good-face-on-it smile," she objected. "Trust me. Phyllis will be studying me, and if she thinks something's wrong, she's not going to think that it's because you're hiding from the mob. She'll think something is wrong with Jar—ay. Or she'll think you're pregnant.''

"Oh, God."

"That's the spirit," Jaron said, not as calm as he pretended to be.

Maureen opened the door. "All right, everybody. Get your game faces on."

Jaron had absolutely no idea what sort of face to put on for this game. He and Sydney had never taken that crucial step of agreeing to marry. But if there had been an engagement announcement, it would have been at an elegant party with toasts of Veuve Clicquot La Grande Dame, certainly not at a country general store. And Jaron didn't think Jay Drake would like it, either.

Jaron got out of the car, automatically offering Bonnie a hand. When she pointedly ignored it, he blocked her so that she couldn't stand up. Angry, she looked up, and their gazes locked.

He spoke in an undertone. "I am not happy about our situation, either, but acting like a spoiled child will not improve matters."

"I am *not* acting like a spoiled child!"

Jaron raised an eyebrow.

Drawing a deep breath, she exhaled heavily. "These are my parents."

"Yes, I know."

"They're people I love. They're not like you and your world, and I don't want you sneering at them."

"I wouldn't do that." How could she think he'd be so ill-bred as to insult her parents?

"You do it all the time. I've read your columns."

"I've been writing for years. You couldn't have read more than a handful of my columns."

"I've read enough to see what you're capable of."

"All I do is hold up a mirror to people. I can't help it if they don't like what they see."

"You just keep your fun-house mirror away from my folks." With that, she took his hand, dropping it as soon as she was out of the car.

"You're going to have to do better than that. You couldn't convince a blind man that we're in love."

Bonnie stared up at him. "Really."

Before Jaron had a clue what she intended, Bonnie placed her hands on either side of his face and kissed him, quick and hard—and effectively—right in front of her parents' store on Main Street.

"Let the gossip begin." She laced her fingers through his and walked toward the door.

Now that it was all over, Jaron's body reacted. *Nope, no more. Settle down.* Oh, great. Just the way he wanted to meet his pseudo future in-laws. He tugged on Bonnie's hand, trying to slow her down, and she tugged back.

How could his body go off on its own like that? He did *not* like her. Sure, there had been a few instances of harmony, but they were completely overshadowed by situations like this.

Maureen had already gone inside, but Cokie was watching them. As they approached, she gave him an all-knowing smile that made his blood run cold.

At least he was ready to meet Bonnie's parents now.

From the moment they entered through the old-fashioned door, Jaron knew the middle-aged couple had seen Bonnie kiss him, and were giving him a disapproving once-over.

Jaron gave them one of his haughtiest looks before he remembered that he was a computer geek from Syracuse, and tacked on a smile. He probably looked maniacal.

Bonnie's mother came forward. "Bonnie, what happened to your face?"

Bonnie put her hand to her cheek. "I'm fine, Mom."

"I told her to be careful climbing around those old buildings."

"Cokie!" Bonnie's mother looked stunned to see her sister.

Jaron automatically compared the two. It was country sister and city sister. Phyllis was younger, he guessed, but Cokie was more polished, so he couldn't tell just how far apart in age they were.

"I've brought you a surprise," Cokie crooned, and leaned to give her sister a social air kiss. Clearly having none of that, Phyllis gave her a good ole country hug.

Jaron looked down at Bonnie. She wore a smile that looked worse than his.

"Bonnie?" Her mother was staring at her. At them. At him. She raised her eyebrows questioningly.

Jaron felt Bonnie tense beside him, and slipped an arm around her waist. It had nothing to do with their act and everything to do with offering support. That he could dislike her and still have these emotions really irritated him.

"Mom...this is Jay. Jay, my parents, Phyllis and Philo Cooper."

Jaron shook hands with both of them, keeping his grip firm and making strong eye contact with her father. Fathers didn't like turning their daughters over to wimps.

Jaron was conscious of Maureen watching them closely. She was probably going to report straight back to Quigg on how well they did.

"Bonnie? Don't you have something else to say?"

Cokie deserved a poke in the ribs for that.

"Mom, Dad...Jay and I..." She trailed off with a look at him.

Anyone else might have thought it was a loving look, but Jaron knew panic when he saw it. She couldn't choke out the lie to her parents.

Fine. He'd be the bad guy. He tightened his arm around her waist, dropped a kiss on her temple and took over. "Bonnie has done me the very great honor of agreeing to become my wife."

There was dead silence, then a gasp. "You're getting *married?*"

Bonnie managed to nod at her mother.

"Philo—Bonnie's getting married!"

"I heard." Philo came out from behind the counter where he'd been standing. He was a stocky man with salt-and-pepper hair and dark eyes that were fixed on Jaron.

"But…when…?" Phyllis looked from her daughter to Jaron. "This is so…unexpected."

He maintained a smile he hoped was both reassuring and loving.

"Isn't it romantic?" Cokie ushered Jaron and Bonnie farther into the shop. "Jay's mother and I are old friends and we'd always hoped…well, we're thrilled. I just had to come and watch your faces when Bonnie told you."

"Yes, who are you and why haven't I ever heard of you?" Philo asked, giving Jaron an assessing look.

"Philo, they met in New York, of course," Cokie informed him. "You don't think I keep Bonnie cooped up all the time when she visits, do you? And Nora is such a good friend. Bonnie's known her longer than Jay, haven't you, Bonnie?"

"I've been to her apartment a couple of times."

Jaron realized she was probably telling the truth. She'd met his mother—and his mother had *still* set them up together. Talk about wishful thinking.

"And any number of luncheons and parties," Cokie embellished. "Jay was usually there, too."

"So you live in New York?" Philo approached them, and to Jaron's total shock, this time it was Bonnie who gave *him* a reassuring squeeze.

"Syracuse." Jaron prayed that Philo didn't know Syracuse.

"Bonnie's never mentioned you," Philo said. "If you live in Syracuse, then what are you doing hanging around your mother?"

"I have clients in New York. And why wouldn't I visit my mother when I'm in the city?"

"Jay is being a good son," Cokie said. "And you can gauge how a man will treat his wife by the way he treats his mother."

Jaron wasn't sure he agreed, but Philo shrugged in acceptance. "What line of work are you in?"

His palms were actually moist. Go figure. "I'm a writer." It popped out and he felt Bonnie tense.

"He writes software for computers," she said.

Nice save.

"So you're one of those guys who've made it impossible for me to work my computer?"

"I beg your pardon?"

"Dang upgrades," Philo grumbled.

"You know how that goes. Have to stay ahead of the competition." Jaron tried a chuckle that fell flat.

"Pays pretty good, does it?"

"Pretty good," Jaron said.

"You're not one of those dotcommers, are ya?"

"No, Dad, he has a very steady job and he works very long hours."

Bonnie smiled up at Jaron, and for a second he forgot that this was only make-believe.

"Which is why he's staying in Cooper's Corner for a while. He needs a break."

"I've got a ton of vacation saved up," Jaron added.

"How much?" Philo asked.

"Weeks."

"Hmm. He's unemployed, Phyllis."

"No, Dad!" Bonnie protested.

Cokie sniffed. "As though I would permit such an entanglement."

"If the man's not unemployed now, he will be when his company discovers they can do without him—and what company was that?"

"Dynameg Computers," Jaron said.

"Syracuse Software," Bonnie said at the same time.

"Dynameg Computers and Software in Syracuse," Jaron clarified, rather adroitly, he thought.

How could they have forgotten to name the company where Jay worked? He'd have to tell Quigg so he could set up an answering machine somewhere.

"Never heard of them," Philo said.

"*Philo.*" Phyllis had been carrying on a murmured conversation with Cokie.

"We don't advertise. Word of mouth within the industry gives us all the business we need." Jaron was getting good at this.

"Philo?" Maureen stood at the counter in the hardware section of the store. "If you'll ring up my order, I can take it with me now."

"Okay, Maureen." With a last suspicious glance at Jaron, he went to the register behind the counter.

Maureen could have jumped in a little earlier, but Jaron was glad he didn't have to come up with any more on-the-fly answers. He hoped somebody was taking notes, because he doubted he would remember everything.

Before Bonnie's mother could start grilling them, the bell over the door rang and a round, black-haired woman came in. "Hello, everybody." She eyed them all, then trained her gaze on Jaron.

Once again, he pasted on his I'm-a-good-guy-computer-geek smile.

"Hi, Lori," Bonnie's mother said. "You remember my sister, Cokie?"

"Yes, from New York. Phyllis didn't say you were coming for a visit." Lori's gaze darted between Jaron and Cokie.

"I decided to surprise her. I'll be returning on the evening train."

"What can we do for you today?" Phyllis asked.

Lori pretty much ignored her and walked over to where Bonnie and Jaron stood with their arms linked around each other's waist.

"Welcome home, Bonnie. I saw you drive up."

Which meant she'd seen the wet one Bonnie had plastered on him.

"Who's your friend?"

"Lori, this is Jar-y Drake." Then she added firmly, "Jay, this is Lori Tubb."

"Of Tubb's Café?" Jaron asked.

The woman looked pleased. Her smile added at least two chins to the collection she already had. "The very same. You've heard of us?"

"Yes." He didn't imagine the subtle, yet definite pinch from Bonnie.

"Well, how about that? So what brings you to Cooper's Corner, Jerry?"

"It's Jay."

"You prefer to go by Jay?"

"I'm not a Jerry."

"But I heard—"

"Mrs. Tubb, I was just nervous." Bonnie gave a very convincing nervous laugh. "You see, I've just told my folks that Jay and I are engaged."

Jaron swore Lori Tubb's eyes grew twice their size. "Well, aren't you the sly one!"

"Yes, sly. That's me." Bonnie giggled weakly.

"And when were you planning to tell Norman Ackers?"

"Who?" Bonnie asked.

"Ed Taylor's second cousin's boy. You agreed to go out with him if he comes for Thanksgiving."

"Um…I guess I'll tell him before Thanksgiving."

Jaron flashed a smile—one of his practiced Jaron smiles. Jay just wasn't up to it. "You'll have to forgive me—I swept Bonnie off her feet."

Lori looked him up and down. "Yeah, you look like you've got a pretty good broom."

"Lori," Phyllis said firmly. "What was it you came in for?"

"What? Oh. Uh, yeast. We're all out of yeast. Can't make the dinner rolls without yeast, so I thought I'd run right over here—"

"A jar? Or will a couple of packets do for now?"

Phyllis sounded perfectly pleasant, but Lori looked at her and something passed between the two women. "A jar."

"I don't have the restaurant size in stock. You do remember that I have to special order it for you?"

"Yes, yes."

"Then should I place an order?" Phyllis asked sweetly.

Obviously reluctant, Lori Tubb hesitated, then gave a quick nod. Bonnie's mother headed for the grocery counter.

"So when's the wedding?" Lori asked.

Now, this one they'd rehearsed. Bonnie laughed. "Oh, not for a while. Now that we've found each other, there's no need to rush."

Mrs. Tubb's speculative gaze dropped to Bonnie's waist. Bonnie was wearing slacks and a bulky sweater, which Jaron tried to pull tighter. All he accomplished was to draw Bonnie closer to him, which wasn't such a bad thing.

"Hmm," Mrs. Tubb murmured.

Cokie worked her way between Jaron and Mrs. Tubb. "I am just so glad that these two finally decided they were meant for each other! Jay's mother and I have known they were perfect for each other for years, but you know how young people can be. Do you have children?"

"Five."

"Then you know exactly what I'm talking about."

Cokie was a master. Jaron was sorry she wasn't staying to run interference with the other villagers.

He thought he'd pretty much pegged Mrs. Tubb. She was the Coopers' competitor for gossip, and Bonnie getting engaged was the prime bit of the season. He was going to have to watch himself around the woman, but if he avoided her she would get suspicious. After all, she owned the only eatery in town.

Great. It looked like he would dine at Tubb's Café, after all.

Bonnie's mother returned. "Here's your yeast, Lori. A small jar to tide you over until your order arrives."

"Thanks, just put it on my tab."

"Oh, I did."

The two women gave each other smiles worthy of the shark-infested waters of the New York social scene.

After Lori left, Phyllis gave Bonnie a high five.

Bonnie laughed. "Way to go, Mom."

"That's right. If she wants gossip, she's going to have to pay for it like anyone else."

"Mrs. Tubb has been ordering her supplies off the Internet," Bonnie explained.

"Found she can get them cheaper, so Philo and I have been driving into New Ashford for dinner. It's nice to have a change."

"Hey, Jay, how about a little free labor?" Philo called. What now?

Maureen walked past them, carrying a large box. "I'm loading my car. There's more in the storeroom."

Everyone except Cokie, who wasn't dressed for lifting dusty boxes, carried supplies out to Maureen's car and quickly filled it.

"I guess I'll come back for the rest of it," she said.

"Just put the rest in the back of my truck and I'll drive up to the B and B," Bonnie offered.

And so, after saying goodbye to Cokie and Bonnie's parents, Jaron found himself traveling not in the black Lincoln Town Car to which he was accustomed, but a white pickup truck with Cooper's Plumbing and a phone number on the side.

It was a stick shift, and Bonnie handled the gears as though it was second nature, which it probably was. "Smile and wave when we go by the café."

They both smiled and waved. "There. You are now officially established with a rock-solid cover story."

"Not quite yet. Stop in front of the café."

"Why?" Bonnie asked, but she stopped.

"Payback." Jaron leaned over and kissed her, right in front of the café's plate-glass window. The gearshift was in the way, but he still managed to make the kiss look good.

"There. *Now* I have a rock-solid cover story."

CHAPTER NINE

SHE WAS THE SCUM of the earth. Not only had she lied to her parents, but some rebellious, foolish, defiant part of her wished the lie were true. Wished that it had been for real when she'd seen the surprise and cautious joy on her mother's face and watched her father grudgingly bestow his approval.

Wished that Jaron…no, *not* Jaron. He just happened to be there filling the role of fiancé. She'd probably feel that way about anybody. Anybody. Definitely not Jaron. Even if he looked very much a part of her world in his country casual clothes, he was not her type. Not…her…type.

Her type was friendly and comfortable and easy to be with. There would be a mutual, deepening attraction, not this inexplicable zero-to-sixty-in-two-seconds sensation she kept getting blindsided with. That was just plain nuts. There was no reason for it.

She could never relax around Jaron. With them, it was a constant struggle to see who'd gain the upper hand. Sometimes she had it, and sometimes he did.

Right now, he did.

The timing couldn't be worse, because nearly everyone in Cooper's Corner was packed into the Twin Oaks gathering room.

The kiss in front of Tubb's window had done it. With both her mother and Lori Tubb burning up the phone lines, word had spread faster than mental telepathy. The result was that Friday afternoon tea at Twin Oaks was the hottest ticket in town. Everyone had come to see the newly engaged Bonnie and her fiancé for themselves.

Correctly predicting something of the sort, Maureen had been prepared for her daily afternoon tea to turn into an impromptu engagement party, and Clint had made extra batches of cookies.

The weather was sunny and mild, with the warmth of Indian summer, which was good, because Maureen and Clint had to serve the overflow on the back deck. And then the people just picked up their cookies and tea and brought them back inside, their voices nearly drowning out the soothing piano music. Bonnie could have used some soothing.

She and Jaron held court by the great stone hearth in the gathering room. She'd changed into a dress. Why, she didn't know. It felt more bridal, she guessed. Jaron was dressed much the same as the other men, but somehow, he'd elevated the plaid shirt and khakis to high fashion. The crease on his pants was particularly sharp. If she didn't know better, she'd have guessed he'd been hitting the starch and iron. And maybe he had, but Bonnie didn't know any men who ironed. She barely ironed herself. In fact, did she own an iron? Or had she just borrowed her mother's and never given it back?

"Bonnie!" A short, dark-eyed woman took both her hands and kissed her on the cheek. "I heard. I'm so happy for you!"

Why hadn't her smile cracked yet? "Aunt Gina, this is Jay."

"The teacher?" Jaron shook her hand.

Gina looked delighted. "Bonnie's told you about me?"

"Yes, and about her illustrious teaching career."

"If she told you about that, then I know this is true

love. I don't think she's ever told anyone." Gina patted his hand—the one she still held.

And Jaron gave her that…that *smile,* the one he'd given to all the women this afternoon. And all of them responded just the way her aunt Gina did, by getting a sparkle in their eyes and a flush in their cheeks.

It was so pathetic.

Watching Jaron charm the population of Cooper's Corner was almost as bad as lying to her parents.

The piano music stopped, and Beth Young, who'd been playing, headed their way. "Bonnie, I just wanted to add my best wishes to everyone else's before you got away."

"It doesn't look like I'm going anywhere for a while," Bonnie said. "Beth, this is Jay Drake."

She gave him a shy smile. "I'm happy to meet you."

"Beth is our local librarian and tea pianist."

"The librarian!" Jaron took her hand. "We *will* be seeing more of each other."

"Oh, are you a reader?"

"I'm a lapsed reader," Jaron said. "But while I'm here kicking back for a few weeks, I intend to go on a reading orgy." And there he went with his smile again.

Beth laughed, cheeks pink, eyes sparkling, the whole nine yards. She was usually shy and quiet and given to playing haunting melodies on the piano. Bonnie couldn't remember hearing her laugh like that before.

"Oh, Bonnie. You're in such trouble." Shaking her head and still laughing, she returned to the piano.

And it was like that with everyone. Jaron was charming and glib and just so not the person she knew he was.

"So you think you'll be here for the Christmas festival?" Grace Penrose, the Cooper's Corner Christmas Festival coordinator stood batting her big brown eyes up at

Jaron. "Because if you are, I'm going to put you to work!"

As Jaron made some comment, Bonnie felt a small tug on her sleeve. Alison Fairchild, the local postmistress, was standing off to one side, slightly apart from everyone.

Ducking her head so her blond hair obscured her face, she said quietly, "Congratulations, Bonnie. He seems very nice."

Bonnie and Alison were the same age and had gone to school together from the time they were in kindergarten, though they were not close. Alison was extremely self-conscious about her large nose, and kept to herself. Bonnie could hardly blame her; Alison had been horribly teased when they were growing up.

"Thank you, Alison. He is nice." *When he's being Jay.* "Let me introduce you."

Alarm flashed in Alison's eyes. "Oh, no!" She pulled away.

But not fast enough. "And who's this?" Jaron looked around Bonnie.

Bonnie urged Alison forward, feeling for her when she lowered her head. "Jay, this is Alison Fairchild. She's the postmistress."

He took her hand and bowed over it. "Greetings, Mistress Fairchild." Straightening, he gave her one of those thousand-kilowatt smiles. "That sounds like a medieval lady of the manor."

Alison gave him a timid smile, which widened as he continued to talk to her, drawing her out, learning that she'd gone to school in Boston and that she was planning a trip to New York City in a few weeks. Once he discovered that, Jaron gave her the name of several less-expensive hotels and areas of the city she could stay.

"Jay spends a lot of time in New York City," Bonnie said. "So if you have any questions, he's the man."

He was being incredibly nice to Alison, talking more to her than he had to anyone else, and Alison was blooming under the attention. Bonnie felt the stirrings of jealousy, which was completely ridiculous. She took a large bite of chocolate chip cookie.

Once Alison relaxed, Bonnie discovered to her surprise that she was actually quite pretty, if only her nose... But that was being superficial, and Bonnie wasn't proud to discover that she'd developed a few superficial qualities lately.

"Jay! Bonnie!" Bonnie's father waved at them and started pushing his way through the crowd.

With a last adoring look at Jaron, Alison stepped away.

"I've been checking up on you," Philo said.

The cookie that Bonnie had just swallowed landed in her stomach with a thud.

"And what did you find?" Jaron asked.

Bonnie clutched at him, but Jaron lazily drew her to him and moved his fingers in slow, soothing circles over her back.

"You're very modest." Philo nodded to himself. "I went to your Web site."

Jaron blinked. Bonnie gripped the handle of her teacup so hard she was relieved when it didn't break.

"You didn't tell me you were one of the owners." Philo withdrew a couple of folded pieces of paper. "I printed off the information so I could show folks. Been bragging about you, Son."

Bonnie stared down at the Web site of Dynameg Computers and Software. Jaron, or rather Jay Drake, was listed as one of the three owners, with a company write-up and product list. Bonnie had to bite her lip when she saw Sorenson's name listed as Chief Security Officer. Maureen must have called Frank Quigg immediately. Still, Bonnie was impressed that they'd cobbled together a Web site that quickly. "How did you find this?"

"I called information in Syracuse and got the number for your company. Nobody answered, but the voice mail said to go to your Web site. So I did."

Quigg was incredible. While Bonnie was glad the police could move so quickly, she was a little nervous at what they'd been able to accomplish. And her father was no slouch, either.

"I've got your bio right here," he said.

"That's an old picture." Jaron's voice sounded funny.

Bonnie recognized the picture—it was his column photo, but his goatee and sunglasses had been removed and his hair was different. The rest was basically Jay Drake's cover story.

Bonnie and Jaron exchanged looks. It was another one of those moments of pure connection when she knew exactly what he was thinking—that it was all fake, but it seemed so real. So convincing. That was exactly as it should be, but…should it have been so easy?

Philo turned toward the piano. "Beth! Give us a ta-da."

Beth abruptly stopped the nocturne she was playing and boomed an attention-getting ripple followed by a couple of loud chords.

All conversation stopped. All eyes turned to Bonnie's father.

"I don't think what I'm going to announce will be a surprise to any of you." Good-natured laughter followed. "But I want to do this up right. Phyllis, where are you, honey?"

Bonnie's mother waved from the back of the room and the crowd parted so she could join her husband. He put his arm around her waist exactly the same way Jaron had his around Bonnie's.

"Now, as you all know, Bonnie, here, is my only baby, and it's real hard to let go of her."

Bonnie felt like she was going to be sick—and this time it wasn't from eating too many chocolate chip cookies. How was she going to get through this? How could she go about her business and look these people in the eye?

"But I have to say that it's easier knowing she's chosen such a fine young man."

"Hear, hear!" someone called.

"So, Phyllis and I want to wish you both all the joy and love that we've found."

Bonnie felt her eyes get hot, and her throat tightened. This was the worst moment of her life.

Her father raised his teacup. "To Bonnie and Jay!"

The toast was repeated by several people in the crowd, and then the rumble of conversations began again.

"Thank you, Mr. Cooper." Jaron held out his hand.

Philo enclosed it with both of his. "You take care of my little girl."

Bonnie's mother pooh-poohed him. "Philo, the child has been taking care of herself for years."

"It's symbolic, Phyllis." He let go of Jaron. "Jay knows what I mean."

Jaron looked down at Bonnie. "You bet."

HE WAS WRONG. Hell was not in New Jersey. Hell was in the picture-postcard town of Cooper's Corner, Massachusetts.

Everybody knew everybody else and everybody else's business. Jaron was going to have to keep a diary and study his alter ego's bio before he made an appearance each day.

There were kids living at the B and B and kids asked questions. The twins—Maureen's girls—didn't look much over three. They wouldn't be a problem, but Clint's boy, Keegan, would be. Keegan's hormones were starting their run toward manhood and he was watching the adults around him for clues to their world. Jaron didn't want to be watched as he learned his new role, whatever that turned out to be. If he made any slips, Keegan would be the one to notice.

Keegan reminded him of himself in a way. Jaron had honed his social skills by quietly observing and quietly listening, just as Keegan was doing now. People tended to ignore a young kid, and the kid always knew more than expected. You could learn a lot by being invisible.

Jaron gazed around the inn's gathering room, where he'd stood for the past two hours with Bonnie. He'd talked so much his throat would never be the same, and he'd drunk more tea than he'd consumed in his entire life up to this moment.

The people of Cooper's Corner were a curious mix. He'd made the mistake of so many from the city in expecting them to be uncomplicated, simple folk. They had a grapevine that put his carefully cultivated network of sources to shame, and once he got past the clothes—if he could ever really get past the clothes—this gathering was just like any one of thousands he'd attended from the time he was nine years old.

He'd quickly analyzed the room—who had the power, who wanted it, who'd once had it and lost it, and who would never have it. Jaron was a student of body language. He could tell who had something to hide and who had something to tell.

If anyone was suspicious, Bonnie would be a dead give-away—and Jaron hoped not literally. One reason he kept touching her arm or her back was because she automatically straightened—to get away from him—when he did so. Otherwise, her shoulders hunched and her head hung down in the classic closed posture. Jaron wanted her looking confident and happy. He figured happy was out of the question, so he was shooting for confident.

Poor Bonnie. He did sympathize with her. She'd grown up with these people and they obviously loved her. They were thrilled that she was getting married. They would drown her in sympathy when the engagement was broken. Jaron had already guessed that when the time came, he and Bonnie would break up, so they wouldn't have to tell the entire population of Cooper's Corner they'd been duped. Breaking up would be easy. One argument in front of Tubb's Café ought to do it.

He was really pouring on the charm tonight and doing it well, judging by the reactions he was getting. Maybe he should hold back some. If he became too well liked, Bonnie would look like an idiot for breaking up with him.

But then the little postmistress waved goodbye and he waved back. He couldn't help it. He knew her story, too. She looked different from the norm, so the norm had attacked her to keep themselves safe. Been there, done that, got revenge in his columns. Jaron had written down the names of all the kids who had made fun of his adult manners and adult clothes. He'd had to wait fifteen years to fit in with them—long enough for them to grow up and catch up with him. And now they wanted into *his* world. He enjoyed the irony; he *was* human.

"Jay?" Bonnie spoke in an undertone.

"Hmm?"

"Where were you?"

"Thinking. Thinking that this party is like a hundred others I've been to."

"You're very good at small talk."

"Of course I am—it's a survival skill in my business."

She nodded, then leaned closer. "What's going to happen about your column?"

He bent his head until his mouth was next to her ear. Anyone watching would assume it was a loving moment between the two. "Bonnie, Bonnie, Bonnie. We're still undercover."

"Oh." Jerking back, she looked around, guilt personified.

"Relax. Angela will print reruns. I have a couple of emergency columns in the can, but as of Sunday, she starts a 'best of' series."

"Did you tell her—"

"No. I said I had some personal business."

Bonnie scanned the room. "How long do you think this will go on?"

"Nobody seems to be leaving."

"Not today—I mean everything."

Jaron shook his head. "As long as it has to, I guess." He touched her shoulder. "Incoming at three o'clock."

"Hello again." Lori Tubb sidled up to them. "Tell me, Jay, where are you staying?"

"Here at Twin Oaks."

"Really? Maureen told me she was completely booked."

"Bonnie's renovating the attic," he began, then realized the trap. *He* didn't care what anyone thought of their sleeping arrangements, but he knew Bonnie would.

This was one difference between the people here and in New York. No one there would give it a thought, but this woman was just hoping to find a juicy bit of what in the boonies counted for scandal at Bonnie's expense.

"Yes." Bonnie picked up the conversation. "I can't

wait to get started. And I'm happy that business is so good for Maureen. I know there have been times when she's been tempted to rent out the sleeper sofa in her suite. I'm glad she didn't.''

Not a lie, but not the truth, either. It would do for now, but come Monday morning, he was going to have a man-to-man with this Seth guy.

Either that, or sleep in the hall.

HOURS LATER, Bonnie not only felt like scum, she felt like confused scum.

Was everyone she'd known her whole life so easily fooled? Weren't they worried that she was rushing into a relationship? And her parents… True, Cokie's vouching for Jaron had helped, but why hadn't they pulled her aside and asked parental-type questions like, ''Are you nuts? How long have you known this man?''

Or were they just desperate to see her married? Had they given up hope? Had she secretly been a town project? It sure put all those blind dates in a different light.

And why did everyone act ecstatically happy? The implication was that Bonnie couldn't possibly be happy without a man, and she didn't like that one little bit.

And Jaron. She sighed. He'd been a huge hit. She should feel relieved, if not glad. Instead, well, if she had to put a name to it, she'd have to admit she was jealous. But of what?

She lay in her attic bed, completely enclosed by walls on two sides and sheets on two others, and listened to Jaron's breathing. It wasn't the slow heavy sound of someone who was asleep. ''Jaron?''

She'd given up on getting an answer when she heard a gruff, ''Yeah?''

That wasn't an I-want-to-talk response. That was an I-want-to-sleep response. Bonnie didn't care. "It went okay this afternoon, huh?"

Another long silence. "Seemed to."

"Everyone liked you."

"Surprised?"

"Yeah."

"Good night, Bonnie."

She hadn't meant it to sound that way. "Wait—"

"Do I have a choice?"

"You don't have to talk if you don't want to."

"Is there any possibility of sex?"

Where was a good scathing remark when she needed one? All she managed was a scathing squeak.

"I thought not. Go to sleep."

"Why do you keep *doing* that?"

"Because you're such an easy target."

"Well, quit it, okay?"

"That goes both ways."

"But it's going more your way than mine. Anything I did was in self-defense."

"That's a very convenient attitude. It must make it easy for you to sleep at night. Why don't you?"

"Fine!" Bonnie flounced over onto her side, her back away from him. She wished the sheets were twelve feet thick.

She heard him exhale.

"I can hear you over there," he said.

"I didn't say anything."

"No, but you're breathing in quivering indignation. I'll probably regret this, but what did you want to talk to me about?"

Bonnie thought about telling him to forget it, but she didn't. "You were nice to Alison."

"I was nice to everybody."

"But you were especially nice to her."

"I'm not used to being nice. Maybe I got it wrong—which one was she?"

"The one with the…" Bonnie trailed off.

"Big nose. Yeah. It doesn't take a genius to see that she's self-conscious about it and that she probably took a lot of grief for it when she was growing up."

"We were in school together. They called her Uglychild instead of Fairchild."

"And probably worse. I know how it can be."

Something in his voice caught at her. "How do you know?"

"I knew I'd regret this."

Bonnie wasn't going to let him off the hook. "What happened to you?"

"Save your sympathy—unless it involves something very specifically physical."

"A kick in the groin?"

He chuckled. "You're not going to be as much fun anymore, are you?"

"It sounds like fun to me. Quit stalling or you will never sleep tonight."

Bonnie half expected him to fling back the curtains and tell her off, but he didn't.

"I had a great childhood, but I didn't have a typical one. You've met my mother. Imagine her the way she is now, but as the single mother of a seven-year-old, one who up to that time relied on nannies for the day-to-day details of child care."

The intimidatingly elegant Nora Darke changing diapers? Nope. She was a nanny mom through and through.

"My dad died when I was seven. He was a lot older and had children from his first marriage, who inherited a chunk of his estate. Let's just say that our income dropped, but our standard of living didn't.''

''Are you saying you were poor?''

''We would have been if Mother had continued spending the way she was. The accountant convinced her to economize.'' Jaron chuckled. ''She didn't have a clue. She did things like have Cook fix macaroni and cheese three nights in a row.''

Bonnie laughed, too.

''She figured it out, though. By the time I was nine, she began taking me to parties with her. She saved on baby-sitting costs—the nannies and servants were gone by then—and fed us both, too. I had dinner jackets and suits and formal wear tailored for me. I was her 'walker.' ''

''I'm sorry?''

''Escort. A lot of women don't like attending functions alone, and an attractive, unattached, well-spoken male is always welcome.''

''You were nine.''

''Only in years. Mother was never a blocks-and-finger-paint mom. This was what she knew and this was what she taught me. It was great. I loved it. I went to art gallery openings, plays, concerts, charity galas, and private gatherings, as well. I'd hit the hors d'oeuvres, make sure I greeted everyone I knew, then plop myself in a corner somewhere and do my homework.''

Bonnie sat straight up in the cot. ''Or eavesdropped and sold what you heard to the gossip columns!''

''Ding ding! Give the lady the stuffed monkey.''

''I want the panda bear. But why did the other kids make fun of you?''

''They thought I was a dork. I was more comfortable around adults and I got to go to parties and they didn't. I liked dressing well, which meant I didn't embrace the styles of the seventies. You know the kid with the glasses, the slicked-down hair and the sweater vest? That was me.''

"Wow.''

"I convinced myself that I didn't care, but I did. Anybody would.''

Bonnie felt awful for him. "Oh, Jaron.''

"Cut it out. You're over there feeling sorry for little Jaron, aren't you?''

"Well, not anymore.''

"Good.''

"It's big Jaron I'm thinking about.'' She winced. Why had she said that?

"What are you thinking?''

She was thinking lots of warm fuzzy thoughts. They'd bonded. "Thanks for telling me.''

"You're welcome. It was only fair. I learned more about *you* than I ever wanted to know today.''

Warm fuzzies turned into cold pricklies. When would she learn? "Jaron? This doesn't mean we like each other any better or anything.''

"Of course not.''

"Good.''

"Fine.''

"So…I'm going to sleep now.''

He exhaled softly. "Good night, Bonnie.''

CHAPTER TEN

FREEDOM. Sort of. If anyone could ever be free once caught in a small-town web.

In spite of his resolution, this was the third morning in a row that Jaron had eaten the huge Twin Oaks breakfast, but the first time he'd eaten downstairs.

Maureen and Clint had a great place here. There were worse places to be stuck. The B and B managed to look old and new at the same time. Too much chintz for his taste, but the mahogany table in the dining room was a wonderful piece and he'd always appreciated fresh flowers.

He and Bonnie had deliberately waited until most of the paying guests had served themselves from the buffet and left for the day. The only dining-room occupants now were a couple with a young girl who'd attracted the attention of the twins, and a rawboned man who ate as though he was starving.

Maureen came through the kitchen to the dining room to refresh the coffeepot. "Here's the money for the chickens, Ed. And for some reason, no one wanted blueberry muffins this morning. May I give you some? Otherwise, they'd just go to waste."

Smiling, his mouth full, the man took the envelope and shoved it into the pocket of his worn jeans. He hesitated, but took the plastic bag Maureen held out to him, looking as though he'd discovered gold.

Sure, the muffins were good, but they weren't *that* good.

Maureen poured a mug of coffee for herself and came to join Bonnie and Jaron. "Ed, I didn't see you at tea yesterday, so you haven't had a chance to meet Bonnie's fiancé, Jay Drake. Ed Taylor is our neighbor and raises free-range chickens."

"Pleased to meet you." Ed stretched a work-roughened hand across the table. "Best wishes to you both."

Jaron gripped it and felt nothing but tendon and bone. The man didn't have an ounce of fat on him.

Maureen stirred sugar into her coffee. "Bonnie, you're awfully quiet this morning."

Beside him, Bonnie held up one finger, then drained her coffee mug. "Give the caffeine time to kick in." She stood and retrieved the coffeepot, pouring herself another cup, topping off Ed's and Jaron's before returning the pot to the sideboard.

"Bonnie feels quite strongly about her coffee in the morning," Jaron said.

"I also feel strongly about Maureen waiting on us like we're paying guests."

Maureen smiled. "If you insist, I'm sure I can find a dish or two for you to wash."

Oh, joy. Not that it wasn't fair, but visions of unending KP didn't thrill Jaron.

"We'll talk," Bonnie promised.

Maureen nodded, sipped her coffee, then wrapped both hands around the mug. "You know the closest outbuilding?"

"The one that looks like an animal shed?" Bonnie asked.

"I'm too much of a city girl to know what it was used for. We've been storing things in it. Anyway, Clint and I were thinking it would be a good place for Jay to stay. There are a couple of electrical outlets in there, but they don't work. Seth would have to take a look at the wiring. The attic is going to be a mess with the renovations and this will give Jay someplace quiet to work." Maureen glanced meaningfully toward Ed Taylor.

A cue. "I really zone out when I'm writing code." Jaron hoped he had the terminology correct. He doubted the farmer would know the difference.

"And if bookings stay as steady as they have been, we might look at converting it into a guest cottage."

"Sounds good." Bonnie dipped the last bit of her griddle cake in syrup. "You know I'm game."

Ed pushed back from the table. "Thanks for the breakfast, Maureen. You're a real sweetheart." He made as though to take his dirty dishes into the kitchen, but Maureen waved him on.

After he left, she grinned. "Guess what's for dinner tonight?"

"Chicken?" Bonnie grinned back. "Jay, you're in for a real treat. Ed's chickens are as natural as you can get. No growth hormones or anything else. Pure chicken."

Okay, so Cooper's Corner wasn't the total backwater he'd thought. "I'm looking forward to it—which brings up a point that's been bothering me," Jaron said. "I can't mooch off you and Clint forever."

"It better not be forever," Bonnie muttered into her coffee.

"One more person hardly makes a difference," Maureen said.

Twin Oaks rented out four rooms and supported five people on the income. One more person *would* make a difference. Jaron had a little cash left, but it wouldn't last long.

"Excuse me a moment." Maureen rose to see off the other family and corral her girls.

"Time to get—" one twin began.

"—the towels?" the other finished.

"Did you hear the dryer buzz?"

They nodded.

"Then okay. Fold the towels nicely, but no jumping in the pile!"

"Okay, Mommy," they said in unison, and ran out the door.

"They're actually a help there." Maureen returned to the table. "And they're learning responsibility, cooperation, how to contribute to the family and a little bit of geometry to boot."

"They're growing so fast." Bonnie had that gooey tone in her voice that women get when discussing small cute children.

It was a tone that made men very nervous, and Jaron was no exception. "Now, about me staying here—is Quigg paying you anything?"

Maureen shook her head. "Bonnie was going to live here, anyway. It's part of her contract."

"Quigg should at least pay for me. I would, but I can't access any of my accounts." Jaron was disgusted. Quigg didn't have to hire anyone to protect them; Bonnie was taken care of—the least the police department could do was pay the Coopers a stipend.

"Don't worry about it," Maureen said.

Jaron had no intention of worrying. He was going to do something about it. He'd already composed a sneering lead for a column on bullying government policies before he remembered that he wasn't writing his column.

He'd write it anyway and have it for backup. But he *was* going to give Quigg a call.

After breakfast, Clint, Bonnie and Jaron went to inspect the building. Jaron had been preoccupied on the way over yesterday and hadn't really seen the full effect of the Twin Oaks drive.

Pairs of magnificent oaks lined the drive and led to a spectacular view of the village and surrounding hills.

"Twin Oaks is named for those trees." Clint Cooper stopped beside Jaron. Bonnie kept walking.

"Each time a set of twins is born into the Cooper family, two trees honoring their birth are planted along the drive. The smallest ones way down there are for Randi and Robin, Maureen's girls." He drew a deep breath and gazed into the distance. "It's really something, isn't it?"

"Yes, it is. Though I'll have to admit, I've got the city in my blood."

"Not me. You couldn't pay me to go back."

"You lived in New York?"

Clint nodded. "Since I was a kid. I was an architect."

They talked buildings and possible mutual acquaintances. Jaron was familiar with a couple of Clint's projects. And Clint, who knew Jaron's real identity, mentioned enjoying his columns. Yet another preconception about small-town people bit the dust.

"So what made you come out here?" Jaron asked.

The other man was silent, staring into the distant hills. "My wife, Kristin, died."

"I'm sorry," Jaron said, even as something niggled at his mind.

"Yeah. Neither Keegan nor I adjusted well. By the time I surfaced from grief, he looked like a street thug, with the attitude and language to match. He was running with the wrong crowd and I knew a clean break would be best for both of us."

"He seems fine now." Not that Jaron knew anything about raising kids.

"There are moments. And we both miss Kristin like

crazy.'' Clint smiled wryly. "But believe me, things are a lot better here.''

Kristin…Cooper. Kristin Cooper. "Kristin Cooper, the art critic, was your wife?''

Clint nodded. "Did you know her?''

"We'd met. I was dating Sydney Pendleton back when she owned the Pendleton Gallery. I ran into Kristin several times at showings.'' Sydney had always been nervous when Kristin Cooper was in attendance. Kristin's opinion could make or break a fledgling artist's career. "She's missed,'' he said simply.

Clint gave him another tight nod and gestured for Jaron to follow him to the weathered building across from the garage. Jaron guessed that they'd painted it when they'd painted the farmhouse, and it looked like the paint was the glue that held it together.

Bonnie met them at the door. "Clint, this would make a great cottage.'' She disappeared back inside. Clint followed her.

Jaron peered in, not at all certain that the place wouldn't blow over in a stiff breeze. But Clint should know. The man had worked for a prestigious firm—and he'd enjoyed Jaron's columns, which meant he had good judgment.

Jaron stepped into the gloom. Bonnie and Clint must have great imaginations. He saw a dirt floor and rotting wood. Mysterious bits of metal and leather were tacked on the unfinished walls. A tarp covered the ceiling at one end, and beneath it were painting supplies and rolls of wallpaper and scraps of carpet. Aged gardening equipment took up the rest of that end.

Clint and Bonnie were talking. Bonnie was gesturing to where she wanted to install the bathroom. "Clint! This view cries out for a Jacuzzi.''

"Bonnie, we're not that kind of place. We need to stick to the family crowd."

"But with a little extra, this could be the perfect honeymoon cottage. Private and isolated…soaking in the Jacuzzi together with just the moon and stars to see you…"

"And anybody in Cooper's Corner with a telescope."

"Okay, if you're not going to go for the Jacuzzi, then how about a double claw-footed tub?"

Clint hooted with laughter. "You've been trying to unload that old tub for two years! Your mother told me so."

"But I just found vintage fittings for it."

"Hmm." Clint examined the beams and pushed at the supports. "I think the bathroom should go over here."

"That's not romantic at all! Clearly, this will be the bedroom and the fireplace should go there." She patted a spot on the wall. "It'll be easier—and cheaper—to access the main sewer line from over by the window."

"What, ten feet less?"

"We could wet vent from there. I haven't measured, but my guess is that this is outside the code distance for wet venting."

He gave a rueful smile. "It figures."

After that, they got even more technical, and Jaron tuned them out. He wandered over to the window Bonnie wanted to make part of the bathroom. This was where he was going to put a table and chair. He could look out as he wrote. He still wasn't a country person, but he might as well try to appreciate it while he was here.

"You mentioned electricity?" he asked them, still looking out the window.

"We'll get Seth to check it out if you're interested."

Interested?

After fighting to get to sleep last night, Jaron was ready to sleep in a tent to get away from Bonnie. He didn't want her knowing *things* about him. He didn't want to talk with her and he didn't want her telling him stuff, either. He didn't want to think about her *or* her stupid sheep pajamas.

As he'd listened to her voice in the darkness, he'd remembered the feel of her pressed against him, the curves she kept hidden beneath the loose clothes—except for that one pair of jeans. And knew that only a flimsy floral sheet—and the utter horror of what would happen if he actually slept with her—separated them. He was not going through that again.

He'd seen her world. Bonnie had grown up with these people and they weren't the type to tolerate no-strings sex. She had more strings than a plate of linguine.

He couldn't believe this was even an issue for him.

She'd contaminated him, that's what she'd done. Everyone knew "flannel nightgown" was synonymous with unsexy. And sheep-covered pajamas was the corollary. So why was he drawn to her? Why did he want to rip down the sheets and count sheep?

So, yeah, this place would do. At least he and Bonnie wouldn't be sleeping under the same roof. He nodded to Clint. "Have Seth check the electricity."

After Clint left, he and Bonnie straightened up the place. Bonnie had been surprised at his determination to sleep there, but he was adamant. Next they'd wrestled the folded cot down two flights of stairs and out the front door.

Maureen met them when they returned. "I need a volunteer to go into town for chocolate chip cookie supplies." She grinned. "Seems we had a run on them yesterday."

"I'll go." Jaron sounded pathetically eager, even to his own ears.

"Take my truck," Bonnie offered. "Do you drive a stick?"

"No." Jaron saw his chance at freedom fade.

"Then take my car." Maureen handed him the keys.

"Bless you," Jaron whispered.

Actually, driving wasn't something Jaron did very often, but he made it to the tiny library just fine.

On Saturday it was open for only a couple of hours, and he had about thirty minutes before it closed. Entering the door, he inhaled the smell of wood and books and smiled.

"Hello again." The pianist from yesterday's tea greeted him. She seemed to be the only person in the room. "I'm Beth Young, the librarian. We met yesterday, but I know you met a lot of people."

"I remember. You played the piano—and quite well."

She dropped her gaze. "Thank you. It's something I enjoy."

"Where did you study?"

She looked startled, then her gaze went blank. "At home. I went to weekly piano lessons like every other kid. Was there something specific you came to find, Jay?"

She didn't want to talk about herself. That was more than fine with him. He didn't want to talk about himself, either.

"I'll just look around and see what you have here." Before he finished the sentence, he caught sight of the wooden newspaper rods by the desk. "Hello—you've got the *New York Times*."

Smiling, Jaron slipped it off the rod and sat at one of the tables. Oh, bliss. He turned to the spot that should have had his column. Which one had Angela run today?

There was his picture, and beneath the byline was a notice: "Jaron Darke is on sabbatical while he works on a novel. During his absence, we'll repeat some of his most popular writings."

A book. Clever of Angela. In fact, not a bad idea at all. He'd always wanted to write a searing social novel, but had never found the time. Now time was all he had. *Thanks, Angela.*

He scanned his column, which was a compilation of the commentaries of several columns, with the outdated social-sightings gossip omitted. That was fine with him. He scanned the rest of the paper, breathing easier now that his reputation wasn't going to take a nosedive.

After finishing with the paper, he decided to check out some electronic and computer books, since he had to maintain that stupid story about being a computer expert.

He found the best ones in the children's section—simple language, lots of pictures. Perfect. He restrained himself from grabbing them all.

It was past noon and he was keeping Beth from closing. "Sorry." He stacked the books on the checkout counter.

"Not a problem." Beth hesitated, then reached beneath the counter and withdrew a form. "You'll have to fill out an application for a library card and I'll need to see some identification."

Damn. His new identity papers hadn't arrived yet. Stalling, he patted his pockets. "I don't have my driver's license with me."

"That's okay. Fill out your address and telephone number and you can show me your license another time." She laughed softly. "It's not like I don't know how to find you while you're here."

Innocent words, but they sobered Jaron. He stared at the form. Did he know what address Quigg had devised for him? No. Did he even know his phone number? No. Business address? No. He should have memorized the one from the Web site. He could put Twin Oaks, but she already knew that. He could put his mother's address, but what if Beth checked? He couldn't have anything of his connected to Jay Drake. And his mother lived in New York, not Syracuse.

He could put a fake address, except he didn't know the zip code for Syracuse without looking it up.

Jaron had taken far too long writing the name "Jay Drake." *Think.* Finally, on the address line he wrote "Twin Oaks" because he had to write something.

And miraculously, wonderfully, blessedly, she took the card and attached a plastic tab with "Drake" written on it, and filed it.

His knees were jittery. His knees were actually jittery! He swallowed dryly as she wrote out a wallet-size card in Jay Drake's name and added a three-digit number.

Jaron watched in fascination as she used the old-fashioned stamp-and-card method of checking out the books. She pulled the blue card from the pocket, wrote his number, then stamped the due date on the remaining white card. No scanning wand for the Cooper's Corner library.

"I can't believe you don't have a computer." He could have bitten his tongue.

"I'd love one, but the library is small enough that I can get along without it. And I'd have no idea how to computerize the checkout procedure or the catalog." She smiled up at him. "Maybe you could teach me."

"Maybe." Why hadn't he told Quigg to make him an accountant? "But I'm more of a software writer."

She pulled the card from *The Friendly Little Computer* and stamped the due date. "Doing some brush-up work?" She smiled as she asked, but to Jaron, it was a loaded question. And unfortunately accurate.

"One of the reasons I've taken so much vacation is that I'm collaborating on a children's computer book. I thought I'd check out the competition." Would she buy it?

She would. "Very wise." She pushed the stack of books toward him. "I'll see you at tea."

Once Jaron was back in the car, he gripped the steering wheel and took several deep breaths. That had been close.

He closed his eyes, and when he opened them, they focused on a quaint—there was no other word for it—tavern. Maureen hadn't pointed out the tavern yesterday. Jaron wondered if he dared stop in there for a…beer, probably, but he'd make it an imported one. He started the car, intending to do just that, but stopped. It was barely past noon. He could already hear the talk about Bonnie's fiancé drinking in the middle of the day.

Nope. No beer.

He gripped the steering wheel and nosed the car across the street toward Bonnie's parents' store. If her parents weren't busy, he supposed he was going to get grilled again. Grabbing the grocery list Maureen had written, he got out of the car.

Man, he hated small towns.

He hated them even more once he stepped inside the store. The general hum of conversation stopped at the sound of the bell clanging. In the few moments it took for Jaron's eyes to adjust to the light, the people inside had the advantage.

Volunteering to come to the only grocery and hardware store in town on a Saturday was not the best decision he'd ever made.

Volunteering to come without Bonnie might become a fatal mistake.

Was the entire population in here? Did they travel in packs, or what? Did he imagine that the smiles were smaller—when they were there at all—and the gazes harder? No, he didn't imagine it.

"Greetings, all." He reined in the wide Jaron smile,

substituted one that was all-purpose pleasant, and went up to the counter, where Philo had spread out an assortment of drill bits.

Jaron was very glad that he hadn't lied on his library card application. These people would have already called for a credit report and had the sheriff, or whoever passed for law enforcement here, check his record.

"Hello, Jay," his future faux father-in-law said. "What can I do for you?"

Jaron was very conscious that everyone in the store— mostly men—was unabashedly watching and listening. He placed the list on the counter. "I'm picking up a few things for Maureen."

Philo glanced at the list and gestured with a nod of his head. "Phyllis is at the grocery counter."

"Ah. Thanks." Retrieving the list, Jaron walked down the center aisle until he'd crossed over into the grocery store. He felt the gazes of each person on his back the whole way.

The conversation was higher-pitched at this end of the building, but the women reacted exactly as the men had. They stopped in midsentence to eye him.

He tried his wide Jaron smile, but only received casual ones in return.

Wow. Without Bonnie as a shield, the villagers weren't as openly friendly. They were reserved and polite, but there was no sign of the open-armed welcome he'd received yesterday.

They couldn't have found out anything about him, could they?

"Hello, Mrs. Cooper." Bonnie's mother was at the cash register, a handsome old-fashioned one—but next to it she had a thoroughly modern credit card swiper and bar code scanner hooked up to a box that printed receipts. Jars of penny candy—actually selling for a penny—were displayed kid height in front of the counter.

"Jay! How delightful to see you!" And she looked determinedly delighted, too.

He figured it was all for show, but wondered why it required such an effort. "Maureen needs a few things and I volunteered so I could have an excuse to see you and explore the town." *Don't oversell it.* Behind him, he could smell different perfumes. The women were drawing closer. Trapping him. Ready to pounce.

"Twin Oaks is lovely, isn't it?" asked a female voice.

"Yes." Jaron wondered where they were going with this.

"Maureen and Clint are doing so well," commented another. "I hear they're completely booked for the whole season."

"Sometimes there are cancellations," Phyllis said.

"Now…" one woman put her finger to her cheek "…I believe I heard her say she had a full house this weekend."

"Are you in one of the rooms, Jay?"

Oh, so that was it. The morality police were on patrol. "No, I'm temporarily in the attic."

"Bonnie's redoing the attic, isn't she?" The women were coming closer and closer, like jackals circling their prey.

"Yes." Jaron glanced over at Phyllis, but she was fiddling with something behind the counter and wouldn't meet his eyes.

"And she's rented her house out, too,"

"That's right."

It was as though they were a Greek chorus, taking turns speaking.

"So where is Bonnie sleeping?"

The million-dollar question. His best defense was the

truth. "She's camping out in a room in the attic." A floral-lined room.

Eyebrows rose as if they were choreographed. "With you?"

They practically held their breath, waiting for an answer.

He tried his best to look scandalized. "No. I'm in the attic, but I'm in the other room."

There was a collective exhaling of coffee-scented breath.

"Or I was in the other room. Once the renovations start, it'll be too noisy, so today we've been fixing up an old shed. I haven't met Seth yet, but I understand he's going to check the electrical wiring."

The smiles were wider now. Jaron's wasn't. What right did they have to judge where he and Bonnie slept? What right did they have to even ask?

"Tell us again how you met," an elderly woman in a silk jogging suit asked.

"Jay, this is Mrs. Dorn, Dr. Dorn's wife," said a relieved-looking Phyllis. "You didn't get a chance to meet them yesterday."

Gently, Jaron took the blue-veined hand in his. "You are a very lucky young man," Mrs. Dorn said. "Bonnie is a special woman."

"That she is." Jaron eased his hand away.

"So how *did* you meet?"

"Mrs. Cooper's sister and my mother are old friends. They introduced us."

"When?"

Jaron had an inspired thought. "I can't remember exactly when it was...I was dating another woman at the time. Sydney Pendleton, the gallery owner. In fact, Clint and I were talking and discovered that I'd met his wife when she used to critique showings there."

Conversation exploded. He was brilliant. He'd given them not one, but *two* pieces of juicy information to gnaw on.

He smugly put the list on the counter, but as Phyllis went to get the supplies for him, his self-satisfied smile faded, to be replaced by a leaden feeling in his stomach.

Jay Drake had never dated Sydney Pendleton.

Jay Drake had never met Kristin Cooper.

Jay Drake had spent an awful lot of time in New York City for someone who lived in Syracuse.

Jay Drake was sunk.

CHAPTER ELEVEN

HOW COULD BONNIE IGNORE Jaron when he wasn't around for her to ignore?

It was just so typically annoying of him. After she'd worked so hard all Saturday—and Bonnie had worked *very* hard, since listening to Jaron's even breathing on the other side of the sheet was interfering with her sleep—Jaron had moved into the shed-cum-future guest cottage. Seth had strung wiring and connected the shed to the main house's power line, and Jaron had made himself a nice little nest. Then he'd gone to ground and hadn't been seen since. Even his meals had been eaten on the sly, or when Bonnie wasn't there.

He certainly hadn't been to tea. It had been four days now, and people were beginning to talk. At first, they were all sympathetic concern. Was everything all right between them? Was he ill? Then they were curious. Where was he? Why didn't he put in an appearance at tea? Had they offended Jay in some way? And then they began making pointed remarks about big-city folk who snubbed locals. And they didn't even know he was really from New York and not from Syracuse.

Beth had told everyone he was working on a book, which mollified them somewhat. Except Bonnie. She wasn't mollified. She hadn't known about the book. Shouldn't he have told her something that important?

Maureen had decreed that all noisy renovation work be

done when her guests were not present in the house so as not to interfere with their stay. That meant that Bonnie and Seth got about four to six hours of work time in the attic. She was finished by teatime every day, which allowed her to respond to the occasional private distress call from Cooper's Corner residents—and skip tea, which she'd done yesterday.

But today, Seth and Clint were adding supporting braces and cutting notches in the wall studs for the DWV pipes— the drain-waste-vent system. Bonnie didn't have to be there.

She had plans. The renters had left her house and she had planned to clean it herself before the next family arrived, saving the cost of the professional cleaners the rental agent would hire. Bonnie was going to roust Jaron from his lair and make him go with her. It was just the sort of supportive domestic activity of which Cooper's Corner residents would approve. Bonnie didn't expect him to do any of the actual work, but he could use her phone line to get on the Internet, or work or whatever, as long as he stayed in the house.

Bonnie marched down the inn's steps, across the drive and down the gentle slope to the future guest cottage. She knocked on the door.

And waited.

She knew he was awake; he'd finished his shower about thirty minutes before.

"Jaron?"

She heard a scraping sound. "Nobody here by that name."

"Very fun—oh."

The door opened and he looked down at her.

Somehow, probably because she'd been irritated with him, Bonnie had forgotten that he'd adopted native dress.

She'd visualized the old urban, black-clad Jaron, the one with the goatee obscuring his strong jaw. It was easier to dislike the old Jaron.

Instead, she was faced with the new and attractively improved Jay, but with Jaron's eyes. Dark eyes that stared at her without a hint of welcome.

"Let me in before somebody sees us."

Silently, he stood away from the door and Bonnie walked in. Two space heaters chased the chill from the fall air. Beneath the window, the precise spot where she wanted to put her double claw-footed tub, he'd placed a folding card table and chair. On the table were a stack of books, his laptop, a desk lamp and...was that a soldering iron? A bright yellow extension cord—the only note of color in the place—ran the length of the room to the newly-working plug, courtesy of Seth.

She could see new plywood patching areas of the roof, and several beams had been replaced. "Very nice."

"What do you want?" He crossed his arms over his chest.

Bonnie remembered his chest. Very well. Pretending to be interested in Clint's handiwork so she didn't have to look at Jaron or his chest, she issued her invitation with all the grace of a draft board. "You haven't been seen lately, and people are beginning to talk."

"Talk about *what?* I've been keeping out of sight."

"That's what they're talking about."

"This place—" He bit off something she knew wasn't complimentary. "Don't you people have lives? How can you stand it?"

Bonnie didn't like the "you people" crack. "It's my home. They've known me all my life and are just concerned."

"They're not concerned. They're small-minded, petty and judgmental."

Bonnie felt her jaw drop. "They were so nice to you!"

"Ha!" He stabbed a finger at her. "*You* weren't around on Saturday. Once they got me alone, it was open season. I was practically accused of stealing your virtue and—" He broke off, shaking his head.

"And what? And what?"

"I thought I'd distract them by—"

"*Distract?* Why didn't you just tell them we weren't sleeping together?"

"Because—" he bit off the word "—they wanted to know precisely *where* we were laying our heads at night. I told them we were both in the attic in separate rooms. I didn't tell them the walls of the rooms were made of sheets."

"They actually asked you that? I figured Lori Tubb would have scotched that rumor."

"Not only that, they asked in front of your mother. And if I hadn't given the right answer, your father was standing by with the lynch mob."

Bonnie ruthlessly suppressed a smile. "It couldn't have been that bad."

Jaron just looked at her.

"Well, I apologize for them."

"I'm not as angry with them as I am with myself," he said. "I started to tell you that I tried to distract them with a couple of facts to chew on. I told them I'd dated a gallery owner and that I'd known Kristin Cooper."

That even distracted Bonnie. "Did you really know Kristin?"

"*Jaron Darke* did."

Bonnie considered the risk. "They're not going to know that."

"All someone has to do is talk to Sydney Pendleton and ask her if she dated a Jay Drake."

Sydney. He'd dated a woman with a chichi man's name. Sydney was a rich and thin name. She'd owned an art gallery, so that made her thin, rich, cultured, and a business woman.

Bonnie was a business owner. But her name was round and down-to-earth and practical. One out of four wasn't going to cut it. "Nobody is going to check up on your past love life." Except Bonnie. She might—no. He could have dated a hundred Sydneys. *She* didn't care.

"I think your father was taking notes."

"He doesn't want me to be hurt. That's his job."

Jaron made a noise. "I also nearly blew it at the library. I had to fill out an application for a library card and the address part stumped me. My nifty new driver's license hadn't come yet."

Bonnie gestured to the books. "So what did you do?"

"Sweated a lot and wrote Twin Oaks. She took it, but wants to see my driver's license later."

"So you've got it now. What's the big deal?"

"The *big deal* is that I nearly slipped up. I've told so many half-truths, I can't keep them all straight. And if that's not enough, that kid knows more about computers than I do. He kept asking me questions."

"Keegan?"

Jaron nodded. "So it's better if I stay here and get a reputation as a recluse."

"Trust me. It's not." Bonnie snagged his denim jacket from the nail he'd hung it on and tugged on his arm. "You're coming with me."

"Where?" He'd taken his jacket, but hadn't put it on.

"My place. I've got to get it ready for the next renters."

"And you want me to help you scrub toilets?"

"That would be 'toilet' singular. I wouldn't say no, but my main goal is for us to be seen together. You can take your laptop."

He looked as if he needed more convincing. They must have done a number on him in town. "You can get on the Internet."

Jaron shrugged into his jacket. "You drive a hard bargain."

IN TRUTH, Jaron was finding his own company very trying. He'd worked his way through the computer books and had written some very simple programs. Then he'd tackled the electronic books and had learned how to solder. He didn't know if anything he'd built actually worked because he was afraid to risk blowing out the tenuous source of electricity. And once the electricity was gone, Jaron would have to move back to the main house. And moving back to the main house meant moving back to the attic and Bonnie and her sheep pajamas and her curves and her lower lip.

He followed her to her truck. They were almost dressed alike. Both wore denim jackets—there hadn't been a lot of choice in the store—jeans and plaid shirts. She looked like Paul Bunyan's little sister.

Paul Bunyan's *cute* little sister. That was fine with him. She could be cute if she wanted; he didn't care.

The leaves were starting to turn color, but it wasn't the peak season yet. Each day he'd stared out the window, he'd seen more and more oranges, yellows and reds on the Berkshire hills. It reminded him of the passing time and the fact that his life was on hold because of a hotheaded Irish mobster and a chintz-loving interior decorator who couldn't keep his pants zipped.

Jaron had been using the Twin Oaks phone to get on

the Internet late at night when the guests had gone to bed, and sleeping in during the day. Maureen got very nervous when her phone line wasn't free. In her position, he would, too.

They'd heard absolutely nothing from Frank Quigg. Sonny hadn't been found. How could somebody with hair that color just disappear?

After a two-minute drive past the village green and its statue of a Revolutionary War soldier, Bonnie stopped in front of one of a semicircle of cottages. He remembered what she'd said about them being planned as part of a hotel.

"This is it." Bonnie got out of the truck and slammed the door, then dug in the back for her equipment.

Bonnie's cottage looked like the rest, except that she'd painted her door red. "Were you in your feng shui period?"

She glanced at him and unlocked the door. "Yes. But that's as far as I got." She stepped into what was one of two rooms. "As you can see, there isn't a whole lot of feng to shui."

One side of the room had chairs and a television, the other held a small table and chairs and the kitchen. Kitchenette, more accurately, though he hated English words that ended in "ette." By turning his head, Jaron could see her bedroom reflected in the bathroom mirror, so he had a view of her entire home from about three feet inside the front door.

Her furniture looked like flea-market finds. Nothing matched, so she'd pulled it all together by painting the wood dark and upholstering all the chairs in a heavy white material. Even the cushions on the wooden kitchen chairs were covered in the same material. "Is this white denim?"

"Yes."

"Very nice." He liked it—not for himself, mind, but he could appreciate a well-decorated home.

"Thanks." Except that a frowning Bonnie stood by one of the chairs. Sighing, she reached for a can of foaming upholstery cleaner from the bucket of supplies she'd brought in. "It looks like they ate pizza while they watched television."

"Maybe white wasn't the best choice for a rental."

"I expected some damage, but still. On the bright side, there's plenty more fabric where that came from. I bought several rolls of it at a salvage sale. The ends got stained in rusty water, but the rest is perfectly fine once you cut off the edges." She squirted the cleaner on the orangy-red smears. "There's a phone jack in the kitchen."

Jaron looked at the wall phone. He'd have to drag a chair over by the small refrigerator and set his computer on his lap. Gee, maybe that's why they called them laptops. "Is that the only jack?"

"No." Bonnie was examining the other cushions. "But the second one is in my bedroom. I'd rather you used the one out here."

They looked at each other, then away. "Right."

"Oh, and every so often, go outside and bring something in from the truck. I want to make sure everybody sees you." Bonnie went back to her bedroom.

By leaning to one side, Jaron could see her stripping the bed. He could also see the crammed bookshelf against the wall just outside her room. Jaron subscribed to the theory that one could learn a lot about a person by reading the titles on her bookshelf. By the time he stood in front of the shelf, he remembered that he didn't want to learn anything about Bonnie.

Colorful paperbacks lined the bottom shelf. They were the usual fiction bestsellers and beach books. The next shelf contained her college textbooks. Didn't she sell them back in the time-honored tradition of poor students? The rest were a mix of books he'd have to say were technical, and dozens that contained photographs of the architectural features of old buildings. He pulled out one, noting the sticky notes she'd used to mark pages. Turning to one, he saw pictures of pull-chain toilets. Bonnie had made notes in the margins about fittings and part numbers and where she'd found parts for the models.

Amazing. He wondered if his mother knew she'd fixed him up with a woman who collected pictures of toilets.

Jaron took out another book and another, becoming lost in the mostly black-and-white photographs of features of New York City buildings he thought he knew, but had never really seen before.

Bonnie emerged with an armload of dirty sheets and towels. "I thought you were going to log on to the Internet."

"I was." Jaron indicated the book he held. "You've got a thing for old buildings."

She dumped the laundry by the door. "I've got a thing for *preserving* old buildings—or at least their bathrooms."

Interesting woman. He didn't want her to be interesting. She had no right to be interesting in a town like this. On her way back to the bathroom, she stopped next to him. He could smell the cleanser she held.

"A lot of people are into architectural salvage. They find an old fireplace mantel, windows, doors and moldings for their house. Then they fill it with antiques—but then spoil it all by putting in a glaringly modern bathroom."

Jaron liked glaringly modern bathrooms. He felt any progress in that area should be encouraged. It wasn't so long ago that houses didn't have bathrooms at all.

"I show them how they can remain true to the rest of their house."

"Why don't you just build an outhouse and be done with it?"

"You have no soul." She marched into the bathroom— not a long march. A marchette.

Jaron marched after her. "I do, too, have a soul. I think what you're doing is great—up to a point. But give me modern conveniences anytime."

He'd reached the door of her bathroom and stopped. There wasn't a lot of room, and the reason there wasn't a lot of room was that an ornate claw-footed tub took up most of it. The tub was surrounded by gauzy drapes, impractical dark wood and a jungle of plants.

Instantly, Jaron had an image of Bonnie, her hair piled on top of her head, soaking in a bubble bath as she extended one lush leg and soaped it with a sponge.

And she was not wearing her sheep pajamas.

Just when the bubbles in his image reached a dangerously interesting level across her chest, reality intruded.

Bonnie, wearing bright blue rubber gloves, began scrubbing out the toilet.

Jaron waved his arm in the general direction of the tub. "This is…nice."

"Thanks." She didn't look up from the toilet.

That tub was big enough for two, if they sat just so. And Jaron was willing to sit just so. A little too willing.

Even Bonnie scrubbing the toilet didn't stop him from imagining himself running his hands over her soap-slickened skin.

He cleared his throat. "I'll take the laundry out to the truck."

"Walk real slow!" she called after him.

After that, he did log on to the Internet, but couldn't

stand watching Bonnie do all the work, so he washed the dirty dishes and wiped down the kitchen.

There was a knock on the door and Phyllis Cooper stuck her head in. "Bonnie? I saw your truck." She noticed him in the kitchen and, in Jaron's opinion, didn't look surprised.

She beamed at him, her whole demeanor different than it had been on Saturday. "Hello, Jay!"

Being caught washing the dishes was a good thing, he surmised.

"We haven't seen much of you lately."

"I've been working and staying out of Bonnie's way."

"I thought you were here on vacation."

"Mom!" Bonnie called from the bathroom. "Leave the man alone. He's on vacation, but I know you've heard he's working on a book. That takes time. Do you think they write themselves?"

"And how's that coming?"

"Fine," Jaron answered, determined to keep it short and simple.

"Well, I just wanted to pop over and see how you two were doing. When you finish, do you want to come by the store for lunch?"

Bonnie emerged from the bathroom and snagged a roll of paper towels. She met his eyes. "What time is it?"

"Quarter to twelve."

"Sorry, Mom. I've got to be somewhere at one and I'm not nearly finished here. Maybe next time."

"Okay. But if you finish early and want to drop by for a sandwich, come on." She waggled her fingers and closed the door.

As Jaron dried a frying pan—which had taken him quite a while to clean because it looked as though someone had fried rubber in it—he wandered to the bathroom door. Bonnie was wiping the mirror and all the shiny surfaces.

"Where do you have to be at one?"

"Nowhere."

"But that's what you told your mother."

"I didn't want to torture you."

"It wouldn't have been torture," he said automatically. *Yes, it would.*

"Yes, it would." Bonnie echoed his thoughts. "I understand how all the questions would get on your nerves."

"Thanks."

"No biggie."

Their eyes caught again. He wished they'd stop connecting like that. When he fantasized about a woman while she was scrubbing a toilet, he knew he was in trouble.

BONNIE WAS BREATHLESS from racing to clean her house. She wanted the job done as quickly as possible. Bringing Jaron here had been a mistake, even though it had accomplished exactly what she'd hoped it would. *And there he was, washing the dishes while she cleaned up for the next rental.* That should stop the talk.

It was just that the minute he'd stepped into her home, it had become small. It *was* small, but a cozy small. With Jaron in it, the house felt cramped small.

He took up too much room, and she couldn't keep enough distance between them, even when she was in the back and he was washing dishes at her sink.

Talk about a surprise. She'd nearly fallen over when he'd offered to help. Maybe he wanted out of the house, too.

She didn't know why she was bothered about him being in her home—she'd rented it to strangers during the past several seasons, and anything of personal or sentimental value was stored over at her parents' for the time being. The only thing other than the furniture that revealed anything about her personality was her books, and that was exactly where Jaron had gone.

She'd left her collection of architectural books on the shelves this season because she figured that the type of person interested in photographs of old buildings wasn't the type of person who would damage books.

Besides, she'd run out of room in the area her parents had allocated to her.

When Jaron had appeared at the door to her bathroom, she'd become flustered, and now the toilet was so clean it could be used as a soup tureen.

She'd seen him looking at her tub. It was the first vintage piece she'd owned and the main selling point the agent used for renting her property. It was also her place to daydream and relax, and now she'd always see Jaron standing in the doorway looking at the tub with an expression that told her he definitely saw the possibilities.

She didn't want to think about possibilities with Jaron.

But how could she not think about possibilities with a man who'd wash her dishes—dishes he hadn't eaten from?

Throwing down the rag and the can of furniture polish, she hauled her chairs around so she could vacuum beneath them.

Jaron had finished the dishes and was sitting at the computer. He wore jeans today. Usually he wore baggy khaki pants, which made him look like most of the other men in town did when they wanted to make an effort with their appearance. But he looked better than most of the other men in town in those jeans. They were new, and hadn't shrunk to fit his body, but it didn't seem to matter.

Bonnie jerked an ottoman over the area rug so hard it left tracks. It was a good thing the rug was there, or she would have scratched the wooden floor. But the physical activity wasn't helping her to stop thinking about Jaron. He was *there*. In her house. Taking up space and occupying her thoughts.

Bothering her.

But apparently not bothered by her.

SHE WAS BOTHERING HIM. Bothering him, and she wasn't even here. But she didn't need to be. Ever since Jaron had seen her bathtub yesterday, images of Bonnie in it had bothered him.

After cleaning her house, they'd driven into New Ashford for ice cream, then decided that they should stick close to home. He'd presented himself for afternoon tea and grilling, and then had come back to his cottage. It was really a glorified shed, but that sounded so pathetic he'd decided to call it a cottage. There, he'd written not one, not two, but three columns, taking out his frustration with the inquisitive village folk by skewering them. And no one knew how to skewer like Jaron.

He might even send them to his editor when this thing was over. If all went according to plan, no one here would ever know he was Jaron Darke.

This morning, he'd restrained himself from gluttony at the breakfast buffet and had begun a fourth column. Conditions were perfect. He was on a roll.

Except, of course, that Bonnie was bothering him.

He gave up and went to find Maureen to demand that she call Frank Quigg and tell him that he had one more week before Jaron was out of there. Maybe less.

He found her vacuuming the gathering room. "Maureen! Have you heard anything from Quigg?"

At the sound of her name, she raised her eyebrows and

turned off the vacuum cleaner in time for "Quigg" to resonate throughout the large room.

"Shh!" She looked all around and Jaron felt like a heel for startling her.

He lowered his voice. "I want to talk to Quigg."

"Why?"

"*Why?* Because I want to know what the holdup is. How can one large redheaded man just disappear and they can't strong-arm anybody into squealing his whereabouts? What about his family?"

"Keep your voice down!" Her face stern, Maureen grasped his arm above the elbow and escorted him to the far end of the room. If she'd whipped out handcuffs from behind her, he wouldn't have been the slightest bit surprised. At this moment, Jaron had no doubt whatsoever that the pretty innkeeper had once been a police detective. "They're watching his home, and so far, it's business as usual. His wife and daughter aren't talking—not surprising because it wouldn't be healthy for them to do so. She's hired another decorator—"

"I don't care about his decorating problems." Jaron stared at Maureen. She may have once been a cop, but she wasn't any longer, and he didn't appreciate being manhandled.

"Oh, and Officer DeMario has volunteered to be on your mother's committee for the Winter Nutcracker Ball."

This wasn't the news Jaron wanted to hear. "Who is Officer DeMario?"

"She's assigned to watch your mom. Apparently this ball raises money that pays for schoolkids to see the *Nutcracker* at Christmastime, and DeMario's little girl has been taking ballet and—"

"Very touching. The next time you talk to Quigg, tell him he has one week before I walk out of here."

"You'll be a dead man."

Jaron thought of Bonnie and the tiny piece of real estate to which he'd been confined. "I'll be a dead man if I stay here."

CHAPTER TWELVE

JARON STARED AT MAUREEN long enough for her to know he'd meant every word, then went up to the attic to tell Bonnie. He didn't know why he wanted to tell Bonnie, or what he wanted her reaction to be, but she was bothering him and he thought he'd return the favor.

He opened the door to the sound of wood striking wood, and saw Seth manhandling a sheet of four-by-eight plywood.

Bonnie looked like she was kneeling in a wooden cage. The framing cut into the once-single room of the attic. Jaron could tell that's where the bathroom was going to be. There was more framing on the other side, probably a closet or a panel to hide pipes or wires or something.

He knew nothing about construction, but it seemed that Seth, Clint and Bonnie had made great progress.

The whine of a circular saw kept them from hearing his approach. Seth, wearing safety goggles, bent over the sheet of plywood now propped on sawhorses.

Yes, good old Seth, Jaron thought sourly. He was the quiet type—but his type didn't need to talk. The tight white T-shirt stretched over a massive chest and arms as big as thighs—not Jaron's, but some men's—said all that needed to be said. Shouted, actually. Shouted to women, silly women who didn't know any better than to admire muscles.

Yeah, Jaron wouldn't be challenging him to any arm-wrestling contests, but he knew he could take him in a five-kilometer run. Bulky muscles were heavy.

He wondered if Bonnie was a silly woman. Did she admire Seth's muscles instead of Jaron's lithe strength?

Seth's type didn't look good in suits. All those over-muscled bulges would spoil the lines. Jaron looked good in suits, not that Bonnie would care, because she clearly wasn't drawn to the suit-wearing type. And that was fine with Jaron, because he didn't care to whom or what Bonnie was drawn.

He advanced into the room. Bonnie was doing something with various-sized pipes. It involved screwing them into fittings and poking them down the wall toward the floor below, bringing them back up, marking them and making a notation in a notebook.

Jaron had known she was a plumber, but there was a huge difference between being told she was a plumber and seeing her actually plumb. He watched, fascinated. Here was a woman who possessed a realm of knowledge that he knew *nothing* about. Why should he? That's what building supers were for. And, no, plumbing didn't fascinate him.

Bonnie fascinated him.

Her dark hair was pulled back into a ponytail and one piece kept falling into her face. Rather than redoing her ponytail, she kept impatiently pulling the piece of hair behind her ear, where it stayed only a matter of seconds before slithering forward to curl against her cheek.

Blueprints were spread around her as well as a larger sketch that she made notations on. Fittings and pipes in plastic, metal and copper were lined up on the floor. She looked competent. Strong. A woman to be reckoned with. And Jaron wanted to reckon with her.

Seth's sawing whined to a stop as Jaron crunched on some stray woodchips.

"Hey. What brings you up here?" Bonnie asked without looking at him.

She had sawdust on the knees of her jeans and wore a white T-shirt that said Cooper's Corner Christmas Festival 1999 in red and green on it. Her T-shirt wasn't as tight as Seth's, but it would do.

Why was Jaron up here? Oh, yes. He was leaving. But he couldn't tell her that, or work up a good dose of justifiable anger with Mr. Strong-and-Silent listening to every word.

"I wanted to see the progress."

On her knees, Bonnie measured the space from the floor to a point on a notched wall stud and marked it, then picked up another length of pipe and bent forward. Her jeans pulled tight. Her T-shirt pulled tight. The piece of hair slithered.

Jaron sweated.

He happened to glance Seth's way; maybe the carpenter's lack of motion registered. Through the safety goggles, Seth met his gaze. The other man moved the goggles to the top of his head, glanced briefly toward Bonnie, then met Jaron's eyes again. The corner of his mouth turned upward before he turned away and dropped the cut pieces of wood on a stack of similar ones.

He'd caught Jaron staring at Bonnie and had given Jaron a yeah-she's-one-hot-babe look. There'd also been an acknowledgment that she was Jaron's territory and he wouldn't trespass. He could, but he wouldn't.

Oh, he thought he could, did he? Jaron might not have his muscles, but he had...absolutely no business thinking like that. It was a fake engagement. No poaching could occur.

"Are you going to stand there all day?" Bonnie stuck a pencil in her mouth and screwed a connector to the end of the pipe. Clearly she'd forgotten the lovey-dovey act.

"Just couldn't bear to be away from you any longer, my love," Jaron said.

Bonnie's eyes widened, then understanding dawned. "How's the book coming?" Her voice was much sweeter.

"I wrote a lot last night. I'm taking a break."

Nodding, she continued doing plumbing things.

"What are you doing?"

"Getting ready to rough in the plumbing. You've heard the saying 'measure twice, cut once'?"

He hadn't, but could see the value of it. He nodded.

"That's what I'm doing."

"Then what?"

"Then I'll hook this soil stack into the main line and fit the hot and cold water pipes here. And then we call in the building inspector to make sure everything's to code." This time, she stuck her pencil in her ponytail as she took the pipe frame she'd hooked together—it looked like old-fashioned tinker toys—and pressed it into the notches in the wall studs.

"Could I help?" The offer slipped out, motivated by a reluctant desire to watch her.

Bonnie made pencil marks on the wall studs. "Have you ever done any plumbing work before?"

"No."

"Well…how about using a saw?"

"No."

"A sander?"

Jaron shook his head.

"Floating and taping?"

He wasn't sure he knew what that was.

"Have you ever done *any* construction work?"

"I assembled a floor lamp." It even worked.

Bonnie sat back on her heels, pulling the denim tight over her thighs. The pencil went back into her ponytail, the movement of her arms pulling her T-shirt.

At that moment, Jaron wished he'd accepted a friend's invitation to go on a Habitat for Humanity building mission, because he desperately wanted to be able to do something to prove himself in Bonnie's world. In Bonnie's world, people constructed things out of other things. They created useful things.

Jaron could visualize Bonnie as a pioneer woman coping admirably, whereas all he could do was write about the experience—not a useful survival skill.

"Well, Jay…" She looked around, trying to find something for him to do, catching her full lower lip in her teeth as she did so.

Jaron felt every pull on her lip deep within him. "I could paint." Anyone could paint.

"We're not at the painting stage."

The fact was, he was totally useless here and they both knew it. He dredged up a cool smile from somewhere. "Never say I didn't offer."

"Okay." Bonnie had already returned her attention to her work. "See you later."

And, feeling completely and utterly worthless for the first time in his life, Jaron went back downstairs.

GOOD. It was time for Jaron to realize what a worthless parasite he was.

Bonnie was feeling very accomplished—both in her work and in her one-upmanship game with him. *She* was making an actual contribution. Once she and Seth were finished, there would be a fifth guest room for the B and B. She and Seth had worked on the original renovations, too.

Bonnie had something to show for her time other than a bunch of snotty comments about people and restaurants that catered to the underworld. She, Bonnie, was a valuable member of society. If she was gone, drains would clog and toilets would overflow. Old fixtures—history—would be destroyed. She both created *and* preserved. Take that, Jaron Darke.

Except…except she'd seen the look on his face when he'd offered to help and there was nothing he could do. She didn't like seeing him look that way.

Yesterday, he'd washed her dishes. He'd charmed her friends and family. He'd tried to protect her reputation.

He'd stood by her on the street when she'd refused to leave. He'd gotten them out of that seedy hotel, calming her when she would have panicked. He'd stayed with her until she was back home.

She touched her cheek, now all healed, and remembered Jaron shoving her into the side of the restaurant and covering her with his body. She'd felt his heart pounding against her backbone.

And he didn't even like her. What would he be like with someone he truly cared for? Truly loved? Bonnie wished she knew.

The thought struck her harder than her cheek had struck the brick wall. *She wished she knew.*

Why? Why did she want to know? Even though he was all those admirable things, and looked okay—more than okay, since she was being fair—he was still Jaron. She didn't—she couldn't… Bonnie's mind refused to form the word.

"Earth to Bonnie." Seth had finished sawing more plywood. "Are you going to break for lunch or work straight through?"

She really ought to work straight through. But she really wanted to see Jaron. "I'm breaking for lunch."

Heading downstairs, she heard Maureen vacuuming in the guest rooms, which meant she probably hadn't fixed any sandwiches for them yet. Bonnie followed the sound, intending to ask if Maureen wanted her to start lunch. Yes, she and Seth both were charging less for their labor in exchange for meals, but Bonnie knew Maureen could barely keep on top of things as it was. Between running the B and B and looking after the twins, Maureen put in full days. Not to mention the stress of wondering if her next guest was a member of the mob in disguise, or the guy who was after her.

Bonnie walked into the room where she heard the vacuum cleaner. "Maureen, would you like—" Breaking off, she stared at the dark-haired man wielding the vacuum cleaner with the careful movements of one who is learning a new skill. "What are you doing?"

Jaron's black eyes were expressionless. "Vacuuming."

"I see that, but why?"

He flipped the off switch. "I'm making myself useful."

Bonnie hardly knew what to say. "You've become quite domestic lately."

"The twins were hungry, so I offered to do this so Maureen could get them something to eat." He flipped the vacuum back on, apparently considering the conversation at an end.

Bonnie stood in the doorway for a moment. There was something extremely sexy about the play of muscles in a man's back as he vacuumed. She'd never realized it before. But had she ever watched a man vacuum before?

Jaron effortlessly moved the bed and vacuumed the area

by the wall. Even she didn't do that all the time. He was rhythmically methodical, with long smooth strokes, and was able to work his way into tight corners. He looked like a natural. At the vacuum. She swallowed and went downstairs to make sandwiches.

After that, Bonnie noticed that Jaron vacuumed the entire B and B every day. He never complained. He complained about a lot of other stuff, but never vacuuming. He didn't visit Bonnie in the attic again, either. It was probably just as well. It didn't stop her from listening for the door all the time, which was likely why she marked one pipe at both ends and ended up with a backward assembly. She was so embarrassed, she pretended that she'd done it on purpose.

With her load lightened, Maureen had lost her haggard-around-the-edges look, and Bonnie could almost believe everything was normal.

And then came the day of the scones. Clint was helping Seth in the attic and didn't have time to bake his traditional chocolate chip cookies.

Bonnie had used Maureen's shower to clean up after she'd finished for the day, and when she stepped out into the hall, she smelled something other than the usual chocolate in the air.

She followed her nose to the kitchen, where Jaron, in another stunning display of domesticity, was pouring a glass of milk for Keegan's after-school snack. Keegan was stuffing something white into his mouth. The twins had a head start on mouth stuffing.

"'Nother one." Randi held out her plate

"Please." Robin just held out her hand.

"Only if it's okay with your mother." Jaron had tied a tea towel around his waist, and flour dusted his wrists. He'd never looked better.

"Just this once," Maureen said from the sink.

"What are those?" Bonnie asked.

"Scones." Jaron pronounced it to rhyme with "gone." "They're traditional with tea. Have one."

Like Robin, Bonnie held out her hand.

"No, no, no." Jaron's eyes twinkled. "Presentation is everything."

Jaron's eyes twinkled. Jaron's eyes didn't twinkle. Ever. He wasn't a twinkly eyed sort of person.

Afterward Bonnie knew it had been a warning. *Alert. Life-changing moment ahead.*

Jaron opened a cabinet, got down a plate and put one of the scones on it, but Bonnie wasn't thinking about scones. She was thinking about eyes that had twinkled when they never had before, and she was waiting for the moment when he looked at her again so that she could see if they were still twinkling or if it had been the afternoon light coming in through the kitchen window.

He must have been holding the plate, but she was searching his eyes and not noticing the plate...and they definitely twinkled. The corners even crinkled. Her mouth fell open. Jaron popped the scone in.

And that was when Bonnie fell in love with him.

Vaguely, she was aware of shrieks and giggles from the twins and laughter from Keegan and Maureen, but mostly she was aware of Jaron, who was not laughing, but smiling as he gazed down at her.

Bonnie took a bite of the warm, biscuitlike scone, and as the decadent buttery taste filled her mouth, she wondered if he knew. Could he tell that she loved him? That his vacuuming and his dishwashing and giving Maureen some relief, and his calculated-to-please killer smiles, and his unexpected kindness, and his coolness in a crisis, and his innate decency, and the strength in his arms had all been gathering together until they spelled *love* in her mind?

"You made these?" she asked when she'd chewed and swallowed. She sounded normal. How could she sound normal?

Looking pleased with himself, he nodded. "I was paired with a celebrity chef for a fund-raiser and he taught me."

"They're fabulous."

He rolled out another thick circle of dough. "Thank you."

"And they're going to be served at tea." Maureen washed the twins' hands and faces and sent them off to play.

Keegan wrapped another scone in a napkin, grabbed his backpack and followed the twins out of the kitchen.

"Keegan! Don't get crumbs on the floor!" Maureen called. "Jay just finished vacuuming."

Now, there was something a person didn't hear every day.

Bonnie munched her scone as Jaron used a drinking glass to cut out more circles from the dough. What was she supposed to do now? How did this love business work? She was pretty sure she shouldn't say anything to Jaron in front of Maureen. And the rest of the time, she barely saw him.

And even when she did get the opportunity, what would he say back?

AT LEAST HE'D FINALLY found something he could do in this rural world, Jaron thought.

He put the latest cookie sheet of scones in the oven, glad he had an excuse to be in the kitchen and not out there on the front lines with the citizens of Cooper's Corner. Not that his being in the kitchen had stopped Bonnie's mother, the Tubb woman and a couple of others from coming to see him in action. Phyllis had basked in the glory of having a future son-in-law who could bake.

Jaron hadn't even known he remembered how to bake these. The event had been a day-long feast for charity, with different chefs and celebrities preparing each course of every meal. He'd drawn tea, and counted himself lucky. A friend had had to hack at chickens and was now a vegetarian.

Bonnie had seemed stunned at his proficiency, but in a good way. He wondered if Mr. Muscles upstairs knew how to bake anything.

Jaron wanted Bonnie to see him good at something. She was good at what she did, even if what she did was plumbing. But there was also her respect for the integrity of old buildings. He'd been surprised at her extensive research library and the sheer volume of notes that hinted at the number of vintage fixtures she'd installed. He'd read some of those notes and seen how she analyzed the ornamentation, suggesting complementary designs for the rest of the bathroom. Her work was as much art as anything that had been in Sydney's gallery.

The plumber as artist—who'd have thought it? His mother and Cokie, that's who.

On the heels of his thoughts, Bonnie came into the kitchen carrying cups and plates. "Hey, you're a hit again."

"Just until the next rumor starts."

"The current rumor is that I'm a lucky girl." Bonnie ran a sinkful of sudsy water. "We're running out of dishes."

Maureen came in with another tray. "Thanks, Bonnie. *Everybody* is here today." She stacked the plates and cups on the counter beside Bonnie.

"Aunt Maureen!" Keegan's voice sounded outside the kitchen.

"That can't be good," Maureen murmured.

He burst through the door. "Your toilet is overflowing and there's water all over!"

"My cue." Bonnie dried her hands and ran off.

"I'd better see where the girls are." Maureen was right behind Bonnie.

So. That left Jaron in charge. He liked being in charge. Not just anyone could take command on a moment's notice. Seth probably couldn't have.

After finishing the dishes, Jaron loaded a tray with the batch of scones fresh from the oven and went forth to charm the citizens of Cooper's Corner once more. Only there were just a few people left in the gathering room. When Jaron didn't recognize any of them, he figured they were guests. He offered them scones, then impulsively decided to bring a couple to Bonnie.

He found her still in Maureen's bathroom. Angry mother sounds came from behind a closed door, and he guessed that the twins had had something to do with the overflow. Two large laundry baskets of wet towels were in the bathtub. The floor was damp, but Bonnie, in a blouse and slacks, was on her knees with a strange device that had a handle she rotated.

"Any luck?" He sat on the edge of the tub, thinking that a large percentage of their conversations took place with a toilet between them.

"Not yet. Super Slide Kelly is stuck down there."

"Who?"

"The twins' toy. I'm trying to pull it back through rather than force it into the pipes."

"What's that thing?"

"A closet auger. There's a coiled wire out the other end that I'm trying to work around the doll."

Good Lord, he was carrying on a conversation about plumbing. "I brought you a couple of scones."

She gave him a quick glance. "I'm kind of in the middle of things here."

Jaron held out the napkin and fanned the aroma toward her.

"Hmm. Are those warm?"

"You bet."

She sat back on her heels. "Maybe just break off a little bit."

He did so and offered it to her. Their eyes met. Desire shot through him, unexpected and fierce. When Bonnie leaned forward and took the piece of scone, he felt her lips against his fingers. She began to chew, and all Jaron could do was stare at her mouth, mesmerized. It was time he acknowledged that he was more than a little attracted to Bonnie Cooper. He was surprised the room wasn't steaming.

She swallowed.

"More?" His voice was a whispered croak.

"I'd better not."

Then she went on doing plumbery things—perfectly unaware that she'd knocked Jaron for a loop—until she pulled a doll with platinum-blond hair from the toilet.

"Should I applaud?" Jaron asked, trying to regain some equilibrium.

Bonnie tossed the doll in the sink. "If you wish." She flushed the toilet and watched the water move through the bowl.

Watching water spin around a toilet bowl with a woman he ached to touch was one of the more surreal experiences of his life. There was definitely something going on between them. Couldn't she sense it? Did she see the swirling water as a metaphor for their emotions?

Apparently not. "Turn on both tub faucets full blast for me, okay?"

"What about the towels?"

Bonnie shrugged and turned on the sink faucets. "They're already wet."

With everything going full blast—not as blasting as Jaron preferred, but he hadn't complained—Bonnie flushed the toilet again. The water noticeably slowed.

"Hmm. I don't like that." She indicated that he should turn off the water. "It looks like Kelly wasn't the first explorer in these pipes. Come on up to the attic. I want to test the pressure from up there and I need your help."

"Does that make me a plumber's helper?"

"Very funny."

Desire will make a man do strange things, Jaron thought as he followed an oblivious Bonnie upstairs.

He was not accustomed to being in a position where he couldn't communicate his desire or ascertain whether it was returned. Clearly now was not the time, but though his mind got the message, his body didn't.

And so after a while, his mind surrendered.

Bonnie was tapping and twisting and doing more plumber things. Jaron was just along for the ride and the opportunity to watch her silky, light purple blouse slide over her skin.

"Okay. I want to listen to the pipes because I think the main line might be partially obstructed, and if I don't get it fixed now, I'm going to have trouble later."

"Can you tell just by listening?"

"I know every inch of the plumbing in this place and I know how it should sound."

"Sounds like a plan."

"If you can help, it'll be faster. See the water shutoff valves where the sink will be?" She pointed.

Jaron nodded.

"I'm going to open the main valve here, and when I tell you, you're going to open those. I'll listen, then I'm going to want everything shut off real fast, 'cause if you don't, water is going to come shooting out. Those end caps are only temporary."

"Gotcha."

"It's not going to be for very long," she warned.

"Understood." It was hardly brain surgery.

"Ready?"

At his nod, Bonnie pressed her ear to the pipe and struggled to open the main cutoff valve.

"Here, let me." Jaron walked over to help her.

"Stay there. I can get it." Bonnie reached into her toolbox.

But Jaron figured a good twist would open it. Bracing himself, he grabbed the valve and sharply turned it. He felt a fleeting satisfaction when he felt it move. He was man. He was strong.

Too strong. The valve head twisted off and ended up in his hand.

CHAPTER THIRTEEN

JARON STARED at the silver knob.

"What have you done?"

A rumble sounded below them.

"I—"

"Get out of the way." Bonnie frantically grabbed a wrench of some sort and began twisting the stub of the valve.

She wasn't fast enough. Brackish water spurted through the pipes and popped off the end cap of the toilet water line, gushing all over them. Jaron pressed his hands over the open pipes, but only managed to spray the water everywhere. Bonnie kept working with the valve, and in seconds the water was a trickle, then stopped.

There was silence, except for drips splatting on the floor.

Soaked, Bonnie drew a deep breath and turned to him. Just then, the two end caps for the sink shot off, and residual spurts of water christened the pile of nearby Sheetrock.

With a furious look at Jaron, Bonnie grabbed one of the garbage bags by the door and dragged it over. "I can't believe you did that."

"I'm sorry." What more could he say?

Using a screwdriver, she stabbed the garbage bag, ripped it open and dumped the contents. A cloud of sawdust rose, then settled and absorbed the water on the floor. Bonnie, Jaron and the Sheetrock absorbed the rest.

"You're sorry." She pointed a trembling finger at the Sheetrock. "That's ruined."

"I'll pay for new," he offered, then had to add, "when I can access my bank account."

"Look at this mess!" She ran a hand through her wet hair, leaving sprinkles of sawdust in it. "I gave you a simple job and you couldn't even do that."

He was not about to be scolded like a child. "Perhaps if you'd done a better job of installing the valve handle—"

"I told you it was *temporary*."

"I've apologiz—"

"Oh, my gosh, the wiring! I suppose it got wet, too." Bonnie rubbed her hands over her wet sleeves. "Congratulations. You've undone hours of work."

That…was…it. Jaron's tongue hadn't been sharpened on the whetstone of his column lately, but Bonnie was nowhere in his league for cutting comments. He was preparing to deliver a scathing comment on uppity plumbers when he got a good look at the wet Bonnie.

Her clothes clung to her in a way that settled the question of her figure once and for all. The satin blouse stuck to her body like a second skin. He could see the outline of her bra. It had lace on it. He hadn't figured Bonnie for a lacy underwear kind of woman.

She glared at him. "It's freezing in here! You could at least get a towel instead of just standing there!"

He could see the outline of what was *in* her bra.

"I can't believe you did this," she babbled as her anger grew. "I can't believe *I* did this."

Jaron closed the gap between them.

"Clint is going—"

She broke off when Jaron grasped her by the upper arms. He would never know what she thought Clint was going to do because he was far more interested in kissing her right then. And just before he took her mouth with his, the look in her eyes told him she was more interested in kissing him, too.

He should be furious with her for being furious with him. Instead, he was very, very glad that his arms were full of wet Bonnie and that her lower lip was once again under his dominion. Just to celebrate, he sucked it gently into his mouth.

She gave a little shuddery moan and wrapped her arms around him as though she never intended to let go, which was a-okay with Jaron. His entire body—well, not his *entire* body—relaxed and shaped itself to her curves.

She fit as though she was made only for him, and she was kissing him back for all she was worth.

Life was good.

She tasted of tea and his scones and Bonnie. Her arms warmed him against the chill of the unheated attic. He splayed his hands across her back to do the same for her. But mostly he just zeroed in on what it felt like to kiss her after trying not to think about kissing her for so long.

He recalled with clarity that she'd found his previous kisses substandard. As a matter of fact, now he did, as well. He knew her now, knew she wasn't his type, and wanted her anyway. Maybe it was because he'd recently realized that his type was basically useless. Yes, the arts were important, but if he had to choose between one of the paintings in Sydney's former gallery or indoor plumbing, he'd choose the plumbing. And if Bonnie installed it, he'd have art, as well. Maybe that was the key to her attraction—Bonnie was a practical artist.

She was also an enthusiastic kisser, and Jaron wasn't about to do anything that might curb that enthusiasm. They explored each other, tasted each other, and breathed with each other. Jaron could feel heat rising from their damp clothes.

They should get out of their damp clothes. Without breaking the kiss, he brought his hand between them and unbuttoned the top button of her blouse. He was working on the second when he realized that the pounding he heard was not the blood in his head, but someone running up the stairs.

The door slammed open and Bonnie and Jaron broke apart. A breathless Keegan stood there, staring at them, obviously trying to decide if he should leave or not.

"What is it?" Bonnie asked in a near normal tone of voice.

Wait a minute. How could she sound so calm? Jaron wondered. *He* wasn't calm. She shouldn't be, either.

"Mom sent me up here to find out what happened." He looked around. "Sh—"

"Keegan!"

He rolled his eyes. "Shoot. There. I said shoot, so you don't have to go reporting to Dad."

"Have I ever reported your language to your father?" Bonnie asked.

"Nah. You're pretty cool. So what happened up here?" He nudged the sawdust pile with his foot.

Jaron was pretty sure he wasn't referring to the kiss he'd interrupted.

Bonnie pushed her damp hair behind her ears. Jaron thought he saw her hand tremble. Maybe she wasn't as calm as he thought. "I was testing the pipes and couldn't get the valve closed in time."

Jaron spoke up. "I broke off the valve." It was his fault. She didn't have to protect him.

"The result is the same. Could you get some more trash bags from Maureen for us?"

Keegan's gaze shifted from one of them to the other. "Okay." He turned and pounded down the stairs.

Jaron heard him yelling the gory details to Maureen and everyone within a four-state area.

"Well." Bonnie looked everywhere but at him.

Jaron touched her chin until she looked up at him. "We're past the awkward stage."

"*You* may be, but I'm not. I mean, if Keegan hadn't come up here..." She put both hands to her cheeks. "Or if he'd come about ten minutes later..." She groaned.

"I'd like a rain check on those ten minutes."

He could see doubt setting in. "Jaron..."

Footsteps sounded again. Keegan, with his usual impeccable timing, had arrived with a box of garbage bags. Until today, Jaron had had nothing against Keegan, but the kid was putting a serious cramp in his progress with Bonnie.

"I'm finished with my homework. You want some help cleaning up?"

That was suspiciously nice of him, Jaron thought.

Bonnie must not have thought so. "Sure." She got the two push brooms that had been leaning against the wall by the day's trash and handed one to Keegan, which left Jaron twiddling his thumbs.

He eyed the Sheetrock. It had acted like a sponge, which was bad for it, but good for stopping the water from doing further damage.

"Don't go near any of the outlets," Bonnie warned Keegan.

"Okay."

"Shall I put the wet parts of the Sheetrock in bags?" Jaron asked. "Some of it's salvageable."

Bonnie leaned her broom against the wall and came over to the soggy pile. "Maybe Seth and Clint can use some smaller pieces." She walked over to Seth's worktable and picked up a small black-handled tool. "This is a drywall saw. Use it to cut away the wet parts."

The saw didn't look big enough to hurt him. Jaron got to work. The drywall was frighteningly easy to cut and the wet parts just disintegrated. And this was the stuff walls were made of?

"Can I ask you guys something?" Keegan had amassed an impressive pile of wet sawdust.

"Sure," Bonnie answered.

"You're engaged, right?"

Uh-oh.

"Right," she confirmed.

"Well…how did you get together? I mean, how did you find each other and know you wanted to get married?"

"Whoa." Bonnie puffed out her cheeks.

Jaron rescued her. "The short answer is that my mother and Bonnie's aunt Cokie introduced us."

"Why?"

"They thought we'd like each other."

"And you did. Wow." Keegan was silent, and neither Bonnie nor Jaron corrected him. "See, that's what I want to do for my dad. He misses my mom."

"I knew your mother," Jaron said quietly.

Keegan's eyes grew round.

"We met at a gallery."

"Yeah, she liked paintings and stuff."

"She was a vibrant woman." When he saw Keegan hanging on his every word, Jaron told a couple of stories about Kristin Cooper.

Bonnie listened, quietly filling a garbage sack with some of the wet gypsum he'd sawed off.

Keegan questioned him until he was satisfied that he'd heard everything Jaron had to tell him. "I want to find a lady like my mom so my dad can marry her and be happy again.''

"Well, Keegan, it's not that simple," Bonnie told him.

"I *know* that. He never meets anybody but tourists, and they don't stick around. There's one lady who stays here sometimes. Dr. Dorn is her grandfather.''

"Oh, you mean Emma Hart.''

"The radio talk-show host?'' Jaron raised his eyebrows. Emma Hart's show was for adults only. Extreme Talk Radio, they called it.

"Yeah. She talks a lot like my mom and she's pretty, so I asked her if she wanted to go out with my dad, but she already had a boyfriend." Keegan slumped over the broom handle. "I'm having a hard time finding anybody for him, so when I do find somebody, I want to get it right." He straightened. "So I want to know what you guys had to do to fall in love.''

BONNIE SMILED, but inside she was laughing hysterically. She hadn't had to do anything to fall in love. Love had come to her with all the finesse of a hit in the head. And she'd barely had time to deal with that before Jaron had kissed her.

No, that wasn't kissing. That was fusing. They'd separated so abruptly, she felt as though part of her had been torn away. And now, Keegan was asking her about love because he thought she was in love, which she was, but Jaron thought she was pretending, which she wasn't.

But Keegan was waiting for an answer, and Jaron, after kindly telling him stories about his mother, hadn't given him one. It was up to Bonnie.

"I believe you have to get to know the person first. It helps if you don't always see him on a date, where you're using your date manners. You need to see him as he really is. How does he treat other people? How does he treat his family? What is important to him? Are those things important to you, and so on. And then, one day, you realize that you're happier with that person than without him and…'' She trailed off because she didn't know what happened next. She knew it wasn't to fake an engagement so it would be easier to hide from the mob.

''And you get married,'' Keegan finished for her, which was good because Bonnie had grown a sudden lump in her throat.

Jaron wasn't thinking in happily-ever-after terms. He was thinking in ten-minute terms. Bonnie didn't want to be a ten-minute fling—and by golly, if she did have a fling, it had better be longer than ten minutes.

''You have to be ready to love,'' Jaron said. ''You have to know who you are first and be comfortable with that before you can love, because love changes you.''

''It does?''

''Hasn't being without the woman he loves changed your father?''

Keegan nodded solemnly.

''When you're in love, you see yourself and the world in a different way. Have you told your father that you're okay with him dating someone?''

Keegan shook his head.

''Try that,'' Jaron counseled.

So Jaron believed that love changed a person. It sounded as if he was speaking from experience, but Bonnie couldn't tell if he thought changes were good or bad.

A little while later, they finished cleaning up the mess and Keegan left, taking one of the heavy trash bags with him.

Jaron closed the door after him and hurried back to Bonnie. "Alone at last." He bent his head to kiss her, but she turned her head and his kiss landed on her cheek.

"What's wrong?"

What was wrong was that she loved him and he didn't love her. "This isn't a good idea."

"It's an excellent idea." His hands caressed her back in warming circles.

"I...I can't." She knew where this was leading— straight to heartache. In spite of her feelings, they had no future. They were too different, and what's more, they liked their differences.

"You could a few minutes ago. I didn't imagine you kissing me back."

"I know." She tucked her hair behind her ears. With it still damp and drying all kinky, and her being soaked and breaded in sawdust, she knew she must look horrible.

But Jaron obviously didn't notice. He was staring at her, and his eyes, which she'd thought cold and opaque until she saw the twinkle, now looked warm and almost unbearably intense. He wanted her.

But he wasn't going to have her, not the way he wanted, just because she was all that was available to him.

Giving her a gentle smile, he drew his fingers down the piece of short hair that kept bothering her and tucked it behind her ear. "Bonnie, there's something between us. I didn't want it, didn't expect it, but it's there."

And how. "And it can stay there."

"Why? What's changed?"

"Nothing. Nothing's changed." She couldn't tell him she loved him, because he'd use the knowledge against her. "It's just not right for me."

He misunderstood. Gesturing around them, he murmured, "Not here, not now. But soon." He kissed her temple.

She pushed at his chest. "Not anywhere at any time. This isn't New York. I don't do flings."

His expression changed, as though a window shut behind his eyes, and they went black and opaque again. "Neither do I. The novelty wore off at least a decade ago."

He dropped his arms. They left a lingering warmth on her skin that cooled all too quickly. "I thought you would have learned that about me."

Incredibly, she heard hurt in his voice. "I didn't mean— but I have to live here with these people. I have to face them and work with them and—"

"And apparently live *for* them as well. Fine. I won't bother you anymore." He took a few steps toward the door, hesitated, then turned back to her, his jaw set. "When you decide—*if* you decide—to be your own person, I'll be in my room. If you come to me there, mean it."

"Since when did being my own person mean I have to have sex?"

He kept walking.

"You're saying that men and women can't be friends?" She should keep quiet. "No middle ground? No discussion? Just have sex with you or stay away?"

At the door, he gave her a searing look. "It would be more than sex. And that makes you afraid. I thought you were braver than that, Bonnie." And he left.

She should have kept quiet. Jaron was right—she was afraid. But she wasn't afraid of him, she was afraid of herself.

BONNIE WASN'T AT breakfast the next morning, which was just fine with Jaron. After a solid—okay, broken—night's sleep, he applauded Bonnie's restraint. Clearly, they were the victims of hormones and circumstance. That she should have been the one to recognize this only pointed out how contaminated he'd become by this environment.

He'd let fresh air and a few pretty leaves dim the memory of honest smog and concrete and steel.

Sitting at his computer—and not looking out the window—he opened a file.

People thought the country was so much better than the city. Just let them try to survive without the city! The worst were those who disdained urban culture even as they took what it offered.

No, the worst were those who fled the city, feeling that real life was in the country, and then proceeded to build mansions with all the urban conveniences.

Or no, the worst of the worst were the country people who catered to them. Take Cooper's Corner with its fake antique facade and people who pretended to be truly living the simple life. Put a man in plaid and he was imbued with the wisdom of the ages.

Jaron wrote for hours, holding nothing back, trying to remind himself of who he was. But even as he tried to extol the virtues of his beloved city, he saw it in a different light, filtered through his experiences since coming here.

Filtered through Bonnie, damn her. The fragments he'd written for future columns lacked the bite of those he'd written before. He couldn't see things in black and white as easily. He'd lost his edge.

THE DAMAGE could have been much worse, both to herself and to the attic renovations. Sheetrock wasn't that expensive, and the water had dried without ruining anything. And Bonnie had made the right decision about Jaron.

She packed away her tools and swept the area, since there wasn't anything more she could do until the building

inspector arrived to give the go-ahead on installing the tub,
sinks and toilet. She was looking at another ten days' work
at the most, and that was if she took her time. After that,
she'd hang around and help, of course, but if circumstances
were different, she wouldn't.

Maybe she could offer to assess the other outbuildings
and help Maureen plan for future expansion. She knew
Maureen and Clint couldn't afford anything else for a
while, but if they were interested, Bonnie could be on the
lookout for more vintage fixtures. There had been some
gorgeous pedestal sinks back in New York.

She winced. Jaron thought he was the one who was most
inconvenienced, but Bonnie's life was on hold, too. She
couldn't risk going back to New York or going antique
hunting around New England until Sonny had been found.

"I'm pretty much done here until the inspection," she
told Seth. "I think I'll go check in with my parents."
Maybe someone else's daughter had flushed a Super Slide
Kelly.

Seth held up a hand in farewell and went back to work.
Bonnie watched him for a moment. It would have been so
convenient if she could have hooked up with him, but the
chemistry just wasn't there for either of them.

Naturally, as she walked down the attic stairs, her
thoughts turned to the one person she did have chemistry
with—Jaron.

They needed to talk, and in spite of what he'd said, there
was plenty of middle ground between an all-out affair and
completely ignoring each other. Eventually, they were going to have to appear in public together, and Bonnie
wanted to have things smoothed over between them before
that happened. The people here knew her too well and
would pick up on any tension in a minute.

Her mother had started fishing for possible wedding

dates. Christmas? Late winter? Spring? Next summer? Twice Bonnie had caught her thumbing through bridal magazines, and then had to pretend an interest she didn't feel.

If she ever did get married, this was the time of year she wanted to do it, when the trees were flaming with color, the air was crisp and the sun was bright. And she wanted to wear a simple long white gown and get married in the village church with Pastor Tom performing the ceremony and the whole town watching.

Jaron would hate it, but he wouldn't be the groom, would he?

At the thought, tears scalded her eyes.

"Bonnie?" Maureen called up to her from the foot of the stairs.

Bonnie blinked rapidly. "Yeah?"

"Would you meet me in my office?"

"Sure."

Maureen and Clint shared an office on the first floor. When Bonnie got there, Maureen immediately closed the door. "I just wanted to give you a heads up. One of the guests has been asking a lot of questions—not that they all don't ask questions—but his... I don't know."

"Yes, you do." Bonnie's heart picked up speed. "That's why Quigg relies on you. Does he have red hair?"

Maureen shook her head. "No, he says he's a social worker from New Hampshire working on a study, but something didn't ring true. Clint noticed it, too."

"What does Quigg say?"

"Nothing yet. But if I have to, I'm sending in his water glass from breakfast so they can check the prints. I'll let you tell Jaron."

There it was. Bonnie's excuse to approach Jaron. She remembered his parting words, but this was different. He needed to know about the iffy guest. "I'll tell him," she said casually, "and then I'll probably go see Mom. I'm done here until the inspector comes."

Maureen nodded. "Be careful."

Appropriate words, Bonnie thought as she made her way to Jaron's cottage. She knocked on the door as soon as she was within reach, so she couldn't change her mind.

"Jaron? It's Bonnie." She swallowed, about to tell him that she wasn't there because she'd changed her mind, but stopped because of an awful thought. *Had* she changed her mind? Her mind was engaged in quite a campaign on Jaron's behalf, replaying that last searing kiss over and over. Bonnie *knew* she was attracted to Jaron, and even worse, she was in love with him. But it wouldn't last. It couldn't. They were too different and too stubborn and—

He opened the door.

The smile on his face was gone in an instant as he clearly read the confusion in her expression. "I take it this isn't a social call?"

She shook her head.

"Then what? A humanitarian visit to see if I've shriveled up from lack of contact with you?"

"Jaron, don't be like that." She pushed her way inside without waiting for him to invite her in.

"Like what?"

"Unpleasant."

"I'm in an unpleasant mood, which, I might point out, I was not inflicting on anybody."

His whole demeanor had reverted to Jaron Darke at his worst. That was good. Anything to make him less attractive.

"Maureen says one of the guests is asking too many suspicious questions."

"I assume they're investigating."

Bonnie nodded. "But in the meantime, she wanted to give us a heads up."

"So we can do what?" he snapped.

"Well, I...I don't know."

"Then think about it." He started pacing. "Are we supposed to dodge bullets? Shoot back? With what? We're unarmed, and I haven't noticed Maureen carrying around her old service revolver. She probably doesn't have it anymore. Say this guest is one of the bad guys—how fast can Quigg's people get here? Hmm?"

Bonnie *hadn't* thought about any of that because it had been easy not to, surrounded as she was by the trappings of normal life. "So what do we do?"

"Not 'we,' babe. *Me.*" He pointed to himself. "I'm going home. If I'm going to have to live life looking over my shoulder, then I'm going to live it in a place that has literate people who know how to carry on a conversation, who appreciate food and wine and music and theater and art and all the things that make life worth living, and who, as a bonus, do not wear plaid."

How dare he criticize her world? Bonnie gladly summoned a quick anger. "In other words, you want to return to the life of the shallow and superficial, because you couldn't hack it in the real world."

"The *real* world?" He threw back his head and gave a bark of laughter.

"Yes, the real world—the one that has real people who do real work. Honest work. Physical work."

Jaron gave her a pitying look. "Spare me from people who think dirt under the fingernails is a sign of holiness. It only means they haven't washed their hands."

Bonnie resisted the urge to check her nails. "You know, Jaron, you think you're going back to your life, but you don't have a life. You watch other people living *their* lives.

At least when I go to sleep at night, I know I've done something worthwhile.''

"Oh, please. You pulled a doll out of the toilet.''

It was the expression of disgust on his face that got to her. Bonnie burst into tears, startling herself as much as Jaron. She couldn't stand it anymore. They were saying such horrible things to each other.

"Bonnie." She felt Jaron's arms go around her. "No. I didn't mean it.'' He hauled her to him.

She buried her face in his chest and sobbed—sobbed because she loved him and everything was so wrong.

"I'm sorry,'' he whispered over and over. "I didn't mean it. Not any of it.'' He rained soft kisses over the parts of her head and face that he could reach. "I didn't want to hurt you, but I couldn't stop.''

"You said horrible things,'' she choked out.

"I know. I'm sorry.''

He was holding her so tightly she had a hard time breathing. "*I* said horrible things,'' she admitted.

"You didn't mean them.''

She sniffed and gave a watery chuckle. "Maybe some of them.''

He pushed her away from him, but still held her arms. "Why, Bonnie Cooper!''

She unearthed a tissue from her jacket pocket and wiped her eyes and nose. "I'm sorry I blubbered all over you.''

"It's a plaid shirt, so it's okay.''

She stuffed the tissue back in her pocket and rested her cheek against his chest, comforted by the beating of his heart.

They stood that way for a time. Bonnie didn't know how long.

"Bonnie?'' His voice rumbled next to her ear and she smiled.

"Mmm?"

"It's time for you to go." He paused. "If you intend to." The gruffness in his voice tugged at a heart that didn't need any more tugging.

She knew exactly what he was saying.

And she knew exactly how she was going to answer.

CHAPTER FOURTEEN

THIS TIME, Bonnie was the one who pulled back until she could meet his gaze. "I'm not going anywhere."

His eyes grew heavy lidded. "That's good, because I don't think I can let you go."

She met his kiss more than halfway. Twin groans sounded in the silence and they laughed.

"Are you sure?" he asked, his voice tight.

"No," she confessed, and his eyes squeezed shut. "But I'm staying anyway."

He relaxed and gave her a hard kiss. "Quit doing that!"

She laughed, then sobered quickly. "Unless—do you have any, uh…"

"Condoms?" He nodded.

"You *do?*" She gasped. "*Tell* me you didn't buy them in my parents' store!"

"I didn't buy them in your parents' store," he assured her. "I bought them that day in Pittsfield."

"That's almost as bad."

"I swear, small towns…"

"And what were you doing buying them, anyway?"

"You'd rather I stole them?"

"You know what I mean."

"Yeah, I do. But I also bought aspirin, Band-Aids, antacid and Neosporin. Come on, Bonnie, I'm losing the mood."

"Ha. You *are* a mood."

"I'll show you mood." He bent and kissed her.

"You think kissing solves everything," she murmured against his mouth.

"Only the important stuff." He nibbled at her lower lip. "The rest doesn't matter."

And because she wanted to—and because he kissed *really* well—Bonnie believed him. She leaned into him and parted her lips beneath his.

Jaron ran his hands beneath her jacket to her shoulders and slipped the denim down her arms. Bonnie let it fall to the floor, then wrapped her arms around his neck.

Jaron scooped her off the floor and carried her toward his bed. "I wish I had a huge bed with feather pillows and silk sheets, but all that's here is a cot."

From her vantage point in Jaron's arms, Bonnie glanced down at it. "Seems big enough."

"That's what I thought." He lowered her to the cot and knelt beside it, just looking at her.

It made her feel shy. "What?"

"You're a beautiful woman, Bonnie. And I mean woman in the truest, best sense. I've never met anyone like you."

"Oh." She blinked.

"You're not supposed to cry about it. You're supposed to revel in your womanliness."

What a good idea. She gave him a look and started unbuttoning the plaid shirt he despised. "So let the revels begin."

"I like the way you think." He carefully leaned down and nuzzled her neck, insinuating a hand between her arms so that he could unbutton her blouse at the same time.

He was better with one hand than Bonnie was with two, but she was distracted by the movements of his tongue as he traced the outline of her lips until they tingled. She sighed, then felt coolness against her skin as her blouse fell open.

It reminded her that she hadn't made a whole lot of progress with Jaron's shirt.

"Wait a minute." She sat up and worked at his buttons.

In the meantime, Jaron traced a lazy finger over the lacy edges of her bra. Goose bumps rose on her flesh.

Bonnie swallowed hard and tried to concentrate on the buttons. "Why don't you take off your shoes or something?"

"They're already off," he murmured, then used his tongue to trace the path his fingers had drawn.

Bonnie could feel her pulse in her head and her fingers and her chest and deep inside her in a place that had been pulseless for a long, long time. She shivered, hot and cold at the same time. "Then take off *my* shoes."

He chuckled. "I already did."

And when Bonnie looked down at her feet, there they were—shoeless.

Jaron blew on the moist trail across her breasts and they tingled. Pretty much everything was tingling. She groaned. "Oh, gosh, I can't do this!"

He froze. "You've changed your mind?"

"No! I mean I can't unbutton your damn shirt!"

In a second, he'd pulled the whole thing over his head.

Sighing, Bonnie ran her fingers over his skin. "I adore your chest. I've fantasized about your chest."

"I was unaware that you and my chest were acquainted." As he spoke he was slowly caressing Bonnie out of her blouse.

"Oh, yes. That first morning—I wasn't asleep and you were standing by the window...." She trailed off because Jaron was placing tiny nibbling kisses along the side of her neck, and she arched to give him better access. He caught her bra strap in his teeth and pulled it off her shoulder at the same time he unhooked the back.

She had a brief moment of anxiety as her bra fell away, but stopped herself from clutching it to her.

"Oh…my… Real breasts." Jaron filled his hands with them. "I'd forgotten how wonderful they feel."

Bonnie was surprised into a laugh. "Well, yes. What have you been dating?"

"I've had a run of fake breasts." He cleared his throat. "Not a long run. And not really a run at all, maybe a walk. A couple of hops at the most."

"Forget it, Jaron, I'm a big girl."

"Yes…you are."

"Except…"

His hands fell away.

"Oh, no." She picked them up and put them right back where they'd been.

He gave her—or rather her breasts—a huge, boyish grin. Men.

"On behalf of the sisterhood, I must point out that a woman shouldn't be judged on the size of her breasts."

"You can afford to be generous."

"Jaron!"

He finally met her eyes, but didn't stop moving his fingers in featherlight circles. "I know that, and it doesn't bother me one way or the other because I'm usually interested in the whole package, *capisce?*"

She nodded, because she could no longer speak, and as far as she was concerned, the sisterhood could take care of itself. She knew the location of his fingers to the millimeter, and that's how close he was to making her explode. Her breathing changed; she could hear it, short little gasps that made him smile.

"Now, having said that, I should also say—" he bent

his head "—that I'm very glad your package comes with breasts."

He filled his mouth with one, and Bonnie let out a long moan that might have embarrassed her if she hadn't been feeling incredibly good.

"You're so beautiful," he murmured.

"Don't talk."

"Bonnie—"

"Talking makes you stop. I don't want you to stop!"

"If I don't stop now, I'll have to stop later."

She glared at him, then became aware that he'd unfastened her jeans. Oh. Right. Clothes. Clothes had to come off. Now was an excellent time. She reached for his jeans, but his arms were in the way. "This will go faster if we each take care of our own jeans."

"I like a slow, lingering—"

"I am *way* beyond slow and lingering." Bonnie shimmied out of her jeans and underwear and was peeling off a sock when she noticed Jaron's dazed expression. "What?"

"You." He looked awed.

She, simple Bonnie Cooper from Cooper's Corner, had awed the sophisticated Jaron Darke. Well. Maybe she could do slow for a bit. She tossed her hair over her shoulders and arched her back slightly, watching him watch her. That was awe, all right. Awe and desire.

And she felt powerful and womanly and daring because of it. Slowly, she tucked the errant lock of hair behind her ear, then ran her fingers down the side of her neck, over her shoulder and slowly over her right breast.

Jaron swallowed convulsively.

She gave a little moan.

"*Bonnie.*" He looked like he was in pain, or starving, or both.

She smoothed her hand down her rib cage and over her thigh.

Jaron clenched and unclenched his hands. Bonnie continued down her calf, then slowly peeled away her remaining sock. Then she leaned back on her elbows and wiggled her toes.

After that, there was no more of that ''slow and lingering'' talk.

Jaron shucked his jeans, giving her momentary pause. Long and lean, he had a runner's body, with strongly muscled legs to match his arms. Bonnie shivered. If she'd known what she'd been dealing with before, she probably would have taken off her clothes anyway. Maybe even faster.

As he covered her body with his, she had a brief thought about the wisdom of setting herself up for heartbreak, but as she ran her hands over his back and flanks, she figured the risk would be worth it.

THIS WAS HIS FIRST TIME. His first time to make love. Nothing else compared. Nothing. Ever. His feelings for this woman threatened to overwhelm him. If he thought about those feelings, they would have scared him, so he didn't think.

Once again, Bonnie had surprised him. She'd been reluctant, but when she'd decided to stay, she'd given herself completely. Generously. Holding nothing back. Jaron was humbled and determined to give her all the pleasure he had within him to give.

She was so responsive. Her moans and soft cries fueled his own passion.

Bonnie. Jaron wanted to bury himself within her forever. And he wanted to do it now. But he held back, feeling his muscles strain with the effort, using his mouth and hands until he felt her shuddering release. Only after holding her until her breathing slowed did he raise himself on one elbow and kiss her temple.

She sighed and stretched her incredible body. Lush didn't come close to describing the curves and hollows he'd explored.

"It's been a really long time, but I seem to remember there's more to this." She opened her eyes and touched his cheek. "Please?"

Jaron lost himself in her eyes and then lost himself in her body. She was tight and hot and perfect. And right now, she was his.

Bonnie wrapped her legs around his waist and Jaron plunged deeper, feeling that he would explode at any moment. She whispered his name and something else he didn't hear, then tugged his earlobe with her teeth.

It sent him over the edge, and her name was torn from him in a shattering release.

She held him as he'd held her, and he discovered that he needed to be held. This need was a new experience for him.

His muscles quivered when he tried to take the weight of his body off her, but she pulled him close with a whispered, "Don't leave."

"Oh, Bonnie," he said, hoping she understood that he was trying to tell her that he had just been through the most intense experience of his life. He couldn't absorb it all, couldn't express himself, so he settled for another whispered, "Oh, Bonnie," and hoped she understood.

When the air chilled his damp skin, he rolled to his side, gathered her to him, covered them both with a quilt and fell asleep.

BONNIE LISTENED to Jaron's even breathing and felt the heavy weight of his arm across her waist. She wasn't sleepy at all. She felt alive in a way she never had before.

And to think she might have missed this.

She didn't have a lot of experience for comparison, but Bonnie was pretty sure it didn't get any better than this.

Jaron was not a selfish lover. If it was possible, he was almost too unselfish. She'd expected him to be controlled and demanding, but his only demand was that she enjoy herself. So she did, a couple of times as a matter of fact. The second one had caught her by surprise.

It had been right after she told him she loved him. She was pretty sure he hadn't heard her, and she hadn't really wanted him to. She'd just wanted him to absorb it into his subconscious. And then maybe his subconscious would plant the idea and he might realize that he loved her, too, at least a little.

She did know he wasn't ready to acknowledge his feelings yet, and if she stayed here any longer, she was bound to blabber on about love and scare him. She knew him well enough to know that he had to think of the idea of love all by himself.

She was going to have to leave, though. Her truck was still out front and Maureen would know she hadn't gone to visit her folks, unless she thought Bonnie had walked into the village.

And as romantic as the cot had looked before, it was still only a cot and wasn't all that comfortable now.

Bonnie carefully lifted Jaron's arm off her and sat up. She looked down at him and smiled, then leaned close and mouthed *I love you* into his ear, in case his subconscious had been concerned with other things and hadn't heard her earlier.

She slipped quietly out of the cot and gathered her clothes. There was a small rug by the bed, but the floor was dirt. Bonnie sat at his desk so she could brush off her feet before slipping on her jeans and socks. It was while she was buttoning her shirt that she actually focused on the monitor and read what he'd written before she'd interrupted him.

And her blood turned cold. She scrolled back to the beginning of the file and read page after page of his observations and comments on her town and the people in it. To be fair, he lambasted the New Yorkers who came to the country, too, but it was his writings about the people of Shekels Square, a thinly disguised Cooper's Corner, that hit home. Nothing he said was untrue, but it was the truth presented in the worst possible light. A mirror held up to people, he'd called it.

So all the awful things he'd said to her he'd really meant. They had no future. There wasn't going to be any love between them, not true love. Bonnie *was* Cooper's Corner, and if he didn't like her home or the people she grew up with, he couldn't like or love her, not fully.

Not the way she loved him.

BONNIE DIDN'T GO BACK into the main house right away. Instead, she walked along one of the bike trails to the village until she came to the spot that looked out on the huge sugar bush. It was a great view, one that photographers had turned into postcards. But to Bonnie, it was her home at its most attractive, a place where she could think.

Unfortunately, there wasn't a whole lot to think about. She couldn't force Jaron to like her town, just as he couldn't force her to like living in the city. She knew this, yet she'd fallen in love with him anyway.

At least she hadn't cried for a while. Any pinkness in her nose or cheeks would be from the cooling afternoon air.

She came back to the house to find Maureen watching anxiously from the front steps. "Bonnie!" She gestured frantically.

Bonnie took off at a run. Had her pipes sprung another leak? Or... Bonnie didn't want to contemplate what that *or* might be.

She pounded up the steps toward the front door, but Maureen intercepted her. "Come around back. I don't want to go through the tea crowd. You worried me! When your mother said you hadn't been to see her—"

"I was walking."

"At least you're safe."

"What's happened?"

"I'll tell you in the office."

When they got to the office, Bonnie saw that Jaron—a rumpled Jaron—was already there. He gave her a questioning smile, but she shook her head and stood on the other side of the room.

Maureen pushed aside some of the papers and sat on the corner of her desk. "Frank Quigg called a little while ago. They found Sonny O'Brien."

"Hallelujah," Jaron said as Bonnie exhaled in relief.

"He was dead. It was almost certainly a mob hit and this time there weren't any witnesses."

"Even better!" Jaron said. "Not that I haven't enjoyed your hospitality..." He stopped as Maureen shook her head.

"You two are still witnesses."

"To what?"

"Quigg is going to try to link this to McDormand," she said.

"Great. More power to him. But it doesn't sound like he's got much of a case. Bonnie and I can place McDormand at the restaurant, but that's all."

"And if anything, he was trying to calm Sonny down," Bonnie added, unable to believe she was defending a mobster.

"Deciding if there is a case is not our job." Maureen continued talking in a flat voice. "Sonny's sloppiness provides a motivation for his killing. You two witnessed that sloppiness and that makes you loose ends. McDormand doesn't leave loose ends. His legendary thoroughness is what has kept him out of jail. So, clearly, you're in more danger now than you were. Quigg is offering you the witness security program until you can testify before a grand jury."

"Offering?" Jaron asked.

"He can't force you into it. There are very specific guidelines for the witness security program. It's written in the U.S. Code. You can read it on the Internet. But I can tell you that it's offered only when the federal marshals consider you to be in grave danger."

"*I* have to go, too?" Bonnie asked.

Maureen nodded.

"But…this is when they give people new identities and they can't ever contact their families…" The entire time Bonnie spoke, Maureen was nodding her head solemnly.

"They're not forcing us," Jaron said.

Maureen looked extremely uncomfortable. "No, but…I can't have you staying here. I've got my daughters and Keegan to consider."

Bonnie thought she was going to be sick.

"I understand, of course," Jaron said. "I'll go pack."

Maureen held up her hand. "I'm not kicking you out tonight, but Quigg wants a decision by tomorrow."

What she didn't say was that she wanted a decision by tomorrow, too.

"You both can stay here and discuss this."

"What's there to discuss?" Bonnie asked bitterly.

"Whether you go together or separately." Maureen slid off her desk and walked to the door. With her hand on the knob, she smiled. "I was in love once myself, you know. I know the signs."

Bonnie stared at the wooden floor as Maureen shut the door. She wished Maureen hadn't said that.

"I woke up and you were gone," Jaron said softly.

Bonnie couldn't look at him.

"Or rather, Maureen woke me up, so I suppose it was good that you were gone if you would rather Maureen didn't... Bonnie, would you help me out here? I'm babbling and I've never babbled in my life."

Her eyes felt hot and she willed herself not to cry. Apparently she didn't do a very good job because Jaron was beside her, his arms around her, in an instant. "I know this is awful, but we'll get through it."

"What do we do?"

"What do you want to do?"

She looked at him and shook her head sadly, then decided to bring it all out, to squelch the will-we-go-together-or-not discussion before it started. "I'm a little bit country and you're a little bit rock and roll."

He frowned. "You're quoting Donny and Marie?"

"Jaron, I read your columns. The ones on your computer."

His face blanched. "Bonnie, let me explain. I—"

"Don't. We don't have time and it doesn't matter. Nothing will change. The point is that you would never be happy here or anyplace like here, and I wouldn't be happy in your world. So, as it stands now, anything we do we'll probably do separately."

He stared at her, his jaw working. "I don't know what to say."

Bonnie knew what he should say. He should tell her that they could make their own world. She looked at him and waited for him to tell her he loved her. If he did, now was the time. If they loved each other enough, they might find a way out of this mess. But if he didn't love her, then there was no point in wasting what time she had left here.

But he said nothing. That was it, then.

"I'm going to go spend some time with my parents. I'll probably stay the night. If you think of anything, give me a call."

How could this be the best and worst day of his life? Jaron was still groggy from sleeping most of the afternoon. He wasn't as sharp as he needed to be, and he was aware that he hadn't been at his best with Bonnie. In truth, he was still reeling from the news. He needed to clear his head.

Home. He needed to go home. If he did decide to go into the protection program, he wasn't doing it without seeing his home one last time.

He walked slowly out of the office and saw Seth loading equipment into his truck. "Seth, I need a favor."

"What's up?"

"I need a ride into Pittsfield."

"When?" Seth slammed his tailgate shut.

"Now?"

Seth shrugged. "Hop in."

Relief flooded through Jarod. He was going home. "Let me grab a couple of things and I'll be right with you."

Jaron got off the train and inhaled deeply. Ah, now there was good solid air. Air the way it should be. When a person took a breath in New York, by gum, he knew he'd breathed.

He started to hail a cab, then stopped. He wanted to walk the streets of the city. He wasn't afraid. It was dark, nobody knew where he was, and he looked very different than he had a few weeks ago.

It was time he faced the fact that he *was* different.

He walked for blocks, slipping into clubs both familiar and new, and stood outside restaurants looking at the people, his people. He went to his mother's apartment building, but couldn't get past the doorman without giving his name, and then realized it was just as well. He walked on, thinking as he went.

How could Bonnie not like the city? She liked parts of it; she had entire books with pictures of its buildings. Couldn't she feel the energy? Jaron fed off it. He felt more alive than he'd felt since…since he'd made love to Bonnie that afternoon.

He'd probably never see her again, and the knowledge left a hole in a place within him that he'd never known was empty.

After walking the streets awhile longer, he decided to go into the witness security program. He had nowhere safe to go here. Whether or not he accepted the protection, he knew he'd have to leave New York, and since that was the case, he might as well go somewhere he wanted to go. Maybe Chicago.

Inevitably, his wanderings drew him back to his apartment. If he was going to disappear, then there were things he wanted to take with him. Keeping in the shadows, Jaron watched the street. After several minutes, he slipped away and walked around the block, approaching from the other direction. He saw nothing. Still, he stayed in the shadows for nearly forty-five minutes, watching the traffic, waiting for the people who owned the parked cars to get in and drive away.

And still he waited, leaving to get a cup of coffee at a place three blocks away that he'd never been to before. He returned, staying out of sight, sipping his coffee and watching the building.

By the time he finished his coffee, Jaron was convinced that there was no one watching for him. Why should there be? It had been weeks. They'd probably given up.

Turning up the collar of his jacket, he remembered what Bonnie had said about changing the way he walked. Shoving his hands into his pockets, he hunched over, shuffling every once in a while.

Jaron's apartment building had no doorman. It relied on coded keys and two security keypads. And then, to gain access to the elevator, tenants had to key in yet another series of numbers. Jaron had always found it a bit of a pain, but not anymore.

Once he got into the elevator, he relaxed, but when it opened he checked the hallway before getting out, not that he'd know what to do if he did see someone. Unlocking his apartment, he slipped inside, leaned against the door and waited for his eyes to adjust to the darkness. Home. It was the first time he'd been back since he'd left to pick up Bonnie for the never-ending date.

He didn't dare turn on any lamps, but decided he could risk opening the blinds just enough for the street light to shine through. He stared down at the street, but noticed nothing unusual.

It was after he turned around that he saw the man sitting in his chair.

CHAPTER FIFTEEN

THE MAN IN THE CHAIR had a shiny gun pointed right at him. "Mr. Darke?"

Jaron didn't know whether it was better to be himself or not.

The man flipped on the table lamp and squinted at him, then consulted a picture. He had dark auburn hair.

Jaron was toast.

"Could you cover part of your chin?"

"Yes, I'm Jaron Darke." If he was going to go out, let him go out with dignity.

"Mr. McDormand will be very happy to hear that."

In the moment the man's eyes met his, everything became crystal clear for Jaron. He loved the city, but he loved Bonnie more, and he wouldn't be happy anywhere, even here, without her.

What fabulous timing for a defining moment. Bonnie would appreciate the irony—and she would never know. It made him angry that she would never know, angry at redheaded mobsters and angry at himself. "I have a final request."

The man was punching a number on a cell phone. "Sure, shoot."

Must be mob humor. "I'd like to write a letter."

Using the gun, the man waved Jaron over to his work desk. "Go for it."

"Really?" He didn't want to turn around and get shot in the back of the head or anything.

The man was already speaking into the phone, so Jaron grabbed a piece of paper out of his printer and a cheap giveaway ballpoint from the newspaper, and began to write. A farewell note of this magnitude deserved to be written with his 1922 Montblanc 6 on engraved Crane writing paper, but he didn't want to ask. He was already astounded at getting this reprieve. He wasn't current on mob assassination rules, but he hadn't expected to find hit men so reasonable.

Jaron wrote as he'd never written before, pouring out his heart to Bonnie, afraid that if he stopped to think, his time would be up. Above all, he didn't want her blaming herself—not that she had anything to blame herself for, but women always found something. He tried to put into words the inexpressible—his feelings as he'd made love to her. Had it been just that afternoon? In trying to describe the wonder of it all, Jaron was afraid he'd purpled his prose, and actually considered whether he really wanted this to be his last piece of writing. But it was too late now. He'd turned the paper over and was running out of room. He wrote smaller and smaller, trying to delay the moment when he'd have to reach for another piece and the man would tell him that was enough and then shoot him. But Jaron needed to address an envelope. How could they get the note to Bonnie if they didn't know her name…? No wonder they were letting him write this letter! It was a trap, and would lead them right to Bonnie.

He flipped over the paper and scribbled out her name from the "My dearest Bonnie" salutation. Maybe they'd leave the letter in his apartment for the police to find or—

Across the top of the page, Jaron wrote, "For my mother." Then he added, "Give it to her." He hoped that the red-haired man would think that Jaron wanted him to give the note to Jaron's mother, but his mother would read it and know it wasn't for her, and would understand she was to give the note to Bonnie.

Jaron was uncomfortable at the thought that his mother would read what he'd written to Bonnie, but by that time he would have died from something other than embarrassment.

He had to end the letter and wrote simply, "I may not have known it for long, but thank you for teaching me what true love really is."

Imagining Bonnie's reaction when she read that almost made him tear up.

Jaron carefully folded the letter and left it on his desk, then turned to face the man in the chair. The gun was still pointed right at him.

"Is that where you write your columns?"

A fan! Maybe he could play on that. "Yes. Do you read my column?"

"No."

Jaron was glad he hadn't offered to autograph a photo for the man.

The silence stretched between the two of them. Jaron was about to go insane from wondering when the end would come, when there was a knock at the door. He looked at the man.

"Yeah, go answer it."

This was Jaron's chance. His only chance. He'd open the door and he'd run as he'd never run before. He'd launch himself down the stairs and hope he'd get enough of a head start to dodge the bullets.

Adrenaline spurting through him, Jaron opened the door without even checking the peephole, ready to escape.

And came face-to-face with Seamus McDormand. Surprise made Jaron hesitate, and the moment was lost, especially since the space behind Seamus was taken up by two very large men.

"Mr. Darke, it's good to see you again." Seamus shook Jaron's rather moist hand.

"Please come in." Jaron wanted to kick himself for being polite at a time like this.

"Thank you." Seamus and his two pieces of "muscle" entered and sat. Rather, Seamus sat and the muscles stood ominously by. "Now, are you writing a book?"

And that would pretty much be the last thing Jaron thought the mob kingpin would say. "No. But I could."

"Ach." Seamus pursed his mouth and shook his head. "I understand that you witnessed some unpleasantness after dinner at Lorenzo's."

"I was there, yes."

"Sonny was a hothead." Jaron noticed he spoke in the past tense. "He'd act without thinking things through. When you're a hothead, you shouldn't be thinking. You should let others think for you."

Jaron nodded, aware that he was being given some information, but had no idea of the significance.

Seamus regarded him and must have picked up on Jaron's cluelessness. "That night, *nobody* was thinking for Sonny. Sonny was mad 'cause the decorator he thought was a flou-flou had been boinking his wife and daughter. You may have noticed that I was trying to calm him down."

"Absolutely. I did notice that."

Seamus spread his hands. "And then the unpleasantness." He shook his head. "Naturally, you told the police what you saw."

"Naturally."

"It's a citizen's duty to report unpleasantness, that I understand. You're to be commended."

Jaron didn't want to be commended. "It was nothing, really."

"And it distresses me that you felt you had to go on..." He snapped his fingers.

"Sabbatical," supplied the man with the gun. "It's a fancy word for vacation. I looked it up."

Seamus quelled him with a glance. "The thing is, you haven't been writing your columns. I don't like that old stuff. I've already read it."

"I didn't have much choice. There was unpleasantness the next day, as well."

Seamus shook his head. "I heard about that. You know, the thing about hotheads is that they're accident-prone. Sonny had just such an accident."

"I'm sorry to hear about it." And he was, because Seamus could only be telling him all this if he thought Jaron wouldn't be around to tell the police.

"So was I, but these things happen. The point now is that Sonny is no longer with us. He won't be around to engage in personal, unauthorized activities that have nothing to do with me."

"It must be a great relief to you."

"It is, I can tell you. So..." He slapped his hands on his knees. "I apologize that you were inconvenienced by one of my associates, even though it had nothing to do with me."

"You weren't even there," Jaron said.

"I was as surprised as you." He shook his head. "But that's in the past. You don't have a problem with me, I don't have a problem with you. You can come back from your vacation now and write your columns."

It took several beats for Jaron to realize that Seamus

was giving him back his life. When he did, he tried very, very hard not to get down on his knees and weep at the man's feet. "I, uh, am going to do that. In fact, I have ideas for several columns already sketched out."

"That reminds me." Seamus removed a card from his breast pocket. "Here's a singer you should hear. I'll read what you think about her in your column."

"Thank you. I'll do that." Jaron didn't have to hear the singer; he could write the column now. She would have the voice of an angel.

Seamus stood, so Jaron did, too. "Also, please convey my apologies to your lovely dinner companion. Will you be seeing her again?"

"Yes." And then, because he was feeling buoyant with the relief of one who has been given a second chance at life, Jaron added, "I'm going to marry her."

A grin split Seamus's face. "Are you, now. Congratulations. Send me an invitation to the wedding."

Jaron made sure he kept his own smile in place. "Thank you. I'll do that."

"Leave it at Lorenzo's." Seamus winked at him and then he and his "associates" left. Backing up, the man with the gun kept it pointed at Jaron until they were all in the hallway.

Jaron closed the door and his knees threatened to give way. Water, he needed water. No, vodka. No—water *and* vodka.

He staggered to the kitchen and gulped a glass of water straight from the tap, no ice. He swigged vodka out of the bottle the same way. His tongue caught fire, so he put it out with more tepid water.

He screwed the cap back on the vodka bottle. No more, though he could probably drink the rest of the bottle without getting drunk, such was the amount of adrenaline coursing through his body.

He was home. He was free. He could sleep in his own bed. Jaron collapsed onto the sofa and leaned his head back. Oh, the relief. And then he thought about the letter he'd written when he'd expected each word could be his last. It was there on the desk, and he got up and unfolded it.

Bonnie. He loved Bonnie. And she didn't know it yet.

He had to go to her. He didn't care about sleeping in his own bed in his own apartment in a noisy, smelly city.

He had to get home to Bonnie.

BONNIE OPENED THE DOOR to Maureen's office and slumped into a chair.

"Have you found him yet?" Maureen's face had been white ever since they'd discovered Jaron was missing.

Bonnie's face was green—she'd seen it in the mirror. She shook her head. Where could he have gone? "And you can tell them that I'm not going into any protection program without talking to him first."

"Oh, Bonnie." Maureen looked as if she wanted to cry, only Maureen never cried. "The man who was here asking questions—he's not a social worker from New Hampshire. We don't know who he is. I've sent the glass to Quigg, but I hope that man didn't have anything to do with Jaron's disappearance."

Bonnie thought she was going to be physically sick, and leaned toward the wastebasket. She'd been awake all night and had come to the decision that she'd rather be miserable with Jaron than without him. Only he wasn't around for her to tell, so she was being extra miserable without him.

What should she do? The deadline set by the marshals

was this morning. What if Jaron had been... She couldn't think about that.

Not telling her parents had been horrible. The one thing she could tell them was how much she loved Jaron, and even then she had to call him Jay.

"Bonnie?" Maureen nodded to the window.

A long black Town Car drove up the oak-lined drive. The last time Bonnie had seen a Town Car, somebody had been shot.

"You stay here," Maureen instructed. "Don't come out whatever you hear."

Bonnie really, really was going to be sick.

The car drove up and parked out of sight of the office window. Bonnie paced and tried listening at the door. She could hear a low murmuring of voices, but nothing that sounded like distress.

Maureen was taking forever. What could be going on? Bonnie was about to ignore her instructions when footsteps approached. There was nowhere to hide except behind the desk, and that would be the first place anyone would look.

"She's in here," a voice said, and then the door opened.

Jaron walked in, wearing his black Jaron clothes.

Bonnie squealed and launched herself at him, firing questions in between kissing him. "Where have you been?" She kissed him so he couldn't answer. "I was so worried. I didn't want to go into the program without you." She kissed him again. "I don't care where I go as long as I can be with you!"

This time when she kissed him, he held her head until she relaxed and moaned and leaned into the kiss. When he broke it, Jaron pressed his finger against her lips. "We don't have to go into the program."

"We don't? Why not?"

"I went to New York last night—"

"Jaron!"

"—and Seamus McDormand paid me a visit at my apartment."

She stared in horror. "You might have been killed!"

"Yes, I might have been. I wrote you a letter telling you all about it. Sometime you'll have to read it."

"What did he want?"

"Well, basically, with Sonny gone, Seamus wanted me to know that he had no beef with me and he was tired of reading column reruns."

"You're kidding."

"No. And he sends you his regards. I asked him to the wedding."

"What wedding?"

"Ours." A corner of his mouth quirked upward. "Marry me, Bonnie?"

"You asked a mobster to our wedding before you asked *me* to our wedding?"

"Yes." Jaron nodded. "It seemed like a prudent idea at the time."

"What if I say no?"

"Then there won't be a wedding, and when he doesn't get an invitation, he'll think I've insulted him and he'll hunt me down."

"In other words, I hold your life in my hands."

Jaron took her hands, turned them upward and kissed each palm before curling her fingers over the spot. "You do anyway. I love you."

Bonnie's heart melted. "Of course I'll marry you! I've been in love with you ever since you pushed that scone in my mouth."

He laughed and pressed his forehead to hers. "I'd better write down that recipe so I never forget it."

"But where are we going to live?"

"The city is part of who I am," Jaron said. "And I know that Cooper's Corner is part of who you are, so I say we live in both places. There's no rule that says we can have only one home, is there?"

"Well, if there is, then I say we break it."

"Actually, there's another rule—this will be a chintz-free marriage."

"You're invoking the chintz clause?"

Jaron nodded.

"Well, if you're invoking the chintz clause, then I'm invoking the no-goatee clause."

"Hey!"

"Because I like kissing you so much better without it." And Bonnie spent a good long while proving it.

EPILOGUE

AS A SYMBOL of their compromise, Bonnie got her simple fall wedding in the Cooper's Corner village church and Jaron got an exclusively elegant reception in New York.

It was the end of October and the leaves were still brilliant on the bright day when Bonnie married Jaron in front of the entire village of Cooper's Corner, as well as her aunt Cokie, Jaron's mother, some of his closest friends and a pewful of redheaded men who arrived immediately prior and vanished immediately after the ceremony. The New York delegation wore their interpretation of country wedding casual and were outdressed by the villagers.

Afterward, the bride and groom's limousine led a caravan of private cars and buses filled with wedding guests back to the city. Even Maureen decided she'd risk returning to New York. She'd stay on the bus, walk into the hotel, then stay in the room where the reception was being held. Afterward, she'd get back on the bus, and would never been seen by anyone except friends and family.

The reception was at an exclusive hotel and was possible only because Cokie and Nora Darke had started planning it from the instant the door closed behind Bonnie and Jaron on their first—and only—date.

The food was plentiful and catered by a wildly popular new Hawaiian restaurant. The champagne flowed, the band was great, and flanking the wedding cake was an enormous bouquet with all best wishes from Seamus McDormand.

Maureen didn't consider herself sentimental, but as she watched Jaron and Bonnie gaze adoringly at each other during their dance together, she felt tears threaten—at least until Frank Quigg touched her arm.

"What's happened?" she whispered. He'd told her he'd have an officer keeping watch outside the hotel, just in case, but she hadn't expected to see him.

"Sorry to intrude. I wanted you to know that the fingerprints we took off that glass you sent belong to a Gene Vogel."

"I don't know the name."

"He's a private investigator from here in New York."

A chill crept over her. "We know he wasn't hired by McDormand. Do you think he was hired by the Nevils to find me?"

Quigg shook his head. "I don't know."

"Well, if he was, then my cover is blown." How could she stand this?

Frank gave her a sympathetic look. "Hang in there. We're working on it."

She nodded to him as Randi and Robin, who had been flower girls in the wedding, came running up. "They're leaving! It's time—"

"—to throw the birdseed!"

Maureen looked down into their happy faces and the happy faces of everyone around them, and hid her anxiety. She took their hands. "Well, come on then! Let's throw birdseed!"

* * * * *

Welcome to Twin Oaks—the new B and B in Cooper's Corner.
Some come for pleasure, others for passion—and one to set things straight...

COOPER'S CORNER *a new Harlequin continuity series continues in October 2002 with* STRANGERS WHEN WE MEET *by Marisa Carroll*

Radio talk-show host Emma Hart thought Twin Oaks was supposed to be a friendly inn, but fellow guest Blake Weston sure was grumpy! Blake had planned to buy an old farmhouse just outside Cooper's Corner, flee the rat race and propose to his girlfriend...until he'd caught her in bed with the real estate agent.

Here's a preview!

CHAPTER ONE

BLAKE STOOD ON THE DECK that overlooked the fields and meadows stretching up the hillside behind Twin Oaks. The night was quiet, as quiet as the nights of his Indiana boyhood, as silent as the deserts of Saudi Arabia or the ravaged Somalian countryside. The stars were high and bright, cold and far away. The scent of fallen leaves and dried grass mixed with the tang of spruce and pine from farther up the hill, and a chill hung in the air, the harbinger of frost before dawn.

He'd been standing there long enough to notice the chill. Turning up the collar of his worn leather jacket, he faced away from the starlit vista of shapes and shadows, his attention captured by the scene in the inn's gathering room, just beyond the French doors.

Emma Hart was sitting cross-legged on the floor, playing dominoes with Maureen Cooper's small twin daughters, Randi and Robin. Blake had met them the evening before when they'd put in an appearance at teatime. He'd avoided tea this afternoon in case Daryl Tubb came by. He didn't want to be in the same room as the bastard.

The twins were three or three and a half, Blake guessed, sturdy little girls with chestnut hair and blue-green eyes that sparkled with health and mischief. They were well mannered and well behaved, but not above wheedling one or two of their uncle Clint's chocolate chip cookies off a guest's plate.

The domino game was proceeding with what seemed to be little regard for the rules. There was much laughter and jumping up and down on the twins' part, and lots of smiles and hugs on Emma's part. From Blake's perspective, she looked to be a natural with kids. He bet she wanted a big family of her own, though how he knew that he couldn't say. It was something he himself wanted in life, and had been yet another sticking point with Heather, who thought two kids were more than enough, and then only someday in the distant future.

Finding her naked with Daryl Tubb had been a blessing in disguise.

For him.

But for Emma Hart, it was going to be a heartbreaker.

If she found out, that is.

Should he tell her?

He couldn't quite see himself in that role. How did you go about breaking a woman's heart? Over breakfast the next morning, perhaps? Just come out with it? *Oh, by the way, that guy you're with—the one you're going to marry... Well, the damnedest coincidence. Remember the guy I told you I found my girlfriend naked with? It's him. Your Daryl. Do you need a little more maple syrup on that griddle cake?*

God, how had he gotten himself into such a mess? He supposed if you thought about it, the odds of him meeting Emma weren't as astronomical as they seemed. Cooper's Corner was a small town, after all. He could accept the chain of events that had brought them into each other's orbits. She'd met Daryl through her grandparents. He'd met Daryl because he wanted to buy property in the area.

Heather had betrayed him with Daryl. Daryl had betrayed Emma with Heather.

And then fate had brought them to Twin Oaks at the same time.

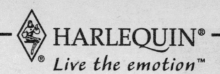

HARLEQUIN®
Live the emotion™

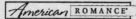
American ROMANCE®

Heart, Home & Happiness

HARLEQUIN®
Blaze™
Red-hot reads.

HARLEQUIN®
EVERLASTING LOVE™
Every great love has a story to tell™

Harlequin® Historical
Historical Romantic Adventure!

HARLEQUIN®
HARLEQUIN ROMANCE®
From the Heart, For the Heart

HARLEQUIN®
INTRIGUE
Breathtaking Romantic Suspense

Medical Romance™...
love is just a heartbeat away

Next™
**There's the life you planned.
And there's what comes next.**

HARLEQUIN®
Presents
Seduction and Passion Guaranteed!

HARLEQUIN®
Super Romance®
Exciting, Emotional, Unexpected

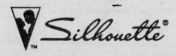

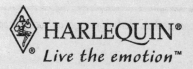

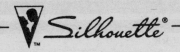

SPECIAL EDITION™

Emotional, compelling stories that capture the intensity of living, loving and creating a family in today's world.

Desire

Modern, passionate reads that are powerful and provocative.

nocturne

Dramatic and sensual tales of paranormal romance.

Romantic SUSPENSE

Romances that are sparked by danger and fueled by passion.

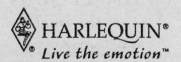

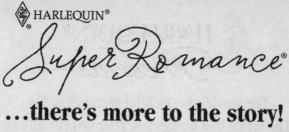

HARLEQUIN®
Super Romance®

...there's more to the story!

Superromance.
A *big* satisfying read about unforgettable
characters. Each month we offer *six* very different
stories that range from family drama to adventure
and mystery, from highly emotional stories to
romantic comedies—and much more! Stories
about people you'll believe in and care about.
Stories too compelling to put down....

Our authors are among today's *best* romance
writers. You'll find familiar names and talented
newcomers. Many of them are award winners—
and you'll see why!

If you want the biggest and best
in romance fiction, you'll get it
from Superromance!

Exciting, Emotional, Unexpected...

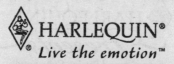

HARLEQUIN®
Live the emotion™

HARLEQUIN®
Presents

The world's bestselling romance series...
The series that brings you your favorite authors,
month after month:

Helen Bianchin...Emma Darcy
Lynne Graham...Penny Jordan
Miranda Lee...Sandra Marton
Anne Mather...Carole Mortimer
Susan Napier...Michelle Reid

and many more uniquely talented authors!

Wealthy, powerful, gorgeous men...
Women who have feelings just like your own...
The stories you love, set in exotic, glamorous locations...

HARLEQUIN®
Presents

Seduction and Passion Guaranteed!

HPDIR104